Bargain with the Bachelor

Bargain with the Bachelor

A SMALL TOWN FRIENDS TO LOVERS FAKE DATING ROMANCE

AN EASTPORT BAY BILLIONAIRES NOVEL

TRU TAYLOR

Contents

About

BARGAIN WITH THE BACHELOR

She's desperate for a temporary place to live. My mansion has plenty of room. So I offer my lifelong secret crush a bargain she can't afford to refuse.

Kristal:

So I've just been kicked out of my family home... by my wicked step-mother. I know, I know, sounds like something out of a fairy tale.

More like a horror movie.

But even I have no sympathy for the poor-little-rich-girl sob story, and I refuse to take charity, so I've traded my camera for a waitress's order pad and put my dream of becoming a world-renowned photographer on hold.

The problem is I can't keep couch-surfing at my best friend's tiny house. I *need* a new place to live—the sooner and cheaper the better.

Hunter:

Thanks to a knack for coding and a whole lot of hard work, I've gotten almost everything I ever wanted growing up poor among the rich kids of Eastport Bay, Rhode Island.

Almost.

I've made my first billion, working with my six best friends is a blast, and women are throwing themselves at me everywhere I go.

Actually, that last thing wasn't on my list.

There's only one woman I've really ever wanted, and she's *still* out of my league. All my money means nothing to her.

But then we end up accidentally spending seven minutes in heaven—in this case a dark room at a high society party—together, and I start to think she *might* not be so indifferent to me after all.

So I offer her a bargain she can't afford to refuse. She's desperate for a temporary place to live—my mansion has plenty of room.

And there's *no way* I'm leaving Snow White out in the cold this winter.

Not when there's even the smallest chance my lifelong unrequited crush might finally wake up and see I'm the prince she's been waiting for.

Bargain with the Bachelor is a full-length hot small town rom com take on the Snow White fairy tale. It's a standalone secret crush, friends-to-lovers, roommates, fake dating billionaire romance.

Enjoy the story...

ONE

Biologically Incapable of Cool

You can't completely comprehend the term "shaken" until you find yourself playing an accidental game of Seven Minutes in Heaven with your unrequited lifelong crush at a swanky society fundraiser. – Hunter Bestia

She looked almost too good to be real, like a mirage—or one of those photoshopped magazine images of models you probably wouldn't look twice at in real life.

I considered taking a sharp detour, cutting across Bellevue Manor's oceanfront lawn and not stopping until I reached my own house several doors down.

But then she lifted one hand in a tentative wave, indicating she'd spotted me too.

My heart lurched forward and slammed against my sternum like the cold Atlantic waves crashing against the nearby cliffs.

Time to man up, Hunter. Talk to her. Show her how you've changed.

I crossed the marble terrace toward her, making my way

through a sea of designer dresses and tuxedoes, my pulse thrumming harder than the savage war drums in one of my brother Jack's best-selling fantasy novels.

Drawing closer, I confirmed it was no mirage. Kristal Bianco, the girl I'd longed for pretty much every day of my entire middle school and high school career, was indeed real and standing right in front of me, looking even more unattainable than ever.

Somehow my voice came out sounding normal, though my belly vibrated with nerves. "Hello Kristal."

"Hunter!" She rose to her toes and gave me a brief hug, laughing brightly. "I thought that was you. How long has it been? Wow, you look incredible."

It took me a few seconds to respond. The combination of her scent, her compliment, the *hug*, and her utter gorgeousness had fried half my brain circuits, leaving me fumbling for words.

"Oh, uh... since graduation. So what is that... eleven years?"

"Twelve. I thought you were a math genius," she teased. "Wow," she said again, shaking her head and looking shockingly delighted to see me. "What are you doing here?"

"My brother Jack and his wife were coming and told me I should make time for it. Support the cause and all that."

She nodded, still smiling. "I know the Charity Relief Foundation *and* my stepmother appreciate it. Still, these things can get kind of dull after a while, can't they? Same old people, same old small talk."

Dull was the furthest word from my mind at the moment. Kristal was stunning, even more dazzling up close than she'd been from afar. Back in high school I'd thought she was the prettiest girl I'd ever seen.

Now... she was ethereal.

Her red cocktail dress hugged her curves and perfectly

complemented her pale complexion and shoulder-length black hair. She wore matching red lipstick, which only made it more difficult to stop staring at her heart-shaped mouth.

Stop. Staring. Say something. Anything.

"Yeah," I pretended to agree with her comment. "I can see that." Then I confessed. "Truthfully, I don't really come to many of these society parties."

"Lucky you," she quipped.

What I *didn't* say was that I didn't have much desire to socialize with the same people who'd looked down on me, treated me like I was some lesser form of human when I was growing up poor in Eastport Bay, Rhode Island, America's first playground of the rich and famous.

I'd only recently begun to be invited to rub elbows with Eastport Bay's elite. My wealth, while considerable, was a newfound thing, a result of the recent launch of Chipp, my tech startup. Most of the attendees at these soirees were old money.

Kristal's people.

No doubt she'd learned ballroom dancing and formal dinner silverware placement at an early age, attending events with her family.

Her family. Finally regaining some sense of composure, I said, "I was sorry to hear about your dad's stroke. How's he doing?"

Her smile fell. "Not too good, actually. It was a major one, and I happened to be out that night. So was Margot—that's my stepmother. He was alone and didn't get to the hospital quickly enough for the TPA to take full effect. His mobility was severely impacted, and he's basically lost his speech. I can tell he's really down about it. He won't even let me take him out in public."

"Oh man. That is rough. I'm really sorry to hear that."

Kristal's father, Richard Bianco, was a wildly successful

attorney and a partner in the state's most prestigious law firm. If there was a high-profile case in Rhode Island, his name was bound to be attached to it. He'd made a fortune.

Losing your speech and a good portion of your mobility would be devastating for anyone, but for a man whose claim to fame was making jury-winning persuasive arguments, it had to be doubly so.

Kristal's gaze flitted to the side then up as she appeared to blink back tears. Her long lashes fluttered rapidly as she swallowed.

"Yeah. It's hard—on all of us. I hate seeing him so unhappy… and feeling so helpless to make it better."

My heart tumbled toward Kristal. It killed me to see *her* so unhappy.

Though she'd been a member of the rich kids' crowd back in school, she'd always been kind to me. Of course, I'd realized it for what it was—common courtesy and simple friendliness—more than I could say for a lot of her friends.

Obviously, I'd never asked her out. She would never have seen me as dating material. She'd been so far out of my league it had practically made me lightheaded to even think about scaling those lofty heights.

So I'd admired her from afar and mustered all my courage just to meet her eyes whenever she'd offered a friendly "hello" in the hallway or classroom. Now, though, I instinctively reached for her hand, compelled to offer some small comfort.

"I'm so sorry you're going through this. I know how hard it is."

She squeezed my hand and gave an uncomfortable laugh, withdrawing her fingers to swipe quickly under her eyes.

"Thanks. You're probably one of the few people who does. We both lost our mothers at such a young age. I guess I'm lucky to have had my dad for this long."

Her soft words knocked all the air from my lungs. She remembered.

It stunned me that she'd paid enough attention to a guy from the poor side of town, a skinny math geek, that she'd been aware of anything personal about me, much less my mother's death from breast cancer. I fervently hoped she *didn't* know about my father's condition as well.

I swallowed hard, getting a little choked up myself. "Yeah, well, you know these things do get at least a little easier with time. Not perfect, but better."

She nodded. "I just feel like I need to spend every minute with him, you know? While I can. He was always working so much, this is the first chance I've ever had to spend significant time with him. I didn't even want to leave him to come here tonight, but Margot is the chairwoman, and she insisted I be here. I'm just trying to get through the night, honestly."

Taking in a deep breath and letting it out, Kristal shook her head and put on a bright smile.

"Let's talk about something happy. Like your success. It's amazing what you've built. I read somewhere that your company was just valuated in the upper millions."

She's read about me? My heart kicked back into a rapid rhythm, my nerves resuming their jittery dance. A sudden scramble of thoughts started a raucous barroom brawl in my mind.

Maybe this is my chance to impress her.

No, don't brag.

But... she did *ask. Maybe if she understands how successful I've become, it would even the playing field. She's used to successful men.*

"Billions, actually," I corrected, attempting a suave smile. "The Wall Street Journal called Chipp the most innovative, must-have tech of the past two decades."

Kristal's smile dimmed. Her tone flattened. "It must be exciting to see all your hard work pay off."

Her eyes drifted from mine and across the vast lawn, searching for something. I was losing her attention.

"And you're leasing the old Weston place," she said, sounding almost bored now. "Are the renovations as spectacular as they say they are?"

"It's pretty nice."

My shrug masked a growing sense of desperation. I felt like a kid who'd been picked first for the kickball team and then put on the bench without warning. What had gone wrong?

"We've been comfortable there," I continued, then doubled down on my attempt to impress her. "But I'm looking into buying my own place. Considering that castle on Atlantic Avenue with nine acres. It's only nineteen million."

Not quite sure what orifice I'd pulled *that* one out of, other than the fact I'd driven down Atlantic Avenue yesterday and had noticed the For Sale sign.

Fuck was I nervous. Honestly, I'd have no use for a place with ten bedrooms, sixteen baths, and an ocean-view tennis court. I didn't even *play* tennis.

Kristal seemed to have barely heard me, literally turning her body away so I was seeing her in profile now as she continued to scan the property.

"Have you seen Harry McAllen tonight?" Flashing her eyes back to me, she said, "He's my boyfriend. Remember him from school?"

Indeed I did. Harry had been my least favorite member of the silver spoon club. I remembered him as an entitled jerk who'd moved quickly from one girl to the next without necessarily notifying the first girl in advance.

When we'd been seniors, Harry had started showing up at the house next door every night, visiting my shy but sweet ninth-grade neighbor, Elizabeth.

When I'd asked her about it, she'd tearfully told me that Harry had claimed to love her but refused to acknowledge her at school. *Dick.*

The next time Mr. McAllen had showed up for a cradle-robbing booty call, I'd been waiting. I'd challenged him to a fist fight in the front yard. Harry had stormed away, slamming his car door and peeling out of the run-down neighborhood in his new Mercedes.

But he'd stopped messing around with Elizabeth.

Harry and I had despised each other from that point on. But that was a long time ago. People changed, right?

All I could say was that Harry must have *really* grown up and turned a corner character-wise to be dating a classy woman like Kristal. It probably hadn't hurt his case that he worked at her father's law firm and was known as Richard Bianco's protégé.

Thinking of the two of them together siphoned the remaining air from my already deflating mood.

"Um... sure. Yeah, I remember Harry. Haven't seen him around tonight. You think maybe he went into the mansion?"

"He said he was going to get us drinks, but he hasn't come back. I think I'll go and look for him." She stuck her hand out and gave me a tight smile. "It was nice seeing you again, Hunter. Congratulations on all your success."

I clasped her hand for an all-to-brief moment before she withdrew it, turned, and left.

"Good to see you too... Kristal," I called to her back, my voice dying off along with all my stupid hopes.

Watching her retreating form, I gave myself a swift mental kick.

Great work, asshole. You really *impressed her, didn't you? Sent her running off in search of Harry-fucking-McAllen, of all people, for more pleasant company.*

When Kristal had complimented my success, I should have

brushed it off, said something humble and self-deprecating. Played it cool.

Apparently I was biologically incapable of cool when it came to this woman.

I was no better at talking to her now than I'd been at seventeen. And she was with Harry.

Fucking fantastic.

Feeling annoyed with myself, and now with the party in general, I wandered back into the house, looking for Jack and Bonnie so I could say goodnight and drop off a check for the Charity Relief Foundation before leaving.

Approaching a few people I knew, I asked each of them if they'd seen my brother and sister-in-law recently. I followed their directions, checking the dessert buffet and then the ballroom, but didn't find the pair. I was about to give up when the woman collecting donations in the grand entry hall pointed at the massive marble staircase.

"I think I saw them go upstairs just a few minutes ago. Some of the second-floor rooms are open for tours tonight. You should go check them out too."

I returned the volunteer's warm smile, thanked her, and climbed the gleaming turned staircase.

Like many people who live in popular tourist areas, I'd never really bothered to explore many of the sights myself, leaving them to the visitors. I'd been to functions at Bellevue Manor on the first floor and out on the grounds but had never actually toured the mansion.

I got something of a self-guided tour as I walked the long second-floor central hallway, peeking into room after room filled with gilded antique European furniture and priceless artwork.

The second level was basically deserted as far as I could tell. Either the other party guests had toured the rooms on the upper floor earlier or they weren't interested in anything beyond the food, drinks, and dancing downstairs.

I didn't find Jack and Bonnie, but I did spot something that caught my interest in a large bathroom adjoining one of the bedrooms. I'd never seen anything quite like it.

The 1920's era bathroom contained the usual fixtures, but there was something extra in this one I wasn't quite sure how to classify.

It looked like a very small bathtub, low to the ground, with water spigots above it for fresh and saltwater. I studied it, walking from one side to the other to view it from different angles.

It wasn't a bidet—I'd seen those before when traveling in Europe. So what was it?

Deciding I'd ask someone when I went downstairs again, I left the bathroom and backtracked through the bedroom, heading for the door to the central hallway.

That's when the lights went out.

TWO

Hide and Seek

Kristal-- Fifteen minutes earlier

Stepping into the house from the terrace, I moved from room to room, searching for Harry. It seemed strange I hadn't seen him in such a long while.

Hopefully he hadn't spotted me talking to Hunter and gotten angry. Harry had a legendary temper.

There was certainly nothing going on, but Hunter was a tall, good-looking, single guy. I hoped my boyfriend hadn't mistaken what he'd seen as something more than two old friends reconnecting.

It *had* been really nice to see Hunter—at first. I'd followed his blossoming software design career with interest, so happy for him and not the least bit surprised. I was proud to say, "I knew him when."

And I'd always known he'd be successful—at whatever he chose to do. It had been obvious in high school he was brilliant, maybe even a genius.

He'd been such a nice guy, though painfully shy. Truth be told, I'd harbored a bit of a secret crush on him back then.

Though a little on the thin side, he was very fit, like a

runner, not to mention his arresting electric blue eyes. He'd been cute in a geeky high school boy kind of way.

Being a self-identified art-geek, I'd thought we might make a nice couple. But he'd never asked me out or really even shown any interest in me beyond general friendliness.

Now I was kind of glad we'd never dated, though admittedly, Hunter had developed into a stunningly handsome man. I almost hadn't recognized him at first glance with the way he'd filled out and matured.

But he was *such* a braggart. I would never have predicted that of him. He'd always seemed so down to earth when he was young.

Then again, I hadn't really known him all that well. Anyway, I had my hands full with Harry—or *would* if I could manage to locate him. I needed him.

The air-kisses and chit-chat were wearing thin, and the melancholy I'd been fighting daily since my father's stroke was starting to creep in again.

I was craving Harry's easy laughter and charisma, the mega-watt smile that always charmed whomever was around.

"Where have you been?" an imperious female voice demanded from over my shoulder.

I spun around to face Margot. My stepmother's unnaturally smooth forehead actually creased a teensy bit.

Boy she really must be perturbed. That skin hadn't moved in at least a decade.

Margot wore a flapper-style dress embellished with allover white feathers. A bejeweled headband with a single matching feather adorned her sleek platinum bob. I assumed she was going for a 1920's look, but she was giving off strong poultry vibes.

"I went outside to get some air," I said. "Everything okay?"

"No. Everything is not *okay,*" Margot mocked my choice of words. "The emcee from the local radio station is *intoxi-*

cated, and the live auctioneer hasn't arrived yet. The auction is supposed to begin in five minutes! If we don't start on time, people will leave before the auction even happens, and the night will be a *total* failure."

"What can I do to help?" I asked.

Margot's arms flew out to the side and bounced up and down. Yep, she definitely looked like a flustered chicken.

"I don't know," she whined. "I'm going to get the emcee some strong black coffee. You can... call the auctioneer's cell phone. Here."

She shoved a business card at me before turning to stalk away in her four-inch stiletto heels. I felt bad for her.

Though we weren't exactly close, I knew the event was important to my father's wife.

Margot had put a lot of work into it, spending long hours every day away from home coordinating things, in spite of her husband's condition. Perhaps because of it.

I'd tried to be understanding about that—people dealt with stress and grief in different ways. Margot's approach seemed to consist of plenty of self-care—long lunches with her girlfriends and lavish shopping trips.

She'd always been a firm believer in money buying happiness.

Recently, she'd shut down a boutique in the Brady's Wharf shopping district and spent sixty thousand dollars in one trip on haute couture and jewelry. I wasn't even sure I wanted to know how much Margot had spent over the years on cosmetic procedures.

While Richard Bianco had gone gray and looked every minute of his sixty-four years, Margot was obsessed with looking young. I'd always thought her a very attractive woman, but Margot was never quite satisfied.

She seemed to consider physical appearance a competition

sport, and her opponents were all other women—including her stepdaughter.

I'd first noticed the friction the year I turned fourteen, when my body had begun to develop. Margot had remarked on my "childbearing hips" and attributed them to my mother, who in her words, had been "pretty in a common, middle-class way."

The offhand cruel remarks had increased as I matured and began to attract the notice and casual compliments of Margot's male acquaintances.

But the things she said were never egregious enough for me to mention them to my father.

He wasn't around enough to witness the animosity, and he loved us both and wanted so desperately for his "best girls" to get along and be friends. I hated to disappoint him.

I would much rather have had a mother figure than someone determined to be mistaken as my sister, no matter how many years passed.

And as far as I cared, Margot could keep the "Fairest of Them All" title.

Whatever gets her through the day.

I only hoped my stepmother was keeping an eye on the household finances. Maintaining and staffing a house the size of the one Dad had built twenty-five years ago on Oceanview Avenue was no small thing—not to mention the taxes—and the task had fallen to Margot when Dad had suffered the stroke.

I'd volunteered to take the financial stuff off her hands—my work at the Art Guild had honed my skills in that area—but Margot had insisted she could handle it and that it wasn't my role.

So I'd focused on the things I *could* help out with, filling in as my father's companion and nurse too whenever the visiting home care nurse wasn't around.

Hopefully after tonight, with the foundation ball behind her, Margot would be more attentive to Daddy. I had no doubt spending more time with his wife would boost my father's spirits.

Tapping in the number from the card Margot gave me, I placed the call to the auctioneer, who answered on the first ring. He said traffic on I-95 had been horrendous, assuring me he was only minutes away. I was about to slip the phone back into my evening bag when the text notification sounded.

Yes! It was from Harry.

-Hey beautiful. It's time for hide and seek. Go ahead and sneak upstairs to the lilac bedroom, and I'll meet you in 5. Don't let anyone see you. Turn out the lights when you get there.

He'd added a comical eggplant and a grinning devil emoji to the end, making me giggle.

I let out a breath, relieved to finally hear from my boyfriend and frankly a little surprised by his suggestion.

Since my dad's stroke, Harry had been acting distant. I knew what it was about. My life wasn't the only one adversely affected by my father's new limitations.

Harry was dealing with the sudden loss of his mentor and idol, not to mention the increased workload Dad's medical leave had caused him.

But his text indicated a return of the old, flirtatious, fun Harry I'd fallen for. He probably thought I'd be tickled at the idea of playing a naughty "game" during this fancy party, and you know... I was.

It was exactly what I needed. A welcome escape from the crowd, from Margot, from the never-ending stress-fest my life had become lately. I couldn't wait.

Peering around surreptitiously, I headed for the staircase, feeling giddy and quite daring.

Not that anyone would care about seeing me go upstairs—the second floor was open to party guests tonight.

But just knowing what I'd be doing upstairs—rendezvousing with my handsome boyfriend for some stolen kisses—made me feel like I was back in high school again.

I'd explored Bellevue Manor several times before, listening to the informative self-guided tour recording, so I knew exactly where the lilac bedroom was.

Featuring a circular ceiling painting of Aphrodite, it had once belonged to the lady of the house, one of the Vanderbilt heirs. Turning right at the top of the stairs, I tiptoed down the long hallway as anticipation turned my stomach into a bouncy house.

Finally reaching the room, I checked up and down the hallway once more, just to be sure I hadn't been spotted.

Then I pushed open the door, stepped inside, and flicked off the light switch, glimpsing Harry's dark hair and the back of his tux before everything went pitch black. He must have been eager too. He'd beaten me here.

He uttered a sound of surprise at the sudden blackout.

"It's me," I assured him. "Where are you? Come here."

Reaching blindly, I grasped the air in front of me. My fingers came into contact with smooth fabric, the lapels of an expensive tuxedo jacket.

Harry's taste for the finer things in life was almost as refined and insatiable as Margot's.

"Mmmm... you feel as good as you look tonight," I murmured, gliding my hands up and down the outside of the jacket, admiring the solid contours of the hard chest and torso underneath.

Harry had clearly been working out more than usual.

He didn't speak, just stood there and let me caress him, his breathing accelerated and enticingly audible in the quiet room. Then with a soft grunt, he slid his arms around me, pressing his palms against the small of my back and pulling me close.

I let out a surprised laugh and inhaled, getting an intoxicating whiff of the masculine scent he was wearing.

New cologne too. Yum. Mr. McAllen has really *upped his game.*

I'd missed this—the closeness, the excitement of being with him in a romantic way, the comfort of human touch. It felt like weeks since he'd held me in his arms. Maybe it had been. I'd been so distracted with my father's care, it was hard to remember.

But I wasn't distracted tonight. I was completely focused on him and completely turned on.

The darkness had been an excellent idea. It made me braver than I usually was.

"Let's see if you *kiss* as good as you feel," I whispered and slipped my fingers around the back of his hard-muscled neck, rising up on tiptoe to press my lips to his.

At first, he failed to respond as expected, going stock-still and letting me take the lead in the kiss.

But after a few seconds, he got with the program—big time. He made a sort of gruff, growly noise and leaned into the kiss, sinking one of his big hands into my hair to grasp my nape, taking control.

His mouth moved with mine in heated, luscious strokes, the fervency of his kisses escalating in a steady ascent that drew me right along with it. His other hand left my back and came up to cradle my jaw with a tenderness that brought tears to the corners of my eyes.

What was happening? Within moments of touching me, Harry was drawing feelings from me I'd never experienced in my life.

He had never kissed me like this before, and until now, I hadn't been aware of how much I'd craved it.

It was the intensity, the focus, the sheer *emotion* behind the kisses that made them more potent than anything I'd ever known.

I wasn't a big drinker, and I'd never tried any sort of illicit drugs, but suddenly I understood the allure of addictive substances. I couldn't get enough.

Though we were in a public venue with scores of other people, and I could hear the low hum of their distant chatter as well as the faint strains of live music, this room felt like a world apart, our own secret hideaway.

Part of my mind was aware the door could open at any moment, exposing our private tryst to the world, but I couldn't seem to dredge up any real concern. I was suspended in some sort of alternate state... weightless, boneless, powerless against the hypnotic spell Harry had cast over me tonight.

The subtle sense of the forbidden seemed to be working for him as well because he pulled me even tighter, large hands spanning my waist and back, enclosing me in his strong grip and drawing my lower body against one *very* impressive erection.

In fact, I'd never felt him this hard for me. Or this big.

No workout in the world could achieve *that* kind of result —it had to be the long dry spell that had him super-sized and raring to go.

His kisses deepened, turning sultry and slow, and my insides melted like cheap candle wax. I'd never imagined lips, teeth, and tongues could produce this much pleasure. When he brought a hand up to cup my breast and coast his thumb over the sensitive tip, the pleasure soared to an even higher level. It was *too* much.

I made a little noise—a whimper for him to stop? A plea to go on? I wasn't really sure.

Whatever it was, it seemed to energize Harry. His lungs

worked in heavy surges, his hands gliding down my sides and grappling in the heavy folds of my dress.

He began working it upward as he backed me slowly across the room. The backs of my legs encountered an obstacle. Oh, it was a bedframe.

Whoa.

The surprise realization snapped me out of the lust-fog that had dropped over me in the past few minutes and obscured all my usual cautionary road signs.

Kissing in the dark was one thing—banging my boyfriend at a public venue would be a whole *other* kind of thing.

I turned my head, disengaging from the kiss.

"Wait." I was fighting for breath as well as self-control. "Wait a minute. We have to stop."

Harry let me go instantly, removing his hands and his mind-altering body heat. After a few ragged breaths of his own, he finally spoke.

"Too fast? Sorry about that. I got a little carried away."

A bolt of terror shot through my chest.

Not Harry!

Not. Harry.

That was *not* his voice. Not even close. This voice was deeper, huskier.

Scrambling back from the man, I fell onto the bed in an ungraceful sprawl. Which the stranger couldn't see, thank goodness, because of the darkness.

Stranger. Oh my God, I'd kissed a stranger.

Who was I kidding? I'd *made out* with him.

In a public place.

At my stepmother's party, which was attended by pretty much everyone we knew in town.

Oh no. What if I knew this guy? What if he was one of Margot's friends? One of my father's friends? Ugh.

What if he was one of *Harry's* friends?

This was so bad. So, so bad. I could hardly bear to think about it.

My chest hurt. Mortification flooded my veins, pushing out the words that had been trapped behind the instantaneous lump in my throat.

"Oh my God, I'm so sorry," I gasped.

"Please..." A low chuckle. "... don't apologize. That was just about the best few minutes of my life."

"No, really. I *have* to apologize. That was a mistake—an accident."

"You sure about that? It felt pretty intentional there for a minute." The man's voice was somehow soothing and taunting at the same time.

That voice. It *was* someone I knew. But who?

"No, I mean the kissing wasn't an accident. It's just... I didn't mean to kiss *you*. I thought you were someone else. Wait... who are you?"

I heard the soft shush of movement, and then the light switched on, causing me to squint against its disconcerting brightness.

Blinking and getting my bearings, I shifted toward the bedroom door to see...

"Hunter! What are you doing here?"

He gave me a wry grin. "I believe you've already asked me that question once tonight. What are *you* doing here?"

"Me? I... well I... Harry sent me a text to meet him, and I did—I mean I thought I was meeting him, but I was meeting you, only I didn't know it was you. I just... I'm not really sure how this happened."

Hunter leaned back against the door, shoving one hand through his disheveled hair—through the hair *I'd* disheveled. His narrow-eyed gaze fell on me like a life sentence.

"You really had no idea it was me?" He sounded incredulous.

"Of course not. It was dark. You had no idea it was me either."

One of his eyebrows lifted.

My jaw came unhinged. "Did you?"

Confusion boiled in my brain. "If you knew it was me, why would you kiss me? I told you I had a boyfriend. I told you I was dating Harry."

Hunter's lips twisted to one side, and he huffed a laugh, his gaze going to the floor, to one wall, then up toward the ceiling.

"I thought you saw me. You came in and said, 'Come here.' You said I looked good. I thought maybe you'd... followed me in here, and..."

The color in his cheeks heightened. He shook his head and laughed again, not a happy sound but a bitter one. One hand came up to cover his mouth and chin then dropped to his side.

"Never mind. It doesn't matter. I apologize too. If I'd realized... I never would have..."

As he seemed at a loss for words and almost as embarrassed as I was, I rushed to let him off the hook. "Don't worry about it. It's no big deal. No harm, no foul, right?"

I forced a laugh. Amusement was *not* what I was experiencing. I felt... stricken. And still a little turned on, which made everything worse.

"You won't... tell anyone..."

Hunter's lips folded in, turning his mouth into a hard, straight line. "No. Of course not. Your secret's safe with me."

My insides curdled. I didn't *want* to have a secret. But even as that thought entered my mind another one superseded it. I would *not* be telling Harry about this.

I wouldn't be telling anyone. Ever.

It truly had been an accident, but how could I possibly explain it? I should have known from the first second it wasn't

Harry kissing me and stroking my hair, touching my face and holding me against his hardness.

His extra-long, extra-thick hardness.

Hadn't I even marveled over how different he was tonight?

But I'd been too lost in the fantastic feelings he'd elicited to pursue that tickle of doubt. I hadn't *wanted* to question it too closely… hadn't wanted it to end.

But now it had to. This mistake, this conversation. Harry would be here any moment—and that meant Hunter couldn't be here.

"You've got to leave," I said, urgency straining my voice.

His head jerked back. "Just like that? You kiss me, scramble my brains, and send me packing?"

"Harry is on his way here," I hissed, dashing a glance at the door. "He can't walk in on us like this."

"Like what?" Hunter's tone was bruised, sarcastic. "You mean with your lipstick smeared and your hair all sexy and messed up from my hands? With me sporting a hard-on the size of Texas?"

Without my permission, my eyes dropped to the front of his pants. He wasn't kidding. The Lone Star state had nothing on *this* land mass.

A dart of sensation shot through my belly. My face heated to feverish temperatures, and my hand automatically came up to smooth my hair. I slid off the bed and moved toward the bathroom door.

"I… need to… I need a mirror. Please go, Hunter. I'm sorry. Please understand."

Grabbing my purse, I fled into the bathroom where I spent the next several minutes standing with my eyes closed and both hands clenching the sides of the sink as I attempted —unsuccessfully—to erase the mental image of Hunter Bestia rumpled and aroused.

I took a deep breath and released it then dug around in my

small evening bag for the compact and lipstick I always kept inside.

"You're going to forget about this," I told my reflection in the mirror. "Just forget everything you saw—and felt—tonight. It didn't happen."

When I re-emerged, Hunter was gone.

Conflicting emotions battled inside me—relief I wouldn't be forced to explain this mess to Harry and also a strange sense of... loss.

There wasn't time to consider it further because Harry came through the bedroom door from the hallway, already loosening his tie and top button.

Seeing me, he stopped short, his eyes going wide. He looked stunned.

"Kristal?"

Oh no. He can tell. I thought I'd done a pretty good job of makeup and hair recovery, but obviously not.

My belly plunged to my feet like an elevator car with a failed lift mechanism. I gripped my hands in front of my belly button, wringing them together.

"Hi Harry. I—"

"What are *you* doing here?" He didn't sound angry like I'd expected. He sounded... confused.

And now I was confused.

"What do you mean? You sent me a text." At his continued look of bafflement, I prompted, "Hide and Seek?'

He froze. Blinked once. Looked around.

"Oh. Right. Yeah, I did." Motioning for me to come with him, he said, "I thought about it, and maybe it's not such a good idea..."

A woman's tipsy sing-song voice rang out from the hallway. "Ready or not... here I come."

Harry's head dropped back onto his shoulders, and his arms went slack at his sides. A second later, a beautiful blonde stepped into the room wearing a naughty smile. She looked vaguely familiar.

Going directly to Harry and putting both hands on his chest, she said, "I was too excited to wait for your text. How long have you been here?"

The woman did a double-take when she spotted me near the bathroom door, her glance bouncing from Harry to me, back to Harry.

"What's going on? Harry? What's *she* doing here?" the young woman asked. "I don't *do* threesomes."

And that was when it hit me.

The text hadn't been meant for me.

Biting his lip and sipping a tight breath, Harry turned to me with a *Don't hate me* grimace.

"Um, Kristal… we need to talk."

He turned to the blonde, whose identity had finally popped into my shock-numbed mind—she was the daughter of one of my dad's law partners. The girl was several years younger than me, barely out of college.

"Laurelynn, would you mind giving us a few minutes, honey?" His voice was gentle and low. "I'll be right down. Promise—this'll be quick."

Harry gave her a little pat on the behind, and she left, glancing back over her shoulder at me suspiciously before disappearing into the dim hallway.

"Why don't we sit?" Harry gestured toward a pair of chairs in one corner of the room.

I shook my head tightly, trying with all my strength to keep the tremor currently vibrating in my stomach from reaching my fingers. As stiff as I felt, inside and out, I doubted I'd be able to bend my knees enough to utilize a chair.

"No. Just say it."

Harry inhaled then let out a loud breath. "Fine. I'm in love with Laurelynn. Now you know."

He huffed a laugh. Actually *smiled*. "It's kind of a relief to say it out loud."

My teeth ground together to suppress a scream. "How long?"

"Well, it's hard to say. My feelings for you have been dwindling for some time..."

"No! How long have you been seeing that... that... *girl*?"

"She's not a girl—she's legal. Laurelynn and I have been together for, what is it? Three weeks now."

"So basically you hooked up right after my dad's stroke." The bitterness leached from my soul into my voice. "Why? Why would you *cheat*? Why didn't you just... break up with me? Why go behind my back?"

His expression was infuriatingly sympathetic. "I wanted to tell you, but your father had just suffered a stroke. I didn't think it would be a good time."

"But you *did* think it would be a good time to come to a party hosted by *my family* and hook up with that *child* in an upstairs bedroom? Right under my nose."

He shook his head, a condescending smile decorating his lips. "She's not a child. She's twenty. Listen, I didn't mean for you to find out this way. I'm sorry for that."

"But not for cheating on me for the past month."

"Three weeks," he corrected.

If I hadn't known the value of the antique lamps and statuary in this room, I would have lifted something heavy and hurled it at his head.

"Get out."

"Babe..." He took a step toward me, his hands raised in front of him in a calming manner. "You had to have known it wasn't working. When was the last time we even kissed?"

"I'm sorry if I haven't been attentive to your needs, *babe.* As you said, my father just had a *massive stroke*."

"He didn't 'just' have it—it's been a month. You've got to move past it—get on with your life."

Now I did move toward the nearby dresser, lifting a solid cut-glass clock and testing its weight in my hands. My voice was quiet but deadly serious.

"Get. Out."

Harry eyed the clock. His gaze moved up to take in my expression.

Whatever he saw there must have convinced him the conversation was over. He left.

Sagging from a sudden release of tension, I set the clock down in its place on the dresser and turned to go back into the bathroom on shaky legs.

I shut the door behind me and climbed into the enormous white clawfoot tub, sliding my back against its smooth, cold surface until I was sitting.

And then I cried.

For my dad. For my relationship—which had apparently ended weeks ago.

I cried out of self-pity and out of shame and embarrassment over what had transpired with Hunter only moments before Harry had dropped his ugly truth-bomb and shattered my faith in men along with my illusions.

My only consolation in this whole twisted situation was that there was no way things could possibly get worse.

THREE
Mirror Mirror

Kristal-- Four months later

My boots sank into the deep snowdrifts, my breath fogging the air in front of me as I trudged across the lawn of Seacliff, my favorite of Eastport Bay's beautiful Gilded Age mansions.

It was a perfect afternoon—cold, obviously, but I was dressed for it. The sun was shining, the skies blue and clear, the pre-sunset light, perfect.

My camera bag bounced against my side as I got into position in front of the property's iconic circular fountain and located the ideal postcard angle.

Seacliff, which was modeled on the Grand Trianon of Versailles, rose from the wintry landscape like a spectacular snow-castle, its white glazed terra cotta exterior contributing to the illusion the grand house was liable to melt along with the snow when warmer climes prevailed.

It hosted gorgeous weddings year-round, and I'd always fancied the idea of having my own wedding reception there someday—not that there was anything resembling a groom on the horizon.

Today, I wanted to capture the spectacular beauty of the home and its meticulously landscaped grounds while the snowfall was fresh and perfect, the natural lighting diffused and warm.

It was exactly the kind of shot that would go quickly at the Sandcastle Gallery where I sold most of my work to its owner, Toni, my best customer over the past several years.

The shop was located in Brady's Wharf and got steady foot traffic from Eastport Bay tourists, many of them seeking a framed photographic memento of their visit to the Village by the Sea, as the town was nicknamed.

Toni had asked me for some new photographs several weeks ago, and I was finally feeling like working again.

For a while my father's death had sapped my energy, my spirit, and any ability or desire I'd felt to be creative, but it was returning, along with a lifetime of good memories.

As I'd walked down Oceanview Avenue to get to Seacliff, they'd swarmed me like moths around a midnight lamp post —my father chasing me through the snow or pulling me on the sled as a child, pushing me on the swing hung from the massive European beech tree in our yard.

For the first time since he'd been rushed to the hospital with a second stroke and passed away, I thought of my dad without crying.

Actually, I felt quite inspired today. Dad had been the one who'd always encouraged my photography, and like me, he'd loved the winter shots best.

While Harry had always referred to my photography work as my "little hobby," my father had praised my talent.

"Keep at it, pumpkin," he'd said. "You're an artist. You've got something special, and you'll find your audience in time."

That time hadn't come—my photography hadn't earned much money—not yet.

But it made me happy to know there were people out

there who were enjoying my work and taking a piece of my beautiful hometown with them when they went back to whatever parts of the world they'd come from.

Late afternoon sunlight fell on the elegant home's arched windows, ionic pilasters, and balustraded roofline, causing it to glow. They didn't call this the golden hour for nothing.

Peering through the viewfinder, I clicked off several shots of the mansion then shifted a few steps to one side then the other, capturing a variety of angles.

Eastport Bay had many more visitors in summer than in winter, but in my opinion, this was its most beautiful season —my favorite time to take photographs.

I checked the LCD screen to see what I'd gotten, and my heart hummed with satisfaction. Even in thumbnail, the images sparkled with promise.

Though there was some skill, training, and practice involved, I had to give the subject and the season their due credit. The newly fallen snow lent a sense of magic to everything it touched.

In fact, after photographing the mansion itself, I was drawn to a tree on the property.

Its bare branches looked like they'd been frosted by fairies, and the twiggy ends held plump puffs of snow that resembled mature cotton ready for harvesting.

Pointing the lens, I zoomed in and captured several tight shots then got some wider shots of the majestic tree. The reddish-gold sunset gave the illusion the tree was illuminated from within. These images I might keep for myself.

Dad would have loved them.

Once it got too dark to continue, I walked home, engulfed in a feeling of pleasure and pride in work well done.

Toni would be happy, I'd earn some money, and maybe, just maybe, one of my new shots would be worthy of submitting to the International Photography Awards.

There was a cash prize involved in the competition, but more importantly, the winning entries received international exposure and an exhibit in New York City prior to the annual awards ceremony.

An honor like that could make a photographer's career, putting them on the map, certifying them as an artist worth taking note of. It would certainly drive up my asking price per photo at the gallery and for commissioned work.

I'd been outdoors for a while and was thoroughly chilled by the time I headed for home.

The Oceanview Avenue house I'd grown up in was large but less formal than its elegant Gilded Age neighbors, the massive stone palaces Eastport Bay was known for. My father had commissioned an architect to build our home in a classic style that would fit in but be more comfortable for everyday living and much more approachable than those stately museums.

In spite of their fortune, my parents had been very grounded and enjoyed simply being together more than anything money could buy.

I'd never understood how the same man who'd been in love with my down-to-earth mother had also been attracted to material-girl Margot, making her his second wife a year after his first, my mom, had passed away.

Perhaps he'd just been lonely, and remarrying had eased the longing for his late wife.

I could certainly understand that. Even after all these years, I missed Mom fiercely.

I felt closest to her when working in the offices of the Eastport Bay Art Preservation Guild, an organization she founded to maintain and preserve works of public art so they could be enjoyed by future generations.

Caroline Bianco had considered it her life's work, her calling, and had specified in her will that I should take over running the guild when I came of age.

As soon as I finished school, I began working there full-time. Since money hadn't been an issue, I'd never taken a salary.

Sharing my mother's love of fine arts, I'd never minded the long unpaid hours. And my father had been delighted to see me carrying on my mother's legacy, assuring me that a trust fund would provide for my future and that my unsalaried work at the foundation and my photography pursuits were the most important things I could be doing with my time.

But I didn't intend to rely solely on my inheritance forever.

No, I was determined to turn my photography into a successful, lucrative career, to *earn* the faith my dad had always had in my talent, and I wouldn't stop until I'd made him proud.

His favorite room had always been the cozy den with its overflowing bookshelves and comfy furniture and oversized fireplace.

That was where I headed now, planning to toast myself in front of the fire until all my extremities were thawed and tingly warm. I was looking forward to a cup of hot tea, a good book, and maybe even a fireside nap.

Margot's car wasn't in the drive, which meant she was out as usual. It *was* Friday evening, but she was rarely at home these days, no matter what time or day of the week.

Which was fine with me. Now that Dad was gone, Margot had basically stopped bothering with civility.

It wasn't so bad. I spent most of my time away from home, anyway, working either at the Guild or doing my photography.

When I was at home, I used very little of the mansion—just my bedroom, bath, and the snug sanctuary of the den, processing my grief one day at a time.

Entering the room, I stopped short, surprised to find Margot there.

The older woman was gazing into the mirror above a console table on one wall, poking at her forehead and cheeks. Based on her frown, there would be another cosmetic procedure in the near future.

She spun to face me, seeming embarrassed to have been caught in self-examination.

"Oh—you're back. We need to talk, and now we don't have much time, thanks to all your wandering and nature-worship." She shot a disapproving glance at my camera bag.

Ooookay then. Don't let her provoke you. Be nice.

Margot was dressed to go out in a sleek St. John metallic knit gown that appeared to be melted onto her body.

"I'll be here all night," I said. "Where are *you* going? Where's your car?"

"There's no time to get into it. My date will be here to pick me up in fifteen minutes, which doesn't give us very long to discuss what's going on."

My lungs went flat. I struggled to draw enough air to speak. "You're going on a *date*? Daddy just died."

Margot rolled her eyes. "It's been *two months*, and if you were smart, you'd be doing the same thing. Believe me, a rich husband solves a lot of problems."

"I don't have any problems big enough to marry someone for their money."

My stepmother smirked. "We'll see how high and mighty you are next week when the bank forecloses, and *your* car is repossessed, and you've got to pay your own way with your little pictures."

My breathing problems worsened considerably. "Forecloses? What are you talking about?"

"The house. We can't afford it. The movers are coming Monday to remove my personal things, the things that aren't being auctioned off. I advise you to spend the evening packing yours."

I staggered and gripped the back of a nearby armchair for support. This couldn't be happening.

The house where I'd grown up, the home my father had built for my mother, the place that held all my memories of the two of them—gone? In a week?

"But... that isn't possible. Daddy made a fortune over his career. And he had life insurance. The mortgage wasn't even that far from being paid off, was it?"

Margot lifted a shoulder in a delicate shrug. "Fortunes come and go. Your father enjoyed the finer things."

My insides ignited. *Margot* was the one with the insatiable lust for material things.

How many times had Daddy told me he and my mom were basically broke during the early years of their marriage and had been blissfully happy?

"Our lifestyle was expensive," Margot continued in a blasé tone. "We took out a second mortgage last year... and then, after his stroke... well, I've never been very good at the whole 'financial' thing."

She curled her fingers into air quotes as she said the word "financial" and then waved her hands through the air as if fanning away an unpleasant odor.

"You didn't pay the mortgage—*mortgages,*" I said. It was a statement, not a question.

That was the only way the bank would have foreclosed. The household bills had gone unpaid since my dad's first stroke.

And I had known nothing about it.

A tide of nausea rocked me off balance, and I collapsed into the chair.

"What about savings?" I asked. "What about all the money that went to you when he died?"

As his wife, Margot had inherited half of Richard Bianco's estate. The other half had been put into a trust for me, accessible only when I turned thirty-five.

My father, who was a self-made man, had purposely set it up with my mother that way when I was very young, determined not to cripple his only child's ambition and desire to succeed with a ready-made cushion in life.

My mother had died when I was only nine, but my dad had told me over the years how pleased he was that I hadn't turned into one of those entitled rich kids who expected everything to be handed to them.

The fact was I'd never been interested in expensive cars, or designer shoes and clothes, or exotic travel. My needs were pretty simple—a camera, some form of transportation, a roof over my head.

Apparently the last thing on that short list would be taken away within days.

"The money is gone," Margot said flatly. "With no new income coming in, taxes and maintenance expenses ate it up very quickly, not to mention our living expenses."

Shopping, I thought as a dull headache began to form behind my eyes.

"I spent what was left on a yacht, so I'd at least have somewhere to lay my head at night," Margot explained.

"You bought a yacht?" I gasped. "Knowing the money was running out?"

"Just a small one. You know I've always loved travel, and I have to have *somewhere* to live," Margot said. "I need something to call my own, something no one can take away from me. I earned that money—all those years with Richard, raising *his* child."

She flipped one hand at me in an irritated gesture. "You're young and healthy. Your whole life is ahead of you. You'll be fine, a pretty girl like you. You can even get a job if you want one."

Grabbing her evening bag from the table, Margot walked toward the door, adding, "My opportunities are limited. I've only got a few years left to find someone new. So, as much as it pains me to say it, darling, you're on your own."

There was no discernable pain in Margot's tone or on her unlined, youthful face.

And why would I expect it? My stepmother had made minimal effort to act interested in my welfare when my father was alive.

Now she had zero motivation to even pretend.

Well, what she'd said was right. I was young. I did have my whole life ahead of me, and I *could* get a job—one that paid.

I wasn't sure where. I had a fine arts degree in photography—had even stayed in school and gotten a masters—but some of my friends from college had told me that a MFA degree was essentially worthless in today's marketplace.

Most of them were working in completely unrelated fields from their majors, some in jobs that didn't require a college degree at all.

Sadly, a lot of them were no longer even doing photography anymore because the demands of "real life" had superseded their passion for the art.

Once again, I realized how fortunate I'd been to have my father essentially underwriting my struggling photography career since graduation, to have been doing what I loved without the pressure of supporting myself.

Well, that was over, obviously. Things were what they were. Photography wasn't cutting it earnings-wise, but maybe I could still do some on weekends or something.

One thing was for sure—my life was about to change big-time. I had to find a full-time job and a place to live, in that order.

Luckily, I had somewhere to stay in the meantime.

My friend Cinda owned a very comfortable couch, and I had no doubt she'd let me stay a few days, at least until I could gather enough money for first and last month's rent on an apartment—and find a roommate.

I left the den, still shell-shocked, and went upstairs to pack my belongings. When I was done, I opened my laptop and created an account on a job-search site.

Unfortunately, there was no category for Over-educated, Under-employed, and Suddenly-desperate.

Scanning the dismal display of local options, I found precisely nothing in my field. Maybe Cinda had an opening in her business, the Fairy Godmother Home Cleaning Service.

I could certainly use a fairy godmother right about now.

Or perhaps a magic mirror.

Mirror, mirror on the wall... happen to know anyone who's hiring?

FOUR

Nice work, Bozo

Hunter

I cruised the waterfront of Main Street, the windows of my Bentley Mulsanne rolled down, inhaling the brisk marine air and taking in the beauty of Eastport Bay's main drag.

On my left stood a historic church where George Washington had worshipped when visiting Eastport Bay. The white wooden structure with its clock tower and tall, graduated steeple watched over the quaint downtown of the colonial-era city.

On my right, the upscale hotels, high-end restaurants, and tony shops and galleries of Brady's Wharf buffered the street from the harbor, attracting tourists, even in this chilly weather.

It was good to be back after several weeks away meeting with business partners and clients.

Seattle and Silicon Valley had been especially fun places to visit, but I would never want to live in either of them. The old adage was true... there really was no place like home.

Feeling hungry and wanting a true taste of home, I took a

right onto Thames Street, heading for the Cliffhouse, my favorite restaurant.

It was a gorgeous winter day, and I had a yearning for an ocean view while I ate. There was no better reward for hard work than good food and great views, and there was no better venue for both than the Cliffhouse.

The historic inn and its award-winning restaurant sat on a rocky bluff jutting right out into the meeting point of the open Atlantic and Narragansett Bay.

Its panoramic water views and dining room were legendary, and though I'd never say it out loud within earshot of my wealthy new acquaintances, it never failed to thrill me that I could actually afford to eat there now whenever I wanted.

Hell, I could afford to buy the place if I wanted to.

Who'd have thought the Science Olympiad nerd from the poor side of town would grow up to be a jet-setting billionaire?

Well, actually, *I* had.

I couldn't have foreseen all the details of my current life, but I'd known I would do whatever it took to change my circumstances, to ensure I'd always have enough to eat and a decent place to live and nice things to wear—and to show all those snooty rich kids who'd made fun of me I was just as good as them, if not better.

And I'd done it. I had it all.

Almost.

Pulling up in front of the historic mansion that housed the restaurant and inn, I gave my keys to the valet—with a hefty tip—and went inside.

Dark wood and antique furnishings created an elegant but welcoming atmosphere, and the smell of delicious food made my stomach growl.

"Mr. Bestia," the hostess, Miranda, said. "So nice to see

you again. Would you like to sit in the main dining room or in the smaller one near the window today?"

I grinned at her. "Either. But you know I want a water view. Always."

Following her to a petite, beautifully set table in the small dining room, I slid into the bench seat, facing out toward the ocean-view window.

Miranda handed me a menu encased in a fine leather folder. "Would you like a wine list?"

"No. I'm jet-lagged already, so I'd probably drive off into the ocean on the way home if I drank anything right now."

I wouldn't get into it with her, but I'd given myself strict rules about drinking—minimal amounts on special occasions only, never on an empty stomach, and never during the day.

For one thing, I had far too much to do and the stakes were too high to ever let myself get sleepy, foggy, or out of control.

For another, I'd grown up with a daily example of how undisciplined alcohol consumption could ruin your life and the lives of those closest to you.

"Okay, your waiter will be with you in a moment," she said. "Enjoy your lunch."

Everything on the menu looked good. I'd taken a six am flight out of San Francisco this morning direct to Rhode Island and had slept through first class meal service. I could probably have eaten one of everything.

As I perused the entrees, wondering how I'd manage to narrow my choices to just one, my attention was stolen by the conversation from a nearby table.

A middle-aged couple, the only other diners in the small four-table space, spoke in low voices, but their affection for each other was evident in their mushy, lovey-dovey tones.

I couldn't stop myself from peeking in their direction. I'd expected to see two people on a first or second date—you could usually tell. But the man and the woman both wore wedding rings on their left hands, which were clasped on the tabletop.

Huh. Married.

The man must have noticed me watching them because he turned to me with a happy smile. "I'm sorry. Were we talking too loudly? We've been here for a while and finished a bottle of wine. It's our anniversary."

His wife giggled like a newlywed. "Sorry. I don't usually drink."

I raised a hand. "No. No. You weren't bothering me at all. How many years?"

"Twenty-five," they said in unison, then laughed again.

"Well, congratulations, and happy anniversary."

They thanked me, and I made a mental note to pick up their tab.

Twenty-five years. I wondered briefly... if my mom had lived, would she and Dad have made it that far?

Would my father's drinking still have spiraled out of control... or would he have been a completely different man?

Maybe the alcohol would still have won out, and he'd have made her as miserable as he'd made Jack and me. Maybe my mother's early death was a merciful escape for her.

Shaking away the unpleasant thoughts, I decided to order the indulgent nineteen-dollar brisket burger—and some earplugs. The sweet talk from the happy couple *was* sweet, but it was making me feel like an interloper into a private moment.

It also made me jealous.

Neither of them looked older than fifty, so that meant that by my age they'd found each other—and obviously had made the right choice in life partners.

I wasn't having any such luck in my own personal life.

Work was great. I had amazing friends and business partners, but dating was... well, it just wasn't much fun.

At the encouragement of my crazy-in-love newlywed brother Jack, I'd been making an effort to get out more, to meet people, ask out women I found interesting instead of spending all my time in front of a screen, working.

The thing was, it all felt like a waste of time. Several of the women had been nice, but we'd really had nothing in common, and the conversation had been stilted and awkward.

Others weren't so nice.

It had been obvious from nearly the beginning of those dates that they'd read up on me and my financial success and that had been pretty much the extent of their interest in me.

No thanks. I'd rather be alone.

I was at the point of telling Jack he'd gotten the last good one in his wife, Bonnie, and even that courtship hadn't exactly been simple.

Jack had gone to *extreme* measures to lock that one down.

There was only one person on earth I'd ever go to that much effort for… and she wasn't available or interested.

"Are you ready to order, sir?"

The sound of a soft female voice jerked my head up from the menu. I'd been so lost in my self-pitying thoughts I hadn't noticed the waiter's approach.

When I saw her, all the breath left my lungs in a whoosh.

"Kristal?"

I was dazed by a sense of unreality, as if my thoughts had conjured her like a genie. Kristal Bianco stood in front of me wearing a crisp white shirt with khaki pants and navy flats.

And a name badge.

"Oh, Hunter. It's you." One of her hands came up to rest at the base of her throat, her fingers fiddling with the top button on her shirt. "I didn't recognize you with your head down. How are you?"

"Good… good…"

I knew I sounded absentminded, maybe even a little clueless, but my head was spinning, and nothing was computing.

What was she *doing* here?

"So... are you ready to order, or do you need more time?" Kristal prompted.

Finally, the fog cleared. "You... *work* here?"

She smiled, a little tightly. "I do. For the past couple of weeks. I'm still getting my sea legs under me, but at least I'm not doing everything wrong now. You wouldn't believe how many glasses I knocked over the first week—and plates I delivered to the wrong table. So embarrassing. It's not as easy as it looks."

I nodded, utterly confused. "Yeah, I'm sure."

At her expectant stare, I said, "'Oh, uh... I'll have the burger. And an iced coffee... *lots* of sugar. I may look like a man, but actually I'm an oversized ant in disguise."

She didn't laugh at my joke, just gave me a polite, professional response. "Great. I'll put that right in for you. Can I get you anything else right now?"

"No. I'm... good. Thanks."

Actually, I wasn't. I watched as Kristal walked away, trying to make sense of the nonsensical.

She'd grown up on Oceanview Avenue with the kind of house and car and lifestyle I'd only dreamed about back in high school.

Now I was living in a mansion on Eastport Bay's version of Billionaire Row—albeit a leased one I was sharing with six housemates for the time being—and Kristal was waiting tables. What a reversal of fortune.

Cursing myself for being so awkward and tongue-tied, (An oversized *ant*? Really?) I vowed when she returned, I'd pull it together and actually talk to her like a normal human being, find out what was going on in her life.

What could possibly have happened?

Her father had died a couple months back, but Kristal was his only child—she should have been all set financially just from the inheritance alone, not to mention the life insurance Richard Bianco must have had.

Maybe she wouldn't want to discuss it. We didn't know each other that well... in spite of that blistering few minutes of intimacy we'd shared last summer at the Charity Relief Ball.

That unexpected—and much replayed—encounter was the reason I hadn't attended her dad's funeral.

It was already undoubtedly such a hard day for her, I hadn't wanted to compound her misery by showing up and possibly making her uncomfortable with her boyfriend and family and friends standing nearby.

I had sent a card and flower arrangement to her house—who knew if she'd even seen it? That had been the last contact between us.

But now... she was here, and I was here, and well... frankly I was going to die of curiosity if I didn't find out what was going on.

Maybe she was just bored and wanted to get out of the house. Did heiresses do that kind of thing?

When she returned with my lunch, Kristal seemed much more in control than she had earlier—or than I felt myself.

"The brisket burger with beer-battered onion rings... and one cup of sugar with a side of coffee. See? I got it right, Ant-Man," she quipped.

"It's perfect," I said, once again kicking myself over my stupid joke.

The happy anniversary couple got up and moved toward the door, and I lifted a hand in a wave to them.

"Enjoy the rest of your day." They beamed at me and left, holding hands.

Kristal smiled at the interaction while I pulled out my

wallet and handed her my credit card. "Do me a favor? Tear up their credit card slip and put their meals on mine."

"Sure." She smiled and cocked her head to one side. "That's so nice. Friends of yours?"

"No, we just met. But it's their twenty-fifth anniversary. In this day and age, that's a monumental accomplishment. It *should* be celebrated."

"I agree. Maybe I should follow them out to their car and ask how on earth they did it."

Kristal's cynical tone made me curious. "How's Harry doing?"

Her expression flattened. "I hear he's fine. He left the firm and went out on his own. I haven't spoken to him in a while. Will there be anything else for you?"

A pilot light flared to life inside me, setting my blood to simmer.

She's not with Harry anymore.

"No. Thanks." Kristal turned to go, but stopped when I said, "Actually..."

"Yes?" She turned back to me, wearing an alert expression.

"I'm wondering... why are you working here?"

Her entire body tensed, her tone adopting a defensive edge. "It's a nice place to work. My dad's old friend runs the restaurant group that owns it. He gave me a job."

I shook my head. "No... I mean I know it's a nice place. It's my favorite restaurant. I just wondered why you're working at all."

She took a step back from the table. Her fingers twisted together, and she slapped on an impersonal smile. "It's a long story. I'll let you enjoy your lunch now."

"Kristal. Wait."

She darted a look at the door, clearly wanting to escape. But I plowed ahead. "Listen... I'm not sure what's going on, but if you need a loan or something..."

Her face went dark pink in an instant. Her expression shut down, going cold. "I'm fine... thank you. I don't need your money. Enjoy your meal."

She turned and fled from the room, disappearing around a corner.

Great. I'd offended her. Again.

Nice work, bozo.

I couldn't seem to stop putting my foot in my mouth when I was around her. I spent the entire meal trying to come up with the right words to say when she came back with the check, something to mitigate the damage.

But she didn't come back. A different waiter brought the check and asked how my food was.

"Excellent. Thank you." I pulled out my wallet and withdrew a credit card once again. "Where's Kristal?"

"Shift change," the woman said with a smile. "I'll be right back with this."

She departed, and I was left wondering how and when I'd be able to talk to Kristal, to explain that embarrassing her was the *last* thing I'd wanted to do. I wanted to *help* her for God's sake. I'd do anything for her.

For weeks after seeing her—and kissing her—at the party, I hadn't been able to go more than a few minutes without Kristal on my mind.

Honestly, the unexpected liaison still popped up far too often on my internal movie screen. It had played a starring role several times in the shower and late at night when I was alone in my bed.

And it probably had a lot to do with *why* I was sleeping alone—my lack of interest in the women I'd been dating.

Who was I kidding? It had everything to do with it.

No matter how nice or attractive or smart they were... they weren't *her*. And my stupid heart had, for whatever reason, decided to fixate on her. It was beyond frustrating.

I couldn't stand the thought Kristal might be in some kind of bad situation. I hadn't been kidding when I'd offered a loan.

As far as I was concerned, we could just call it a gift and forget about it. My net worth was so high, just the interest on my bank accounts alone brought in nearly three million dollars per day. I'd never even notice a few hundred thousand dollars.

And in spite of her poor taste in boyfriends, Kristal was a good person. I wasn't sure what kind of trouble she was in, but I had a strong suspicion it wasn't her fault.

Whatever the problem was, I wanted to fix it.

Signing the credit card slip, I added a brief note and decided to stop by the Bianco family's house later after Kristal had had a chance to make it home. I could apologize for my idiocy, tell her I was there if she needed me.

Maybe she'd invite me in, and we'd talk. Even if she wouldn't let me help her financially, I could still be a friend.

Before walking away from the table, I pulled several hundreds from my wallet and tucked them inside the small leather folder with the signed slip and the restaurant's pen.

Then I walked quickly to the exit before anyone came back to collect the payment and outrageous tip.

If I wasn't there, Kristal couldn't refuse to take my money.

It was the least I could do.

FIVE

Pity for the Win

Kristal

I peeked from the kitchen door, releasing a sigh of relief as the back of Hunter's head disappeared through the front exit.

When I'd walked into the small dining room, and he'd lifted his head from the menu, I nearly had a heart attack. It was the first time I'd seen him since the *incident* at the party.

He looked just as yummy as he had that night—maybe even better, with a light scruff and dark, windblown hair, wearing jeans and one of those off-white cable knit fisherman sweaters that made even an average guy look like a Kennedy.

Hunter was *not* an average guy.

He was remarkable in every way—including his arrogance at offering me a loan.

Maybe it hadn't been arrogance. Maybe it had been pity. I wasn't sure which was worse.

I jumped back as the kitchen door pushed inward suddenly and nearly smashed my face.

Jana, who'd saved me by agreeing to take over Hunter's table, came in wearing a huge smile.

"Get a load of this," she said, opening the check folder and holding it up to me. "Looks like someone *really* appreciated your service."

Seeing the stack of hundreds, I shook my head in confusion. "He paid in cash? I thought you took his card."

"He did pay with a card. This is your *tip*, girlfriend."

I gasped. "What? That's more than the entire bill—by a long shot."

Jana lifted her shoulders in a happy shrug. "These rich guys—who can figure 'em out? Maybe he was showing off. Maybe he's just nice. Anyway, I'll take his table *anytime* you don't want it."

Lifting the bills, she fanned them under my nose and giggled.

Wonderful. Now my humiliation was complete.

Hunter had decided I was a charity case, and really, who could blame him? He'd made such a phenomenal success of his life. I was couch-surfing and serving his burgers.

Pity for the win.

Although, all things considered, my life wasn't *that* bad. The couch-surfing had been limited to one house—Cinda's.

It had been wonderful to see my friend on a daily basis and get to spend time with Cinda's adorable four-year-old son, AJ.

And working at the restaurant had been fun once I'd gotten the hang of it.

Jana was an awesome new friend, the view couldn't be beat, there was free food, and I was slowly saving toward that apartment deposit.

If only Eastport Bay wasn't so damn expensive. This entire region, in fact, was one of the least affordable in the whole country.

Of course, I would have loved to make a living with my photography, but there was far less demand for art photography than there was for portrait photographers, which I had no experience in.

Even if I could learn the new set of skills required, starting a new business would take a capital investment I simply didn't have.

I'd been scouring the job listings, applying for any and every opening I might come close to qualifying for. So far, no takers.

My classmates had been right about that MFA not being worth the paper it was printed on. Everyone seemed to want applicants with degrees in STEM fields—people like Hunter.

Worry squeezed my neck muscles in a now-familiar sensation. I hated to think about leaving my beloved hometown.

All my memories of my parents were here. The scenery I most loved to photograph was here. My best friend was here.

But as sweet as Cinda was and as much fun as the extended sleepover had been, I couldn't continue to impose on her and her son indefinitely.

I was an adult, after all. It was important to be able to stand on my own two feet, and I was more than a little ashamed I'd never attempted it before now. I mean, yes, I worked hard, but if I'd had a "real" paying job earlier, I wouldn't be in this position.

At some point, I'd have to expand my job search beyond Rhode Island and maybe even beyond New England. I'd lick my wounds, pack up my meager belongings and... leave.

Collecting the cash, I handed it to Jana. "Here—it's yours."

The other waiter held her hands up, shooting me an are-you-crazy look. "I can't take that. It was your table."

"Yes, you can. I gave him to you." I pushed the money at her.

Like Cinda, Jana was a single mom, though her situation

was the by-product of a divorce and an ex-husband who was a dead-beat dad.

The father of Cinda's child didn't even know AJ existed.

She'd fallen in love with him one summer while working at Kingsley Beach. At the end of it, he'd left without a goodbye. She'd found out she was pregnant a few weeks later.

Anyway, if Jana accepted Hunter's ridiculous tip, it would be a gift. If I took it, it would be charity.

"Honey, if you could *give* me a man like that, I'd take him," Jana said with a smirk. "But I have a feeling he's already taken. You should have seen the little-lost-puppy look on his face when I showed up in there instead of you. Believe me... he's *yours*."

I shook off the insinuation, and we ultimately agreed to split the cash.

While sliding his credit card receipt into the register, I noticed Hunter had written more on the paper than his signature.

Pulling it back out, I read the manly scrawl across the bottom of the slip.

Kristal, my offer of help stands. Anything you need. Anytime. Hunter.

He'd added his phone number as well. I frowned at the words and numbers. I didn't ask for him to swoop in and play Santa Claus, and I *really* didn't need a sugar daddy.

My mind flashed back to that dark room at the party. A mixture of shame and pleasure filled my insides.

Did this have something to do with our kiss? Did Hunter think I'd be open to an... *arrangement*?

Mortification set my face and body on fire. Needing to cool down, I retreated to the walk-in freezer and pretended to look for something inside.

No matter what I had to do or where I had to go, I would

not stoop to my stepmother's level and use my "feminine wiles" to get a rich man to bail me out.

If Hunter Bestia thought his shiny new billions could buy me, he had another thing coming.

The next time he came into the restaurant, I really *would* give his table to Jana.

And maybe add a hefty dose of salt to his coffee.

SIX

A New Approach

Hunter

I walked into the living room and fell into the corner of one of the oversized leather sofas with my laptop.

"Doc!" My co-workers/housemates/closest friends from high school called out my nickname.

It was bestowed upon me because I was always trying to get them to eat better and take exercise breaks instead of mainlining coffee and donuts while spending twelve hours straight in front of a computer.

Five of them were there, hard at work—everyone but Tuck, who was basically a bat, staying up all night and sleeping during the day.

Whenever we managed to cross-over early morning work hours with him, he yawned through every conversation.

Since people referred to us as the Seven Dwarves, the guys had nicknamed him Sleepy.

Aiden, Josh, Paul, and Reid all looked up from their own laptops and offered greetings.

Hap, who occupied the other end of the couch, gave me

his trademark ultra-white grin. He'd been a child star on TV in his youth, and the Hollywood glow still surrounded him.

"Hey Doc, welcome home." Now there was a guy who was cheerful, no matter the time of day or night.

I did not share his mood today. "Hey."

"So... how was the trip?"

"Fine," I replied, opening my laptop and starting to work. I had a lot to catch up on, and I wasn't in the mood for chit-chat.

Hap snorted. "You must be jet-lagging—hard. Whenever I travel from the West Coast, I'm wiped."

"Yeah. I'm pretty tired," I agreed because I didn't want to get into it.

Fatigue was *not* the reason for my funk.

On the way home from the restaurant, I'd driven by the Bianco family's mansion and nearly wrapped my Bentley around the trunk of an old-growth beech tree.

There was a Lila Delman Real Estate *For Sale* sign out front.

Stunned, I'd swung the car back around and pulled into the drive, getting out and walking up to the front door, intending to knock.

A heavy, black lock box hung from the door. I knocked anyway and rang the bell. No answer. Stepping to the side, I'd peered in through a window.

The house was empty. All the furnishings were gone. They'd moved out.

Baffled, I'd dialed the realtor's office and found out the mansion had been repossessed by the bank.

Repossessed. I didn't get it. How could this have happened? I'd driven home, my belly tumbling with worry and disappointment.

Hap shrugged at my terse response and went back to his work, but I never managed to fully immerse myself in my own tasks. I'd wanted to apologize to Kristal tonight. Now I had no idea where to find her.

And there was a bigger concern. Where was she living? Was she okay? I couldn't stop thinking about it.

"Hap?"

My friend lifted his head. "What's up?"

"Remember Kristal Bianco from high school?"

"How could I forget? You drilled her name into my brain back then. Kristal this, Kristal that. Why? You two going out?"

"What? No. I just saw her… at the Cliffhouse."

Hap's interest increased. "How's she look? Still hot? Or did she peak in high school?"

"Hardly. If anything, she looks better. Have you heard anything about her? Like, about her family fortune being blown or something?"

The other guys had all stopped working and were listening now as well.

"No." Hap looked around the room as if seeking input from the others.

Each one shook his head no. Hap looked back at me. "Why?"

"She's working there… as a waitress."

Hap's jaw went slack. "Wow. That's weird. I haven't heard anything, but I can ask around. Hey—you gonna ask her out now that she's fallen from the clouds down to the level of us mere mortals?"

I shook my head. "Nah. She's not interested."

Hap waggled his brows. "I *always* thought she was interested."

Seeing my instant glower, he clarified quickly. "In you, dude, not in me. Whoa—get a grip. You're dopier than Dopey when it comes to that girl." He hooked his thumb at Josh.

"I hate that nickname," Josh said in an I've-told-you-this-a-thousand-times tone.

One of our best friends from high school, Josh was literally a genius, but sometimes the minutiae of real life eluded his understanding.

In other words, he could be a real airhead. He could finish a thick book in an hour and write complex code like he was making a grocery list, but he often wore mismatched clothes and almost never got a joke.

"Sorry, Josh," I said before turning back to Hap. "You're wrong. She wasn't interested then, and she's not interested now. I blew it today at lunch. I was just as tongue-tied and awkward as I was back in high school. I think I might have even insulted her. There's no hope."

Hap slapped his own leg. "I *knew* something was wrong. You didn't even gripe about that bag of nasty fast food on the coffee table."

"Hey—" Reid wore his usual glower. "Those were *my* clam cakes, and they were damn good."

Hap ignored our grumpy friend, keeping his focus on me.

"You know what your problem is? You're the *man*—you always have been—but you didn't believe it then, and you don't believe it now. More money's not gonna fix that. You've gotta realize you've always had everything you needed. The right woman's gonna see that—if she's not right for you, no amount of money will matter."

"Nothing matters," Reid growled. "If she's not interested, she's not interested. You can't *make* someone love you."

I felt bad for the guy. At one time, he'd been as happy-go-lucky as Hap, but Reid hadn't been the same since his high school sweetheart Mara had left town without warning and had refused to even speak to him since then.

If anyone understood the pain of unrequited love, it was me, but for my friend's sake, I hoped Reid would get over it soon.

Mara had been gone for years—last I'd heard she was a TV

reporter in Mississippi, of all places, and hadn't even returned to visit her mom in years.

Paul sneezed loudly then blew his nose with a honk before speaking in his perpetually congested voice. "She's taken, anyway. I heard she's with Harry McAllen."

"They broke up," I said.

"Oh." Paul sneezed again. "Where'd you say she works?"

* * *

The party was almost over.

I'd spent way more time here than I would have liked and made far more small talk than I wanted to—I had too much work to do to waste time hobnobbing with the Eastport Bay elite.

But I couldn't leave. Not until I made absolutely sure Kristal wouldn't show up.

I'd gone to the Cliffhouse a couple more times over the past week, but both times I'd been told she wasn't working that day.

Knowing better than to ask for her number or home address, I'd asked the waiter who'd taken over for her at lunch the last time—Jana—when Kristal's next shift was.

She said she wasn't sure.

I would just keep trying to catch her. I needed to tell her I was sorry for making her feel like a beggar, and I needed to find out what could possibly have happened to cause the foreclosure of her family's home.

When I'd gotten the invitation to tonight's cocktail party, I'd immediately RSVP'd *yes*, hoping she'd be here. The hosts were her family's long-time next-door neighbors.

So far, she was a no-show. Unfortunately, the one Bianco I *didn't* want to see *was* here and had just spotted me.

"Hunter Bestia," Margot said, slinking up to me and

sliding a hand around my arm. She squeezed my bicep and raised a brow in apparent appreciation for its size and firmness. "Just the man I wanted to see."

"Hello Mrs. Bianco."

She pursed her lips and gave me a simpering smile. "Call me Margot. *Please.* No need for such formalities any longer. We're both adults now—not even that far apart in age. I married *very* young."

The older woman ran her eyes up and down my body, making me shudder.

"And my, my... how you've grown up. You know I always told my stepdaughter *you* were the one to watch, but she's such a silly—"

I interrupted Margot's flirtation. "Where *is* Kristal tonight?"

Her Botox-ed eyebrows made a valiant attempt to draw together, and her over-filled lips pouted.

"How should I know? Anyway, as I was saying..."

I shrugged away from the long-taloned hand stroking the front of my jacket. "Don't you live together?"

Apparently getting the message—finally—Margot straightened and lifted her lipo-suctioned chin.

"Not as of the past few weeks. I've decided to downsize. Who needs all that room anyway? Now I'm free to travel and not worry about running and maintaining a large household. *You* must be doing a lot of traveling."

She smiled and stepped close again, renewing her transparent attempt to be seductive.

Ignoring her question, I pressed for information. "Where's Kristal living then?"

"I don't know," Margot snapped, clearly annoyed now by my persistence and lack of response to her come-ons.

"I think she's been staying with some friend or another... 'couch-surfing,' I believe the term is. All the kids are doing it these days. We grown-ups prefer more luxurious accommodations. I've got a yacht at the Eastport Bay Marina. It's brand new and *gorgeous*. The master suite cabin is absolutely to die for. *Enormous* bed. You should stop by later and see it."

I frowned in frustration. Margot had no idea where her stepdaughter was living. Kristal could be at a homeless shelter for all this woman cared.

"Sounds nice," I said dismissively. "I see someone I need to speak to, if you'll excuse me."

It hadn't been a lie. I *had* spotted someone I knew—and it might be exactly the person who could help me connect with Kristal.

Liam Paolini, the owner of the restaurant group that managed the Cliffhouse. The man had been a close friend of her father Richard, according to what Kristal had said.

I walked up and offered my hand. "Liam—Hunter Bestia. How are you, sir?"

Paolini smiled. "Ah, Hunter. Yes. Good to meet you. Congratulations on your company. You guys are making some big moves over at Billionaire Bachelor House."

I laughed. "Billionaire Bachelor House? Sounds like some kind of reality show."

"That's what some of the locals are calling it now. I understand you've got kind of an early-days Facebook situation going on over there, and it might turn out to be just as big."

"Not sure about that, but yes, it's going well. We're really happy the hard work seems to be paying off."

My tone shifted to business. "Listen, I wonder if you could answer a question for me. I'm a friend of Kristal Bianco's from school."

That might have been overstating it—"admirer" was closer to the truth than "friend," but I didn't want to freak the guy out.

"I'm concerned about her. I saw the family home up for sale. I heard she's working for you now?"

"Yeah, it's a crying shame what's become of Richard's estate," the guy said. "His wife drained the accounts dry after his stroke, and I talked to one of his law partners who said even his daughter's trust was in trouble."

My attention riveted to him, and my heart rate increased. "What do you mean?"

"Well, they're looking into it, but apparently someone got ahold of the secure passwords and raided it. The entire account's been liquidated, which means Kristal's flat broke."

Harry. He'd been Richard Bianco's protégé and Kristal's boyfriend. No doubt he knew all about the trust and probably had access to Richard's computer at work.

"That's awful. Do they know who did it?" I asked, seething inside.

Kristal's boss shook his head. "Not sure. Last I heard the investigation was ongoing. Hopefully the poor kid will get what her father intended for her eventually—all he cared about was providing for his family. But cases like these can take years. In the meantime, she asked me for a job. She's a hard-worker, that one, just like her dear old dad."

"Do you happen to know where she's living? I mean—I just want to make sure she's okay."

There were plenty of spare rooms at the "Billionaire Bachelor House," not that I had any chance of convincing Kristal to move in.

Dream on, bro.

"I think she's been staying with a friend," Paolini said. "Amanda and I invited her to stay with us—our kids moved out years ago—but she turned us down. Said she didn't want to impose. She wouldn't take a loan, either, though we offered to help her get on her feet. She insisted she didn't want charity, so I put her to work. Least I could do."

* * *

The following night, I showed up at the Cliffhouse near the end of the dinner shift—Kristal's regular shift, according to Liam.

He said she'd be closing tonight, and I was determined to speak to her, even if I had to wait there until midnight to do it.

A hostess I didn't know greeted me. "Good evening. Welcome to the Cliffhouse. Dinner for one?" She looked around. "Or are you meeting someone?"

Yes, but she doesn't know it yet. I shook my head and smiled. "It's just me."

The woman had already invited me to follow her and started walking toward a table when I said, "If you wouldn't mind... could you seat me in Kristal Bianco's section? She's a friend."

The hostess beamed at me. "Sure. No problem."

Leading me to a table along the ocean-facing window in the main dining room, she handed me a menu. "She'll be right with you."

But when my waiter appeared, it wasn't Kristal. Instead it was a man who greeted me.

"Good evening sir. My name is Robbie. May I start you off with something to drink?"

He was a young-ish guy, early twenties, lanky with big feet and hands, reminded me of myself back in high school.

His most distinguishing feature was his eyebrows. Heavy and dark, they rested low over his deep-set eyes, making it look like he was knifing me a death glare. Since I'd never met him, I knew that couldn't be the case.

Robbie just needed a little grooming to prevent the resting-serial-killer-face he was currently sporting.

The big question was, what was he doing here? Confused, I asked, "Is this not Kristal's section?"

The waiter's posture changed, tensing. He stood a little more erect and looked down his nose at me.

"She has a very large party to take care of, so *I'll* be serving you tonight. Are you ready to order, sir, or should I give you some time with the menu?"

The death glare was still there. And based on the tone of his voice, maybe it *was* intentional.

"Oh, uh..." I gave the prix fixe menu a cursory glance—I wasn't here for the food. "I'll have the oysters, the grilled lobster, and the house made ice creams and sorbets."

"Very good, sir," he said sternly. "And to drink?"

"Just water."

So I *was* sitting in her section—she just wasn't going to serve me tonight. I had a sudden suspicion the "shift change" the other day hadn't been a coincidence.

She's avoiding me.

Fine. I was a patient guy.

As I waited for my meal to arrive, I perused the room, looking from table to table. None of the parties seemed inordinately large. There was one table of six, but that was it.

Yep, she definitely asked this guy to take over for her.

Based on the waiter's body language, he had a crush on Kristal and was more than happy to run defense.

Finally I saw her. She came in holding two plates, which she delivered to a young couple across the room.

All my senses went on high alert. Kristal wore serviceable clothing—another combination of white shirt, khaki pants and flat shoes—and she looked beautiful.

Her shiny, dark hair was pulled back in a low ponytail, revealing her high cheekbones and slender neck.

Though I knew she'd been going through her own personal hell these past few months, she showed no sign of it, laughing at something the diners said and giving them the wide, sunny smile that had stolen my breath and warmed my soul so many times throughout our younger years.

No wonder Robbie was smitten, poor guy.

Kristal interacted with her fellow restaurant staffers in the same way, being her smiling, genuine, helpful self.

I knew, because I watched her like a lion stalking a fat wildebeest throughout the rest of the evening.

If she noticed me there, she gave no indication, never looking my way and certainly never making eye contact.

And if she was hoping I'd get bored and leave, she didn't know me at all. I had no trouble sitting for hours while working on a single intricate bit of code. Waiting out the dinner crowd was nothing.

Of course, if time was money—and it was—I was wasting a fucking fortune tonight.

Worth it.

When I'd finished the appetizer, dinner, and dessert courses, I ordered a cheese plate and a cup of coffee, lingering until all but one other table had cleared. Kristal still hadn't even glanced in my direction.

She's almost as stubborn as I am. I smiled. *Almost.*

Robbie the waiter returned. His voice this time was even less polite and held an unmistakable note of hostility.

He darted a glance across the room at Kristal. "My shift is ending soon. Will that be *all*, sir?"

I leaned back in my chair, lacing my fingers over my overly full stomach. "It's been delicious, Robbie, but I'm thinking of an after-dinner drink—how about a bottle of the 2014 Domaine de La Romanée-Conti, Grand Cru?"

The French chardonnay was the most expensive thing on the wine list at six-thousand-two-hundred-and-fifty dollars a bottle.

There was no way the waiter would refuse me and kick me

out—the restaurant manager would have his hide—and the guy's tip on the wine alone would be over a thousand dollars.

Suddenly Robbie's demeanor changed, his gallant attempt to shield Kristal from me coming to an abrupt end.

"Very good, sir. Right away, sir."

As he walked away, I called out. "Robbie? I intend to savor it, and I don't want you to have to wait around. You can go ahead and bring me the bill with the bottle. I'll settle up, and you can go home."

The waiter nodded and sped away toward the wine cellar. I kind of felt bad for the guy.

Kind of. He'd no doubt only been doing what Kristal had asked of him, and who could blame him for carrying a torch for her? He *deserved* a good tip after all the shenanigans I'd put him through tonight.

But the waiter's irritation—or jealousy—wasn't my chief concern. Kristal was.

I'd thought about her all day today, how she'd lost her father then lost her home, how she'd gone from wealthy to basically penniless without warning.

The only part of last night's revelations that hadn't shocked me was that she had turned down any offers of charity, insisting on paying her own way in the world.

While some of the other rich kids in her social circle had been entitled, Kristal had always worked hard in school, earning a merit scholarship to college instead of relying on her father's money to foot the bill.

Since learning of her situation, I'd been wracking my brain for ways to help her. I'd even considered underwriting a large raise for her here.

But even if the restaurant group's owner had been willing to accept my money and funnel it to her, Kristal would be mortified if she ever learned of my donation.

Still, I had to do something.

Finally, when Robbie and the rest of the staff had left, along with the last table of diners, Kristal walked over to me, giving the barely-touched bottle of wine a hard stare before meeting my eyes.

"We're closing."

"I know."

Her eyebrows lifted in a sardonic expression. "Would you like me to bring you a funnel… or may I cork that for you, *sir?*"

"I was hoping to speak with you."

Kristal's shoulders stiffened, and she glanced at the exit. "It's been a long day. My feet are tired. I'm ready to go home."

"Why don't you sit down a minute?" I gestured to the empty chair across from me, joking, "I'll be happy to share my bottle of liquid gold with you. At least I hope that's what this stuff is made of at the price they charge for it."

"What do you want, Hunter?" she asked bluntly, clearly not impressed with either my wine budget or my joke.

Okay then. Cut to the chase. "I want to know why you're avoiding me, why you're having your co-workers take *your* tables whenever I come in."

Kristal's cheeks colored. Her eyes flicked to the side. *That's right, sweetie. You're busted.*

Her gaze came back to meet mine, looking stronger, more determined. She lifted her chin in defiance.

"I didn't appreciate that tip you left last week at lunch."

"Not big enough?" I quipped.

Her tone scolded me. "You know it was way too much."

"Listen, Kristal, it's not that big of a deal…" I wasn't trying to impress her this time but to make her feel better.

She cut me off before I could finish.

"I already know how well you're doing. You don't have to flaunt it," she snapped.

"Is that what you think I was doing?"

She gave the wine bottle a significant glance. At her isn't-it-obvious expression, I changed my tone from cajoling to sincere.

"I'm sorry it came across that way. When I saw you at the Charity Relief Ball, I admit... I *did* want you to know about my success."

I rolled my eyes in a self-deprecating way. "The wine tonight was just a ploy to keep your wanna-be boyfriend from kicking me out. But as far as that tip goes, I'm a generous tipper—sue me. It wasn't that long ago that I was bussing tables every night and on weekends, then waiting tables all through high school and in college. It's hard work, and so many customers leave stingy little tips—or none at all. I was *trying* to be nice."

Kristal's whole body seemed to sag, and her face softened. "I'm sorry. I'm having a rough day—a rough month, actually."

Pouring several ounces of fragrant golden liquid into a wine glass, I pushed it across the table toward her.

"Maybe a couple thousand dollars' worth of chardonnay will take the edge off. Come on. If you make me drink this all by myself, I'm going to get the world's most expensive hangover. Or get mugged on the way home for my bladder contents."

She snickered. "I *have* always been curious about what that wine tastes like."

Sliding into the chair opposite mine, she lifted the glass, bringing it to her nose and inhaling. "You've never ordered this before?"

"Of course not. It's ridiculously overpriced."

Kristal laughed, making me feel like I'd won a prize. I wanted to earn more of her laughter, to see her beautiful smile.

"I still shop at Marshall's and look at the price tags. Old habits die hard," I said.

She parted with a reluctant grin. "So, the old Hunter *is* still in there."

And still just as in love with you as ever.

"Always," I said. I watched her take a sip, close her eyes, and hum. "Good, huh?"

Her eyes opened. "Yummy. Not sure it's worth six *thousand* dollars, but definitely good."

Kristal swirled the wine around in the glass and took another sip.

"It's funny. My dad could afford extravagance like this, but he was never that into 'conspicuous consumption.' Margot was, of course, which is why I'm sitting here with you now."

For the first time ever, I felt a flicker of good will toward Margot Bianco.

"So... you gonna tell me what's going on? Or do I have to order another bottle and stay till dawn?"

Kristal gave me a rueful grin. After a moment's hesitation, she said, "I'm broke."

She laughed, and the sound was a shade desperate. "It feels strange to say it out loud, but it's true."

So it really was as bad as I'd heard. I'd been hoping the rumors were unfounded. "Oh man, Kristal. I'm so sorry."

Her smile stayed in place, but her eyes watered, and she shook her head rapidly.

"No, it's fine. Really. I was never one of those people who needed to be rich, you know? Not like Margot. I think she'd literally rather die than be poor... or even get a job. But I like working. And I don't really need that much—just a place to live, a way to get around..."

She paused and sipped her wine again, licking her lips afterward before joking, "... and this six-thousand-dollar chardonnay."

"I want you to cork it and take the rest of the bottle home."

"*No.* I was just joking, Hunter. I wouldn't take your liquid gold."

"You can share it with the friend you're staying with. Who is it, by the way?"

She gave me a wary glance, her earlier humor dissipating. "Heard about that, did you? It's Cinda. Remember her from school?"

"Cinda Brown? Yeah sure—though that's probably not her last name anymore. I heard she had a kid."

"No. It's still Brown. She's not married."

I had a feeling there was more to that story, but my interest at the moment was focused solely on Kristal and her financial crisis.

"You moving in with her?" I asked.

"Nooooo." She smiled, dragging out the word with humor in her voice. "We get along great, but her house is tiny, and she has a four-year-old. They need their space. I'm going to get my own place as soon as I can afford it."

"How's the money here?" I asked sincerely.

It was an expensive restaurant, but I hadn't been kidding earlier when I'd mentioned stingy tippers. From what I'd seen since joining their ranks, rich people could be some of the most tightfisted.

Kristal lifted her shoulders in a delicate shrug. "Not bad. I'm saving everything I can, but I needed transportation to get to and from work, so I spent some of my earnings on a bike."

I gasped. "You don't have a car?"

She stiffened at my appalled exclamation. "The one I used to drive was leased—Daddy liked for us all to drive new vehicles, thought it was safer—so he leased cars for me and Margot and himself and switched them out every year. When he had his stroke and Margot took over paying the bills... she didn't. They repossessed it."

My insides were in turmoil. Kristal was putting on a brave face, but this had to be horrible for her. I could hardly stand hearing about it. I sat forward, my brain buzzing with potential solutions.

"What about getting a job in the art field? You have a masters, don't you?"

She nodded. "I'm surprised you knew that. Yes, and I've been applying, but I haven't been able to find anything. Everybody seems to want people with technology or math-related degrees. If I'd majored in engineering, I'd be in great shape. Photography? Not so much."

She sighed, swirling her glass again, watching the golden liquid spin instead of drinking it. "I'm probably going to expand my search beyond Rhode Island soon, especially with the cost of rent around here. I hate to move away, but you know... you've gotta do what you've gotta do."

Looking up, she gave me a weak smile to go with the cliché.

Panic compressed my temples. Leave Eastport Bay?

I couldn't let that happen. If Kristal moved away, we'd never get to know each other better, which meant I'd never have a chance with her. She would create a whole new life for herself somewhere else.

With someone else.

A sudden thought popped out of my mouth before I'd even turned it over a couple of times for consideration.

"Work for me."

Her head jerked back. "What?"

"Yes. Doing photography. We need someone to take photos for our website, publicity stuff."

Honestly, my partners and I had never discussed publicity shots, but we might need some at some point, right? I could certainly find *something* for her to do.

Kristal's forehead creased as she stared at me. "I don't need your charity. I told you before—"

"It's not charity. It's work. You're a photographer. We need photographs."

"Hunter." Her arms folded in front of her as she shook her head back and forth. "I appreciate what you're trying to do, but there's no way you need a full-time photographer on staff at a software company. Anyway, I don't do that kind of photography. I'm an art photographer. I shoot landscapes. I'll just keep looking. Something will turn up somewhere."

Somewhere. Possibly out of state. She had no living family here now. An out-of-state move would mean I might never even see her again.

"You know..."

A new idea percolated inside my brain. A new approach. "There is a way *you* could help *me*."

"What do you mean?"

"You could move in with me."

SEVEN
Snow White

Kristal

"Excuse me?"

Either the wine had gone to my head in record time and I was hallucinating, or Hunter Bestia had just made me an indecent proposal.

He kept going, speaking in his deep, matter-of-fact voice. "You said there's not enough room at Cinda's place. My house is *huge*—way more space than I need. You could move in, stay as long as you want—rent free."

Flames of indignation licked at my skin. "I'm *not* going to be your mistress!"

Hunter's dark eyebrows shot up. He raised both hands in front of him in a *Whoa there* gesture.

"No, not like that." He laughed. "I live there with six other guys. And before you make assumptions, I'm not proposing a reverse harem situation either."

"I don't even know what that is."

He swept a hand through the air as if erasing his last words. "Forget I mentioned it. Anyway, the mansion is divided into five condos. Each one has several bedrooms. We've got tons of extra space. You could live there, keep your job here while you look for something else... and you could keep taking your photographs around Eastport Bay."

Most of those things sounded great, but I still wasn't clear on the living arrangements—or why he'd make the offer.

"With all of you guys there and how well Chipp is doing, you can't possibly need help to pay the rent."

He lifted a finger. "I already said you wouldn't have to pay anything."

"Right. So, what's the benefit to you of having me move in? I don't get it. How would I be helping you?"

Hunter held my gaze, and a few beats passed before he answered. "Well... here's the thing... one of my housemates—Hap Bailey, remember him? He was the president of the drama club."

I nodded, and he went on. "He's not part of Chipp. He's living there while he gets his own company off the ground. He's a director and producer now—he's actually had a couple projects, a documentary and a short film, do very well."

"That's cool. I remember he acted as a kid—his sister Jessica too, right?"

"Right," Hunter said. "But he hasn't acted in years. He prefers being behind the camera these days. His latest project is a reality show, a competition, and he's planning to film the pilot at the mansion—kind of a demo to shop around to the networks. We're all happy to help him, but we need a woman."

Oh no. I was getting a bad feeling about this.

"If it's anything like The Bachelor or Big Brother, I don't want to go anywhere near it."

"This one's different. Hear me out."

"Okay fine, but I can't see being in *any* kind of reality show."

"Like I said, this one's totally different," he continued, undeterred. "That's why I think it'll be a big hit. It's called

Tech House. Groups live together and work on inventing new tech—kind of like what we've done with the Chipp software. Then they put the finished products up against each other in front of judges—like a Shark Tank situation. Viewers watch week after week as the work is done and the teams live and work together in the competing houses. Hap's really talented. I know he can pull this off and make it great. I'm his major backer, so of course I want it to succeed. That means appealing to a wide demographic—which means having mixed-gender teams. You'd only be pretending to work on the software, of course. Really, you'd just need to be there."

I narrowed my eyes, studying him for signs of duplicity.

"It's a little hard to believe you couldn't find *any* other woman willing to move into a *mansion* with seven millionaires..."

"Six millionaires and one billionaire," he corrected with a cocky smile. Why did I find that look a teensy bit appealing on him?

"Right," I said. "Not exactly a hard sell. So why me? Surely one of you has a girlfriend who'd be willing."

He gave a casual shrug and lifted his hands to the sides, palms up. "We're all single at the moment. Filming is supposed to start next week, so we're running tight on time."

Hunter offered the same charming grin that had stolen my breath at the party a few months ago.

"Plus... we know you. You wouldn't steal our code and run off with proprietary information or anything. Wait—would you?"

I laughed at his tease. "No."

"And you need a place to stay," he continued reasonably. "While you're there, maybe you could shoot a few photos for Chipp and maybe for Hap too. I don't know that much about show production, but they probably need stills from time to time."

I *did* need a cheap place to live. Free was even better.

No doubt there really was plenty of room to spare. I was familiar with the subdivided mansion they lived in, and it was massive. And if I was truly helping him and his friends, it wasn't charity.

And I could stay in Eastport Bay.

Everything he said made so much sense—if you put aside the small detail that I'd be *living with seven guys.*

"It's just temporary," Hunter added, "until the pilot is done, and you've saved enough money for your own place."

That was what sealed the deal for me. It *wasn't* forever. I could live there for a few weeks while I got back on my feet. I could still take my winter photographs around Eastport Bay.

You could get to know Hunter better.

No. No, that wasn't a consideration. Hunter was being kind, offering me a mutually beneficial deal. This had nothing to do with what had accidentally happened between us at the charity ball, and I wouldn't—would *not*—let my mind go there.

Where it's gone over and over again since that night.

More than once I'd drifted off to sleep satiated and buzzing after fantasizing about those moments with him in the dark. Though it hadn't lasted long or gone all that far, really, that accidental interlude had been the most sensual, electrifying experience of my life.

Which meant I should *definitely* say no to his offer.

"If you're sure it's not an inconvenience, and it would really be helpful to you..."

"I'm sure," he said instantly. Then his posture relaxed, and he graced me with that spectacular carefree smile again. "It would be a win-win."

I pressed a fist against my stomach to quash the sudden quivery feeling. "Then I accept. And I appreciate it. Truly."

"Don't mention it. I can send some movers over to Cinda's house this weekend to pick up your stuff," he said.

"There's not that much. Almost everything went in the auction."

Hunter frowned. "I'll send a small van then."

In a brilliant flash, the smile returned. "You know of course, you're going to get a new nickname out of this?"

"How so?" I hoped he didn't mean it would ruin my reputation in town, though after the house auction and the repossession of my car, I wasn't sure I had one of those left anyway.

"Well, you know my brother Jack refers to us as the Seven Dwarves."

"He does?" I giggled. "But you're all so tall."

"He does indeed. Which makes you..."

I laughed again. "Snow White."

"Exactly. So be on the lookout for wicked witches bearing apples," he teased.

"I just hope a handsome prince doesn't come along and catch me sleeping. The last thing I need in my life right now is the complication of a relationship. He'd probably demand a refund anyway." I laughed. "Harry said I was a bad kisser."

Hunter's expression had gone rather solemn, the happy smile disappearing.

Oops. I shouldn't have turned the conversation so heavy. This was a good night, and I had a lot to celebrate.

Reaching across the table, I covered one of Hunter's hands lightly with mine. "Thanks for this, Hunter. I'm really grateful. You've always been a good guy, and I'm glad we're friends."

Before I could remove my fingers, Hunter flipped his hand over, squeezing mine gently inside its warmth. The unexpected contact shot darts of heat up my arm and down to the tips of my breasts.

"Harry is an idiot." His voice was quiet and deadly serious.

"And for the record... you *deserve* a prince. Don't ever doubt it."

For a second, we held searing eye contact that made my heart do a double somersault in my chest.

I hastily extracted my hand, reached for my purse, and stood.

"We should go. I don't want to get in too late and wake up Cinda and AJ."

EIGHT

The Pact

Hunter

I'm glad we're friends. Friends. Whoopee.

The phrase echoed through my mind all the way home.

I'd offered Kristal a ride to Cinda's house since *no way* would I let her ride her bike through the streets this late. But she'd already called an Uber, and it was waiting for her as we'd exited the restaurant.

She seemed kind of eager to get away from me anyway.

I kicked myself for that prince comment. I'd never been much of a poker player. Oh well, the game wasn't over. I'd have at least a few weeks with Kristal in my house every day to show her I was the right man for her.

We'd parted with a plan for her to move in on Monday. Which meant I had to go home and break it to my housemates that we were getting a new roomie.

A new *friend*. Ugh.

I'd waited on pins and needles for Kristal's answer to my proposal, and for just a few minutes there, after she'd agreed, it had felt like all my dreams were coming true. My hastily concocted plan had actually *worked*.

And then she'd slammed me right back into the friend zone with a few words.

It was high school all over again. She'd obviously forgotten all about our "seven minutes in heaven" while I had dwelled on it non-stop since that night a few months ago.

But still... I couldn't get *too* down about things. She was moving in with me.

With me and six other housemates, but whatever, it was a start. And she wasn't moving out of state. So there was still a chance for us.

There was also a chance Hap was going to kill me.

He was the first person I sought out when I got home. Hopefully my old friend would still be awake—and be willing to go along with the ruse.

Part of the story I'd told Kristal had been true—Hap *was* looking for his next big project, and he *had* mentioned the idea of a reality show.

The rest had been pure invention. *Yeah, we're going to call it "invention" because "lie" has such an ugly ring to it.*

At worst it was a white lie because I'd told it for the very best of reasons—to convince Kristal to accept my help.

I found Hap in the kitchen making a midnight snack—an enormous tuna sandwich. As Kristal had declined my offer to send the unfinished bottle of wine home with her, I plunked it onto the counter beside Hap's plate.

"The sommelier recommends French chardonnay with tuna salad on whole wheat."

Hap picked up the bottle, checking the label. "Looks fancy." Pulling out the cork and sniffing the open neck, he said, "Smells expensive."

"It was," I said. "Consider it a bribe."

Hap shot me a suspicious look. "A bribe, huh? What's going on?"

"You know how you've been looking for the right show to produce?"

"Yeah..." Hap took a big bite of his sandwich but kept his eyes on me, paying attention.

"I've got an idea."

Hap swallowed and swiped his mouth with a napkin. "Okay, shoot."

"It's a competition. Different teams live and work together, competing to produce the most innovative tech. An expert judging panel picks the winner from the competing houses and helps them market their finished product as the grand prize. Call it Tech House."

My friend's eyes brightened. "That's not half-bad. There's nothing like it in the market, but it's not so different that no one would understand what it is. You gotta sell these things with one sentence, you know?"

Hap spread his hands apart in the air like he was visualizing a marquee. "It's like Big Brother meets Shark Tank meets Robot Wars."

"I haven't seen that last one," I said.

"It's on BBC. Kinda fun. Nerdy guys building big boy toys."

"Sounds familiar," I joked. "So what do you think? Is it something you could pull off?"

Hap leaned back against the counter, lifting the wine bottle and taking a pull. "Whoa." Giving the label a closer look, he said, "This stuff is *good*."

"It should be—that's a six-thousand-dollar bottle of wine you just swigged like Coca Cola."

"Sweet."

He took another drink then focused his attention back on me.

"I can definitely see how it would play out. It's interesting, might even get picked up by a network. But it would be expensive—film crew, lighting, set decoration, location rental for at least two different houses, wardrobe, makeup, editors. I'm not interested in working on a shoestring budget and turning out a rinky-dink product, so I'd need to find some co-producers and associates to help foot the bill."

"I'll pay for it."

"What?" Hap pressed one finger behind his ear and inclined his head toward me. "Not sure I heard you right."

"I said I'll pay for it—everything. Whatever you need, just let me know, and I'll write the check."

Hap looked around, as if addressing an audience, though it was just the two of us.

"*Those*, ladies and gentlemen, are the magic words. And... Action!" He slapped his hands together like a film set clapperboard.

"I'm not joking, Hap. I really want to do this. Soon."

Getting serious again, Hap studied my face. "What's *really* going on? Why the sudden interest in becoming an executive producer? Does this have anything to do with that debutante you've been moping around about? You trying to impress her or something?"

"Not exactly."

I told Hap about my conversation with Kristal earlier tonight, about her need for a place to live and the white lie that had popped, fully formed, out of my mouth when she'd mentioned moving out of state.

"That's why one of the Tech Houses has to be this one," I explained.

Hap shook his head, laughing. "Oh man. Most guys, when they want a girl to live with them, buy a ring. You're gonna underwrite an entire TV show just for the chance to be near her?"

I rubbed my forehead and laughed right along with him. "I know. It sounds a little crazy. But I've already told her we're doing it, and she's agreed to move in. It would only be for a few weeks. Besides… it's too soon for a ring. It might scare her off."

Hap's laughter increased in volume, and he slapped me on the shoulder.

"Boy… you have got it *bad*. But why the hell not? Let's do this thing. Maybe we can put the other house in Boston, so I can drive back and forth easily. I'll make some calls in the morning."

Tucker wandered into the kitchen, yawning and stretching, clearly having just woken up and ready to embark on his nocturnal workday.

"What's going on in here? Oh man, you made tuna?" he said, spotting Hap's half-eaten sandwich and sounding envious until he noticed the wine. "And paired it with a 2014 Domaine de La Romanée-Conti? What are you thinking?"

At his offended glare, we burst into laughter again.

"We're celebrating," Hap said.

"Celebrating what? Another Fortune 500 company sign on?" Tucker asked.

"No. Even better," I said. "We found Snow White."

* * *

The rest of the guys didn't find it so amusing.

There were nothing but scowls around the large dining room table the next morning. Even the donuts and assorted pastries I'd provided instead of the healthful breakfast I usually insisted on hadn't sweetened their moods.

"We don't need another roommate," Josh said. "Especially a woman. I won't be able to walk around in my boxers."

"We've lived together nearly a year, and I've never seen you walking around in your boxers *once*," Hap pointed out.

"Yeah, but I might want to at some point. Now I can't," Josh complained.

I hadn't expected back handsprings and Friday Night Lights cheers from Reid, but my grouchy friend's annoyance seemed to be more with the show than the prospect of a female housemate.

"There are going to be cameras around all the time. I hate cameras. I like my privacy."

"I don't want to be on TV either," Aiden said, blushing at the idea of it. "You grew up in front of cameras, Hap, but it's going to be weird for the rest of us."

His shyness didn't surprise me. "Look, it'll probably never make it to TV. It's nearly impossible to get past all the hurdles to get a show on the networks—even cable or streaming is a longshot. It's just a pilot."

"You'll get used to it in no time," assured Hap. "The guys I work with are really good. They know how to be unobtrusive."

"That's what I'm worried about," said Reid. "We'll get so comfortable that someone's going to say the wrong thing while wearing a mic and let out proprietary information."

"Hap and I will have final say on the edits," I told him. "There won't be any leaks."

"What about my allergies?" Paul sniffled and wiped his nose. "All those people in and out dragging pollen and dust through the house."

"We'd enforce a strict no shoes policy indoors—or we'll make the crew wear those little bootie things over their shoes," Hap said, lifting both arms in a pleading gesture. "Listen guys, it's just for a few weeks. You'll be helping me to possibly get a new show off the ground. Tuck gave us the thumbs-up even though you know the production schedule will wreak havoc with his wacky Interview-with-the-Vampire sleep schedule."

"Not to mention what you'd be doing for Kristal," I said, pulling out the big guns and going for the sympathy vote. "You remember how nice she was to all of us when the rest of her clique teased us for being geeks or just ignored us entirely. How often did she say hi and ask how your day was back in high school—Paul?"

"Every day," he admitted reluctantly.

"Josh? Did she ever call you an airhead? No—she called you by your name, which she took the time to learn, by the way."

"You guys call me 'airhead' all the time when you're not calling me 'Dopey,'" Josh complained.

"Yeah, but we're your friends," Reid said. "We insult you because we love you." To me he said, "You're right. She *was* super-nice."

"She still is," I assured them. "And she's had the year from hell. Her dad had a stroke, then he died. Her boyfriend broke up with her. Her greedy stepmom blew through the family fortune in record time and lost their house and cars, and someone apparently wiped out her trust fund. Kristal's waiting tables, riding a bike to work, and sleeping on a couch at Cinda's house."

"Cinda Brown?" Aiden asked, his interest clearly piqued. "Is she still single?"

"Yeah, but she has a kid," Josh said.

Aiden shrugged. "So?"

"Hey..." Paul's tone indicated a sudden realization. "*Kristal*'s single too."

There were a few nods and looks of interest. My hands fisted instantly, and the hairs on the back of my neck rose.

"No. *No way*. You heard what I said. She's been through a lot lately. The last thing she needs is her roommates sniffing around her. Kristal is strictly off-limits."

Reid's eyes narrowed in a calculating expression, and an

evil grin sneaked across his face. *Including you?* his challenging gaze seemed to say.

Out loud he said, "I completely agree. Let's all make a pact right now—Kristal is our friend. We're doing this to help her out, and *none* of us..."

Here he stared pointedly at me "... will make a move on her. *Everybody* got that?"

All the guys made some kind of verbal agreement except for Paul, who nodded and lifted a hand while going into a sneezing fit.

When he finished, he asked, "Whose condo will she sleep in, because I don't think my allergies make mine the best choice... unfortunately. She might wear perfume or something."

"Mine," I answered immediately.

At the silence and blank looks, I explained. "Reid and Aiden are already sharing. So are Josh and Tuck. Paul has to have his own. That leaves mine."

"And Hap's," Josh pointed out, oh-so-helpfully.

Hap blinked a couple of times, then came to life. "Yeah, but I'm gonna have some crew from California crashing with me. They'll probably fill up all my bedrooms plus the sleeper sofa."

I shot him a grateful look. "Exactly. So, it's settled then. She's moving in on Monday, and production of Tech House begins as soon as Hap can pull the crew together." I beamed at all of them. "Let's make a TV pilot."

And win the girl, I added silently, smiling as I congratulated myself on my brilliant plan.

NINE
Friends and Housemates

Kristal

What a stupid plan.

My bike glided to a stop, and I set my feet on the ground, standing astride the bicycle and giving the billionaire bachelor house an uneasy once-over.

The mansion itself was gorgeous, a brick Tudor revival. An impressive arched alcove entry was surrounded by historic stonework and topped by an intricately carved stone crest.

On either side of it, rows of tall, leaded glass windows let in the light and featured colorful stained-glass inserts.

Though from the outside the spectacular manor home looked like a single residence, I knew it had been divided into five condominiums with a shared central gathering space for parties, or in the case of these guys, for use as a common work area.

They must have all been home at the moment because it looked like I'd stumbled upon a luxury car show or a billionaires' convention with all the pricey, flashy sportscars parked in the circular front drive.

What was I thinking?

My belly swam like a tide pool full of minnows. Was I really doing this? Perhaps the more important question was… could I afford *not* to? Inexpensive accommodations in this town were rare—free was a godsend.

Not that Hunter was a god.

He might *look* like one, but he was definitely human and in possession of flaws just like everyone else. I just hadn't located his yet, unless you counted overt confidence.

Brilliant, charming, and incredibly good looking, he must have had *some* negative qualities.

No doubt living with him would reveal them in short order. Familiarity bred contempt, right?

Very few people got *better* upon closer inspection—I'd learned that lesson well thanks to Harry.

And skyrocketing from modest means to having billions of dollars at your disposal didn't typically *improve* someone's personality, though I had to admit, Hunter had been pretty darn charming Friday night.

As we'd sat together in the deserted restaurant, chatting and sharing the obscenely priced wine, I hadn't been able to prevent myself from marveling over the changes the years had made in him.

Like a master artisan, time had layered just the right amount of weight onto his frame, turning tall and thin into muscular and manly, and chiseling the most appealing laugh lines at the sides of his eyes and mouth.

I hadn't consumed nearly enough wine to affect my judgement, so I could only blame my extreme attraction to him for knocking me off kilter long enough for me to say "yes" when I probably should have said "no" to his absurd suggestion.

I'd gone home that night and promptly dreamed about the amazing kiss we'd shared—in glorious detail—and had done so every night since then.

In fact, some of my dreams had taken it far *beyond* kissing.

It was mortifying and completely inappropriate, but what could I do? Dreams were dreams.

I banished the butterflies that insisted on parading a circle around my belly button every time I thought of that look in Hunter's eye when he'd declared Harry an idiot.

What had he meant? Was he speaking in general terms? (In which case I wholeheartedly agreed) Or had he been referring specifically to the kissing thing?

It doesn't matter.

When I got to know Hunter better, this ridiculous crush I seemed to have developed would pass, and we'd live platonically ever after—or at least for the next few weeks.

We weren't likely to see a ton of each other anyway—he was busy running a company.

I would stay busy as well, working at the Cliffhouse, looking for a new job, and trying to squeeze in some photography. I was still trying to help the Guild's interim director get up to speed too, so all my free time would be filled.

Besides, we might be sharing a house, but it was a *big* house—seventeen thousand square feet divided into five individual units. It wasn't like we'd be under each other's noses all the time.

And it's not like I'll be under him, *as I am every night in my dreams.*

With those fortifying thoughts empowering me, I walked up to the mansion's front door and let myself in with the key Hunter had sent over with the movers.

At least I wasn't nervous about seeing the *other* guys again—they'd all been really nice in school, the kind of boys you'd trust to date your little sister or go into your house while you were on vacation to pet-sit and water your plants.

Hap met me in the entryway. "Kristal! So good to see you again. Wow—you've hardly changed."

"Hey Hap." I returned his brief cheek kiss. "Great to see you too."

He'd changed—a lot. Like Hunter, he'd filled out and looked much more grown-up than he had back in school, though he'd always been cute.

As a child actor, Hap Bailey's curly hair, sparkling eyes, wide grin, and funny lines had made him a favorite on family TV as well as a "safe" outlet for little girls and pre-teens to direct their puppy love.

By the time he'd moved to Eastport Bay and started high school, he'd developed into a quick-witted, if somewhat awkward-looking teen, gangly in that way adolescent boys raised to an art form.

The gangly was *gone.* Tall and well-built, Hap had grown into a very handsome man.

Though I'd heard his interests leaned more toward behind-the-camera work these days, he looked like he could easily slide into a leading role on television or in the movies.

"Come on in. The asylum can always use another lunatic," he joked as he led me through the warmly lit stone foyer into the main gathering area.

It did look like a madhouse. There were people everywhere. All of Hunter's housemates appeared to be present, stationed in various spots around the room with their laptops.

Camera operators, grips, and production assistants moved through the space, setting up equipment, adjusting lighting, and rolling out cables.

A stylist fussed with the messy mop atop Tucker Donnegan's head. He appeared to have just woken up.

He'd changed a lot since high school as well, but I recognized him instantly.

Yawning widely, he spotted me and lifted a hand in a wave. He rolled his eyes as if to say *Can you believe all this?* before his mouth stretched in another wide yawn.

Reid Nolan, another classmate of ours, wasn't quite so laid back about the situation. He was literally growling at a makeup artist who stood in front of him, holding a powder puff in one hand and a brush in the other.

"I just have to knock the shine off," she protested, reaching toward him.

"I'm going to knock someone *out* in a minute," he replied, his glower making his icy blue eyes even more wintry.

"Not you of course," he assured her. "But no one said anything about makeup. I want a word with our *glorious leader.*"

Though Reid was a few years younger, I remembered him from school. He'd been a generally happy guy who'd loved computers, golf, and his high school sweetheart Mara—and not in that order.

Mara had always come first in his life, which had made me and all my girlfriends envious. That kind of devotion was compelling.

Today, he looked anything *but* happy. "Where *is* Hunter anyway?" he snarled.

That was a good question. I scanned the room, looking for him, but he was nowhere in sight.

From the sofa nearest me, I heard a quiet, "Hello Kristal."

I turned to see Aiden Gleason, a guy who'd suffered from such crippling shyness in high school that these were literally the first words he'd ever spoken to me.

Aiden might have been the biggest ugly-duckling-to-beautiful-swan story in the room.

Tall and sculpted now, with thick, dark auburn hair and clear, tanned skin, he would have caused a stampede of estrogen back in school if he'd looked anything close to this.

"Hi Aiden. It's so good to see you again."

Paul and Josh were also on that side of the room and offered their greetings. I addressed the three of them.

"Thank you so much for agreeing to give me a place to stay."

Aiden blushed deeply—something that *hadn't* changed since school. "Oh, no problem. We're all glad you're here."

"Yeah. Especially Hunter," Josh said and giggled like a little boy.

Paul sneezed. "Speak of the devil..."

I turned to see Hunter enter the room. He wore jeans and a polo today, somehow managing to make the casual attire look even more dashing than the button down and dress pants he'd been wearing at the restaurant.

He didn't appear to have noticed me yet, but every cell in my body came to full attention at his presence. He radiated energy, confidence, and a charisma that seemed to increase the wattage of the lights in the room.

Walking over to Reid, Hunter reassured him about the makeup thing then spoke quietly with Hap before going to the long dining table. He picked up a greasy takeout bag, peered inside, and snorted in disgust.

"Whose is this?" He held it up. "Guys—come on. Don't eat this garbage. I made egg-white omelets and Kodiak waffles with kale-mango-chia smoothies."

"Sorry, Doc," Tucker called out. "But if I'm gonna be dragged out of my bed and forced to be awake this early... there's gonna be some bacon and cheese involved."

There were laughs throughout the room, and all the guys, Tucker included, got up and moved toward the kitchen.

"He nags us like a mother, but he *is* a good cook." He winked. "We like to give him a hard time."

"What *exactly* is in that shake?" Paul asked as he passed Hunter. "I want to make sure I'm not allergic."

"You're cool, man," Hunter assured him with a hand on his shoulder. "A hundred percent allergen-free."

When the other guys had all disappeared into the kitchen, Hunter finally turned to me.

My belly flipped as those unbelievable turquoise eyes met mine, zeroing in with a concentration that seemed to penetrate down to my soul.

"Welcome home," he said with a warm smile and walked toward me. He had this relaxed and easy way of moving, which probably should have set *me* at ease.

Instead, the closer he got, the more my nerves vibrated. By the time he reached me, I was a jittery mess.

"Yes, well, it's just temporary—but thanks. Where should I put my stuff?"

"The movers have already put your boxes in your suite upstairs." He reached for my suitcase and overnight bag. "I'll take those. Follow me. I'll show you the way."

We walked toward a staircase lined on one side with rich, walnut paneling and a highly detailed hand-carved wooden balustrade on the other. A window wall of stained glass lit the landing and reflected kaleidoscope colors onto the shiny wood flooring.

"I'm staying in this unit?" I asked, trailing him up the stairs. "Whose is it?"

Without turning back, he said, "It's mine. It's the largest and has several bedroom suites. I hope you'll like yours."

Oh. Wow. I released a long, shaky breath, willing my nerves to settle. "I'm sure it'll be great."

Following him into my suite, I took in the large bed, the low dresser, and the cozy sitting area in front of floor-to-ceiling ocean-facing windows, which featured a long, padded window seat.

The room smelled fresh, like new carpeting, and looked like it had been torn from the pages of a home decorating magazine.

The size of it amazed me. Apparently, the guest rooms in

this place were the size of a typical master suite. And the view was incredible. I was instantly drawn to the wall of windows and walked over to look outside.

"This is beautiful. Even nicer than the room I moved out of at home." I turned to Hunter. "Thank you."

He was beaming. "I'm glad you like it. I want you to be comfortable and feel at home here. As I said, you're welcome to stay as long as you like. Anything you need here, just let me know."

Something about the tone of his voice worried me. He sounded... proud, almost proprietary. I really hoped he wasn't attempting to pick up where my father had left off and trying to take care of me.

Though, admittedly, I wasn't in the best financial state, I didn't want his pity, and I *certainly* didn't want Hunter to view himself as my guardian or caretaker. I'd never allow myself to be in that childlike position again. I was no one's responsibility but my own.

To make sure Hunter understood that, I said, "Thank you, but as *I* said, it will only be for a few weeks—just until I can save enough money to find a place of my own."

His smile dimmed. "Of course. And we all appreciate you being here and helping out with the show. We should be filming most every day over the next few weeks, but don't worry about the schedule—it's supposed to emulate real life, so you just go to work when you need to, do your thing, and Hap can shoot your parts whenever you're here."

"I still only have part-time hours at the Cliffhouse, but I'll be trying to do as much photography as I can too," I said. "I'm trying to increase my output so maybe I can earn a little more that way."

"I've seen some of your shots in that gallery at Brady's Wharf. Beautiful stuff. You're really talented."

Warmth bloomed in my chest and migrated to my cheeks.

Hearing that Hunter admired my work filled me with bubbles of iridescent happiness.

Down girl. He's just a friend.

A friend who was helping me out with a place to stay. A friend who was now my roommate. So, *no.*

"Thank you. If only the judges at the International Photography Awards would agree with you, I wouldn't be bumming a place to stay," I said.

"Oh, you're entering?"

"Yes. *Again.* I should probably give it up, but desperation makes for amazing motivation. If I were to win my category, it would really drive up the asking price for my photos and prints."

"Well, good luck," he said. "And I don't want to belabor the point, but you're welcome as long as you need a place to stay. I'm glad you're here—we all are."

Hunter paused, his eyes dropping to my mouth. My belly clenched, and my toes curled inside my heavy socks and boots.

"Listen... about that night at the Charity Relief Foundation Ball," he said, "I don't want you to feel uncomfortable..."

I jumped in before he could let me down *easy*. "I know—it meant nothing—absolutely nothing. I mean, it was a total accident. I've barely even given it a thought since then."

Unless you count every day and almost every night.

"I'd nearly forgotten it happened until you mentioned it just then," I lied.

Hunter's lips flattened into a thin line. "Right. An accident. Same here. We're friends, so you don't have to worry about me trying to make any moves on you or accidentally-on-purpose running into you leaving the shower or anything."

My mouth went suddenly dry at the mental image, and I felt a twinge of disappointment.

What was *that* about? I was a *mess*. I would have to watch myself around him over the next few weeks, so I didn't embarrass either one of us.

We were friends. We were housemates. That was it.

"Right. Good. Good to know. Thank you for clearing that up. I'm so glad it won't be awkward between us. Just really, really happy." My words trailed off at the end, but at least they'd been the right ones.

Hunter's mouth opened with a smack, and he began to move toward the door. "Okay then. I'll leave you to get settled. I think Hap wants to shoot some kind of opening scene, let's-meet-the-team kind of thing tonight, so whenever you're ready, come on down and we'll... pretend to be strangers."

He left and shut the door behind him.

Staring at it, then looking around the unfamiliar room, I felt like we were.

TEN

Sheer Torture

Hunter

Well, at least I knew where I stood with her.

When Kristal had stepped into the house—my house—I'd felt a swell of hope and excitement that had nearly knocked me off my feet. I'd literally had to suppress a victory whoop.

After all the years of wishing and dreaming, Kristal Bianco was *living* under *my* roof. I would get to see her every day.

But with a few words, she'd made it abundantly clear—she was not and had never been interested in me.

I'd just been saving face with that "Right, same here," comment, but Kristal was "really, really happy" we were *friends*.

She'd forgotten what to me had been a mind-blowing, unforgettable kiss, said it had meant "absolutely nothing."

All that hope now felt like a sandcastle drowned by high tide, drifting away grain by grain until there was nothing left but a sad little blob on the shore.

My *brilliant* plan to win her over was doomed right out of the gate, and now I would get to live with the humiliation and frustration. Every. Single. Day.

I went back downstairs where six pairs of eyes turned toward me.

"Well?" Paul asked.

"Well what?" I barked back, highly irritated at my friend's all too obvious interest in Kristal.

"What did she say?"

"Yeah," Aiden said. "Does she like it here?"

"How could she like it here?" Reid growled. "You guys drooled over her like a pack of puppies. I wouldn't blame her if she never unpacks her suitcase. She's probably climbing out of one of the upstairs windows to escape right now."

"She likes it fine," I said. "She said her room was nice." Shooting a grateful look toward Hap, I added, "Thank the set designer, would you?"

I'd prevailed on Hap's friend Mary Ellen to redesign and furnish my own suite in preparation for Kristal's arrival. It looked great to me, but what did I know? Kristal had seemed to like it, and that was all that mattered.

"Thank her yourself," Hap said. "She's coming over in half an hour to make over everyone else's rooms. She mentioned being extra eager to get a look at the *master* bedroom," he added with an exaggerated eyebrow waggle.

"She already has. That's where Kristal is staying," I said.

Paul shot up out of his chair. "You moved her into your bedroom?"

Rolling my eyes, I bounced my hands in front of me in the universal sign for *calm down*. "I moved *out* of it, idiot. I'll be staying in a guest room while she's here."

Josh gave me a bewildered glance. "Why did you give her your room?"

"Because it's the nicest one. I'm being a good host." Not wanting to discuss it further, I changed the subject. "Now can we try to get some work done before the film crew comes back from lunch? We're behind."

"And whose fault is that?" Reid asked.

Hap and I pointed at each other simultaneously then burst out laughing.

* * *

By the end of the second week we were settling into a new normal.

The filming seemed to be going well, and everyone was getting along. The guys' fears about having Kristal living there seemed to have been replaced by sheer delight at her presence.

But I couldn't share in it.

Not that I didn't love having her around. I did. *Too much.* She was even sweeter, and funnier—and sexier—than I'd realized.

Having known her for so long—but only from afar—it seemed almost surreal to see her walking around the house in cutoffs, a flannel shirt, and a pair of fuzzy knee socks.

Did she have any idea how alluring the thrown-together casual ensemble was?

Everything about her was captivating, from her throaty laugh, to her sharp and funny conversation, to her bewitching green eyes and beautiful smile.

And she seemed to be totally unaware of any of it.

It was sheer torture. After a few days it became obvious I wasn't the only one of the "dwarves" who was harboring a severe crush on Kristal.

Paul followed her around like a puppy dog, always managing to get hungry whenever she was in the kitchen and sitting next to her on the sofa in our home theater whenever we all crashed after a hard day's work to watch movies or reruns of *The Office*.

My housemates had started dressing better, and someone

—I hadn't pinpointed the guilty party yet—had started wearing cologne.

Anytime Kristal said something remotely funny, all the guys laughed like they were at a stand-up comedy show. When she'd admitted her love of animated films, they'd "confessed" to their own secret "kid movie" favorites.

She basically never had to get her own drink refill or carry her own laundry up from the lower level where the washing machine was.

But Kristal didn't seem to notice the pandering and drooling that got on my every last nerve.

She treated *all* of us with kindness and friendliness. Nothing more.

Just like in high school.

And she was a good sport about the Tech House show, playing her role for the cameras so well Hap started musing aloud about her potential as an actress.

"You've already got the waiting tables part down," he joked. "You're basically ready to move to Hollywood."

"Sounds good." She laughed, playing along.

"She doesn't want to be an actress," I harrumphed. "She's a photographer."

"What crawled up your ass and died?" Aiden asked. "We're going to have to re-distribute the nicknames around here cause you're out-grumping Reid these days."

He leaned back in his chair to put himself in Reid's sightline. "Hey, you wanna be the new Doc?"

Without looking up from his computer, Reid said, "I want to move *out* of this madhouse altogether. This show better not get picked up by the network. I'd rather die than have Mara see me on it."

He pointed a warning finger at Hap, who laughed. "Well, that *is* kind of the idea. But if it does get picked up, they'll shoot it with a new cast."

"They'll never find a cast of bigger idiots than these," Reid muttered.

Josh laughed. "Nah. He's still Grumpy."

Unable to get into the jovial mood of the others, I headed for the door. "I'm going for a run."

I put in my earbuds and hit the street, headed for the open waterfront where I could clear my head and wear myself out physically.

Though I had on lined athletic pants and layered shirts, it was bracing near the water. The icy air and ocean spray hit my face like a hard slap.

Good. I needed a slap.

This whole crazy situation was my fault. Reid was right—the filming was disruptive to our work. We'd gotten less done in the past couple of weeks than we had since starting this venture. The whole idea behind living and working together was to get *more* done.

I felt bad for luring Kristal here under false pretenses and forcing everyone else to go through the stupid ruse of filming the reality show for *no* reason.

I felt even worse for myself.

She hadn't magically fallen in love with me, and she wasn't going to.

Which made it torment to live with her. We were together all the time physically but miles apart emotionally. It was almost worse than not seeing her at all.

No matter what I did, I just couldn't seem to manage to view her as a friend. I'd tried, but it was impossible, and I wasn't sure what to do about it. Maybe *I* should be the one considering moving out instead of Reid.

Returning to the house covered in sweat, I jogged up the stairs and headed straight to the shower, still ruminating on the situation.

My wireless earbuds blasted old-school Stones as I moved

on auto-pilot through my room toward the bathroom and shucked off my pants. Then I stripped my damp shirt and sweatshirt over my head.

I realized my mistake when the garments dropped to the floor just inside the bathroom door.

Beside a small pile of women's clothes.

Included among the items were an incredibly sexy pair of hot pink panties and a matching bra.

My heart stopped then resumed beating at a new, much more erratic pace.

Kristal's clothes. Kristal's room. *Fuck.*

Before I could grab my sweaty clothes and flee, the shower door opened, and Kristal stepped out.

Her hair was twisted up in a towel. Other than that, she wore nothing but a look of utter shock.

"Oh," she squeaked, her hand clamping over her chest as she scrambled for the towel hanging on a hook just outside the shower stall. She hurriedly wrapped it around her torso, but it was too late—I'd seen everything.

And I do mean *everything*. All that smooth skin. Full breasts that made my fingers flex on the thin air around them.

The tempting dark triangle at the apex of her thighs.

Obviously, I should have apologized and left immediately, but my body was frozen in shock.

Even though she was now wrapped in the towel, I couldn't stop my eyes from cataloguing the glorious details in front of me.

The flushed cheeks, the feminine curves, her long, bare legs, the adorable little feet with those bright red toenails.

All that combined with the clean scent of her skin and the sounds of her rapid breathing filled my senses and tumbled my brains.

Nope. Just-friends would *not* be happening today. Or ever.

Kristal stared at me, her wide-eyed gaze dropping to take in my sweaty—completely naked—form.

Which caused me to look down at myself.

Fuck.

That Texas-sized erection? It had added California to its territory and was threatening to annex South America.

Finally managing speech and motion, I bent and snagged my clothes from the floor. Holding the shirt in front of me and the pants over my ass, I blurted, "Sorry," and fled the room before Kristal could scream, "Get out" and grab a can of mace or something.

I berated myself all the way to my *new* living quarters.

How could I have been so stupid? I'd done *exactly* what I promised Kristal I'd never do—accidentally run into her coming out of the shower. Now she was going to think I did it on purpose.

So much for not making things awkward.

After my own shower—which was of the ice-fucking-cold variety, I opened my laptop to look at real estate listings.

Our lease on the mansion was up soon anyway. Even if the other guys wanted to stay here, it was high time I found a place of my own.

Naturally, I'd keep paying my portion of the lease so Kristal could keep this unit as long as she needed, but either way, this living arrangement had to come to an end—the sooner the better.

Until then, the only thing I knew to do was avoid her as much as possible.

If I couldn't be her friend, I'd just have to be a ghost.

ELEVEN
Secret Peach

Kristal

Hunter was acting weird.

I sat at the long dining table with all the guys. While most of them were in a lively mood, chatting and laughing, Hunter was in his own world, brooding and silent throughout lunch, looking down at his phone more than he looked up at the friends surrounding him.

Maybe, like Reid, he was weary of the ever-present camera crew. But even later on, after they'd left for the day, he stayed quiet, keeping to himself as he worked on his laptop in the corner of his favorite couch.

Maybe it was the lingering aftermath of Shower-pocalypse?

We'd discussed it, laughed uncomfortably at the mishap, and vowed to move past it days ago.

God knows I'd tried to. Unsuccessfully.

The sight of him naked had been engraved into my mind's permanent record like carvings on a marble monument.

And what a monument it was.

I'd never thought of Harry as lacking in that department.

But after seeing Hunter's full package… well it was hard for mere mortals to compete.

If the incident had affected him the same way, Hunter was hiding it well. More likely his aloofness and absence was due to the stress of work. It was all these guys seemed to think about.

Hunter, being the founder of the company, took a larger load on himself than any of them. He'd been working insane hours the past week.

That worried me.

My father had been obsessed with work, staying at the office late into the night most weekdays and rarely even taking an entire weekend off.

There was no doubt in my mind his driven, workaholic nature had contributed to his stroke and early death.

Getting up from my own chair in the great room, I walked over to where Hunter was working. I lay a hand on his shoulder, and his body tensed instantly.

"Take a walk with me," I said softly.

He barely looked up. "Can't. Too much to do."

Having expected him to say exactly that, I was undeterred. I wrapped both my hands around his forearm and tugged playfully.

"You've been working non-stop all day. Have you even *looked* outside? Online commerce will survive without you for an hour. Come on."

I leaned back and pulled, succeeding in shifting Hunter's large body mere inches.

Finally, he looked up at me, his sea-blue eyes colder than I'd ever seen them before.

Whoa. He really *was* stressed.

"Someone else can walk with you," Hunter grunted.

"I'll go," Paul said, followed by a loud sneeze.

"You probably shouldn't go out in this cold," I told him

then turned my focus back to Hunter. My mind scrolled for a suitable lure.

"Besides, Hunter mentioned a secret beach he knows of that I want to check out for my next series of photographs," I said. "Toni at the Sandcastle Gallery wants some new ones, and she specifically asked for nautical shots."

I gave Hunter a doe-eyed smile and *might* have added an extra note of persuasion to my voice. "Come on—it's nearly the golden hour, and I *really* need some new shots."

Heaving a defeated sigh, he closed his laptop and set it to the side. "Fine. I'll show you where the beach is, then I've got to get back. Grab your coat."

Victory.

Unfortunately, it was a short-lived one. The drive in his car was painfully silent. Workaholic that he was, Hunter must have still been thinking about all the things he needed to do.

Well, I'd *force* him to lighten up and have fun, if that was what it came to.

Pulling the Bentley down a narrow gravel and shell road, he parked facing the water and came around to my side to open the door.

"How did you find this place?" I asked as I got out and looked around.

"Jack and I used to ride our bikes all over when we were kids—we had a lot of empty hours to fill," he explained.

I had a feeling there was more to that story. Hunter always avoided conversations about his childhood.

"We'd check out any interesting trail we found, exploring," he said. "One day we found this beach. No one else ever seems to come here."

Grabbing my camera bag from the back seat, I followed him down a rocky path to a gap in the cliff wall. From there we picked our way over the dark rocks down the sharp slope to the water.

The hidden beach was gorgeous. Natural and untamed, it featured interesting rock structures and frost-tipped seagrass that protected it from the view of passing drivers or nearby homes.

"Wow. This is amazing." I clicked off shot after shot, finding fresh inspiration everywhere I turned.

As I worked, Hunter stayed silent. Several times I called him over to share an exquisite angle, to see a particularly intriguing shell, a comical hermit crab waddling across the pebbled sand.

He gave me murmured responses, remaining stoic, before going back to gazing silently out at the ocean.

At one point, I aimed the camera lens at him, hoping to capture his profile or at least elicit a response from him. He must have seen me in his peripheral vision because he held out a spread palm, blocking me from getting a shot.

Laughing, I took a picture anyway then zoomed in and clicked off several shots of Hunter's hand as I moved around him, pretending to be a fashion photographer and faking a bad English accent.

"Oh yeah. That's it, baby. Give it to me. Show me that palm. Okay, now the knuckles. Oh yeah. Beautiful. Gorgeous."

That managed to elicit a chuckle from him. "What's got you in such a good mood?" he asked with a reluctant grin.

"What's got you in such a bad one? You've been in a funk for the past week."

"Nah. Just have a lot on my mind. This is nice though. I love the beach in winter."

"Really?"

Hunter nodded. "This is my favorite time of year. It's so quiet and peaceful, and the spare beauty of it just sort of speaks to me."

He lifted his shoulders and let them fall. "I've always been a minimalist, I guess."

For a moment I just stood with my jaw hanging open and my heart pounding.

Who *was* this guy? And how could he be so perfect? It was like he'd been designed in the Made for Kristal Factory.

"What?" he asked when he noticed me staring.

"I can't believe you just said that. It's like you just read my mind and spoke my thoughts out loud. No one ever agrees with me about the winters here. They complain they're too long, too cold. They run off and spend a few months in Florida or California to avoid them."

I turned my eyes toward the sinking sun and its purple-pink reflection glowing on the gently swaying ocean. "But I'd never want to leave here in winter. It's always been my favorite season. It's so beautiful. It's like magic."

Suddenly self-conscious about my effusive language, I laughed. "I always thought it was just me, that I must be a little crazy."

Hunter waited a long moment before saying, "It's not just you."

TWELVE

Sponging Off the Chipp Charity Fund

Hunter

And I was *definitely* a little crazy. Or a lot.

As Kristal gazed out at the water and talked about her love of Eastport Bay winters and their indescribable beauty, I'd moved closer to her, drawn in by hers.

She was magic, and I was a helpless mortal, captured in her spell, apparently for life.

It didn't matter that she saw me as only a friend. It didn't matter how hard I tried to avoid her, tried to pretend indifference. I was absolutely mesmerized by this woman, and there seemed to be nothing I could do about it.

Pathetic.

No doubt I should have been taking advantage of all the women throwing themselves at me. I should probably have accepted one of the numerous offers of no-strings-attached sex and slept with someone—anyone—to help me get past my obsession with Kristal.

But I hadn't. Not once since she'd moved in. Other women bored me. I just couldn't get interested in anyone who didn't look like her, sound like her, laugh like her, move like her.

"What do you mean?" she asked softly.

Looking down at her upturned, expectant face, which was exquisitely lit by the sunset, I was vaguely aware I was probably supposed to respond.

But the only words I could come up with were *You're beautiful*, and the sole thought in my mind was how much I wanted to kiss her.

What would she do if I tried? Push me away? Slap me?

Or worse… laugh it off?

Would she tell me it was a mistake, as she'd labeled our first kiss at the charity ball?

Even with all those fears ricocheting through my brain, my head bent, bringing our faces into closer alignment.

I couldn't stop myself—I was going to do it again.

Please don't let me screw this up…

Loud hissing accompanied by a strangled sort of honking noise startled us apart. From the corner of my eye, I detected something big and white approaching at an alarming rate of speed.

"Watch out!" Throwing an arm around Kristal, I pulled her behind me and spun to face our attacker. Whoever he was, he'd have to kill me to get to her.

Oh. It was just—

"It's Romeo," Kristal shouted. "Run!"

Grabbing the back of my shirt, she started pulling me toward the nearby cliff wall. "Hurry, Hunter. He's vicious."

I laughed out loud as my feet stumbled backward thanks to her persistent tugging and the shifting pebbles underfoot. "He's a swan, not a Rottweiler."

The "harmless" swan let out an explosive snort and lifted his wings, spreading them to their full span as he charged us.

"Oh shit!" I took Kristal's advice and ran, turning to

scramble behind her up the cliff while Romeo extended his neck and nipped at my heels.

At the top we both turned to look down, breathing hard.

There below, floating just off the beach, was the reason for the bizarre attack. Romeo's mate, Juliet.

Eastport Bay's resident lovebirds were frequently seen around town, swimming in the harbor that bordered Main Street or in the town park's pond. I'd even spotted them in the bay from my bedroom window once or twice.

This was the first time I'd shared a close encounter with the swan couple, though. If I had my way, it would be my last.

"Wow. He is *serious* about protecting his woman," I said.

Kristal grinned. "A very heroic quality. Mute Swans can be quite aggressive when it comes to defending their mates and their territory. I guess your private beach is actually *their* private beach. Are you okay? Did he nip you?"

Craning my neck to see the backs of my legs, I said, "I don't think so. The skin doesn't seem to be broken. Thanks for the warning, by the way. I'm not sure if I could have taken him man-to-man."

She laughed. "I don't know... with the right motivation I think you could be pretty badass."

Warmth washed over me, sending blood to my muscles—and to my cock, which was apparently determined to take every little kindness from Kristal as some sort of cosmic sign.

But it wasn't a sign. She was making a joke—simple as that. We'd been driven off the beach by a swan, and she was making light of it.

My cock was an idiot.

And so was I. I'd come perilously close to making a fatal mistake—attempting to kiss Kristal when she'd made it clear time and time again she only wanted friendship from me.

Saved by the swan. I owe you one, Romeo.

Feeling like my feet were made of lead, I commanded myself to turn away from her and started walking to the car.

"We should get back," I called back over my shoulder. "The good light's almost gone, isn't it? Or if you want to stay a while longer, I'll leave you the car and just run back to the house."

Once I'd said it, I fervently hoped she'd take me up on that offer. I was filled with a charging energy I had no outlet for. A run would do me good.

But of course I wasn't that lucky. Behind me I heard Kristal following.

"No. I got a lot of good shots," she said. "We can go back together."

If the ride there had been quiet, the drive home was silent as a tomb. I was aware of every shift in Kristal's posture, the sound of her breathing, the soft scent of her body lotion wafting across my nose as the car's heating vents kicked in.

What was she thinking over there?

I wished for just a few minutes I could read her mind, find out what had been going through it as we'd stood there on the beach, facing each other only inches apart.

Had she *wanted* me to kiss her? If I hadn't been swan-blocked and had succeeded in making a move and taking her into my arms, would it have annihilated our friendship and our living arrangement?

What a fucked-up mess I was.

Apparently wallowing in unrequited love all throughout high school hadn't been enough for me. I'd had to go and ruin my adult life as well.

Something would have to change soon. I couldn't take much more.

Back at the mansion, I parked in the driveway. Instead of obeying the urge to leap from the car and run away from her, I compelled myself to act like a *sane* person and go around to the passenger side to open Kristal's door.

"Thank you. And thank you for taking me," she said as she stepped out of the car and walked toward the house with me. "I know you were busy, and it was a lot to ask."

I shook my head. "No problem. You were right. I needed a break. To be honest, I think we're all going a little stir-crazy. It's been over a year of non-stop fifteen-hour workdays for all of us."

"No wonder you've made such a success of your company. You drive yourself—and everyone else—so hard."

I gave her a sardonic look. "Are you saying I'm a mean boss?"

"I'm saying I don't think I've ever met anyone who expects so much of himself and others and has such ambition—for success, power, respect—except for maybe my father."

My brows lowered. "You say that like it's a bad thing."

"No, not really. It's just... well, he missed out on a lot of good things in life. And the doctors said stress contributed to his health crisis and premature death."

Stopping at the front door with my hand on the door pull, I turned to her. "If I didn't know any better... I'd say you were worried about me."

Kristal's tone didn't match my facetious one. Instead, she sounded completely sincere. Her big green eyes seemed to penetrate down to my soul. "I do worry, Hunter. I care about you."

For a second, I couldn't breathe. What was going on here? And why hadn't we started *this* conversation a little earlier before reaching the front door?

"Well... you don't need to worry," I said cautiously. "I've got everything under control."

A crashing noise from within the house made me jump. Pulling the door open, I ran inside to find pure chaos.

Reid was on a rampage, red-faced and shouting at Hap.

"You *said* you were going to get a different cast! Now the network wants to keep going with *us* in the show? There's no way. I'm a programmer, not a trained monkey.

"I'll move out. I'll quit," Reid threatened. "I should be spending more time at my *own* company headquarters anyway. And my apartment in Providence is looking *real* attractive right about now. Did you know someone dropped a key light on my laptop this morning?"

"I told you I'd pay for it. Please. It's just a couple more weeks till filming is done," Hap pleaded. "We're screwed if you leave and we have to start all over or try to edit in some other dude as a replacement. Come on, man."

Being the peacemaker that she was and never having witnessed Reid in this state, Kristal walked right up to him, getting way too close to his impassioned hand gestures for my comfort. I followed closely behind her.

She put a hand on Reid's arm. Without turning to see who had touched him, he jerked his arm away, knocking Kristal's hand aside, which caused her to stagger back from the unexpected force.

Instinctively, I moved forward, my hackles rising. Reid was my friend, but he'd just crossed a line.

He spun around, spotting Kristal, and did a double take. He held his hands out to her. "Sorry."

In my opinion, he didn't sound sorry enough. My hands clenched into fists at my sides.

"It's okay, Reid... just calm down," Kristal soothed. "What happened?"

"Nothing," he snarled.

Her tone softened even more, and she moved toward him again, reaching out to touch him like a powerless child trying to comfort an aggressive bear.

"Did you hear from Mara?"

Instead of calming him, the question had the opposite effect on Reid. Anger flashed hotly in his eyes as he stepped back from her touch.

"*Of course* I didn't hear from her. Even when I had my PR department send a press release to her TV station and a personal invitation for her to cover my company's IPO announcement ceremony on Wall Street—which she turned *down*, via email. I guess she's too busy covering fender benders and county fairs down there in Po-dunk, Mississippi to come cover news about the fastest-growing social media network in the fucking *world*."

The volume of his voice had grown with each successive word, and so had his passionate gesticulations.

I didn't like Kristal standing so close—not when Reid was clearly distraught over the most recent snub from his long-lost love and behaving like a volatile powder keg. I moved to stand beside her, placing a hand lightly on her back.

She ignored me, keeping her focus on Reid. "I'm so sorry," she said. "I don't know why she's acting like this. It doesn't seem like the Mara I remember from school. All I can think is she must be hurting in her own way."

Reid's face deepened in color, and his expression grew stormy. "I'm not *hurt*. I'm pissed. And you're no better—moving in here, getting everybody worked up."

"Hey man," I said in a warning tone, holding up a hand in an attempt to silence him.

Kristal's head jerked back in surprise. "What are you talking about?"

Reid went on. "Hap's always trying to shoot around *your* schedule. Paul's pouting twenty-four-seven."

He flipped a hand at me. "You've got this guy so twisted up he doesn't know whether he's coming or going. Even poor Josh has fallen under your spell. It's what you women *do*. How long are you gonna stay around messing with their heads and sponging off the Chipp charity fund anyway?"

Kristal's gasp was loud in the sudden silence of the room. Even Hap was dumbstruck.

That's it.

My temper flared like a wildfire finding fresh fuel. Moving between Reid and Kristal, I got in his face.

"That's *enough*. Look, I know the 'press opportunity' didn't turn out the way you wanted. I know you've been unhappy these past few years, and we've all put up with your pissy moods and one-word answers because we're friends and you're a programming genius who *has been* an asset to the company. But Kristal is an invited guest. If you have a problem with that, maybe it *is* time you moved out."

Kristal made a distressed noise. "No. I'll move out. I don't want to cause problems."

Turning to her, I spoke calmly but firmly. "No. You're staying—as long as you want to. This isn't about you—it's about Reid and his unresolved issues with another girl."

Other voices came from around the room, supporting the statement and encouraging Kristal to stay.

"*Please* don't leave." Hap clasped his hands dramatically. "I *really* can't re-cast two of you."

Some of the blustery wind left Reid's sails. "It's true."

He let out a long breath, and when he continued, he did sound repentant. "It isn't about you. I just... lost it for a minute there. That had nothing to do with you, Kristal."

Turning to Hap, he said, "But I do need to be spending more time in Providence. I've been doing a lot online and by phone, but it's my company—I've got to start putting in more face-time."

Reid held up his hand with two fingers extended. "Two weeks. Okay? Two more weeks... and then I'm out of here."

Looking around the room at all our housemates, he said,

"No offense guys. I love you, but I'm not good company for anybody these days." Then he turned to Kristal. "I'm sorry. Really. I shouldn't have said that."

She nodded, still looking as if she was on the verge of tears. "Okay."

It definitely *wasn't* okay, and I had a lot more to say to my longtime friend about it, but here in front of everyone wasn't the place. I put a hand on Reid's shoulder, squeezing hard.

"I was about to grab a beer and sit out on the terrace. Want to join me?"

He met my eyes, understanding from my look and tone it wasn't a request but a *strong* suggestion.

Reid grimaced. "Sure. Sounds good."

I shot Kristal a quick glance that held a one-word promise —*later*—then steered Reid toward the back door where a beverage cooler and some serious straight talk awaited.

THIRTEEN
Like Siblings

Kristal

As soon as Reid and Hunter stepped outside, the entire room seemed to sigh in relief.

I looked around, feeling more awkward and uneasy than I had on my first day here.

Was there any truth to what Reid had said? Had I caused problems in the house? The thought of it made my stomach cramp.

Smiling as if nothing at all unusual had happened, Josh got up and walked toward me. "There's pizza in the kitchen if you're hungry. I'm going back for seconds."

"More like thirds," Hap corrected.

"Want me to get you a plate?" Josh asked.

"Oh. No... thanks. I'm just going to heat up a microwave dinner and take it upstairs. I need to shower, and then I'm going to turn in early. I have to work the breakfast and lunch shift tomorrow."

As I moved past him, Hap's hand tapped my arm, stopping me. He spoke in a low voice. "Don't listen to Reid. He's a bonehead. Everybody likes having you here—*including* Hunter."

I tried to read his loaded, raised-brow expression. "Are you sure?"

"Of course," Hap said. "You're like a sister to us all. Sometimes siblings fight, but in the end, you're still family."

I nodded and walked away, eager to get my food and retreat to the privacy of my room where I could think. I truly hoped I wasn't the source of some sort of rift between the guys.

I'd grown to care for all of them. Hunter most of all. The thought that my presence might somehow hinder his new company's growth or upset his long-standing friendships tore me up inside.

What was it Reid had said? *You've got him so twisted up he doesn't know whether he's coming or going.*

What did that even mean? If he was suggesting Hunter was hung up on me, he was dead wrong. Since I'd moved in, Hunter had acted like nothing but a friend.

Or as Hap had suggested, a brother. *Ugh.*

Even this evening on the romantic private beach when I'd stared up at him in the sunset glow and basically begged him with my eyes to kiss me, he'd done nothing. Felt nothing.

The heated moments we'd shared at the Charity Relief Foundation Ball were clearly a faint memory for him, if he even remembered the incident at all.

I, on the other hand, was tumbling deeper and deeper every day. And when Hunter had gotten in Reid's face and stood up for me, shielding me with his body and his words?

Oh Mama. That had *done* something to me.

This was bad. Instead of getting less attractive on closer inspection, Hunter had only gotten better.

He was smarter, funnier, kinder, and more handsome than

I'd even realized. How could a woman *not* fall in love with him?

In fact, I was falling for all the guys—in a fond, sisterly sort of way when it came to the others.

As an only child, I'd always longed for a sibling. Living here, I'd felt a sense of family that had been missing from my life since early childhood.

And that was also bad. Because this was only temporary. I couldn't let myself forget that.

As much as I might want to at the moment, I couldn't move out immediately. I wasn't quite there yet on the necessary funds. But the time was coming, and I needed to prepare myself to see all of them less, perhaps almost never.

A jagged shard of loss scraped my heart. When I thought of the possibility of not seeing Hunter every day, the scrape deepened, becoming a gouge, stinging around the edges and aching at the center.

I *definitely* needed to prepare myself for that separation, because if I didn't, the wound was likely never to heal.

Climbing into bed, I tried to relax enough to fall asleep, but my mind wouldn't turn off. So I went with it, letting my thoughts go where they wanted.

Predictably, they turned to Hunter. Which meant my fingers went where *they* wanted to go, sliding beneath the covers toward the waistband of my panties.

No. Not helpful.

I gave myself a mental slap and folded my hands together over my stomach *on top of* the covers.

Ugh. I was never going to fall asleep this way. I needed to shift my thinking.

Instead of fantasizing about and longing for something that was obviously never going to happen and keeping my focus so pitifully trained on Hunter, I needed to start looking in other directions.

Maybe I'd finally accept one of the offers I occasionally got from restaurant customers to go out for coffee or dinner.

Yes, that was it. I needed to start dating.

* * *

My thinking must have been along the right lines because the next morning it was as if the universe manifested the perfect opportunity and seated him in my section.

Tall, and strawberry blond, the man smiled up at me with a dazzling set of teeth and eyes the color of ripe blueberries.

"Good morning," I said. "Do you know what you want, or would you like to hear our breakfast specials?"

"I would like to hear about anything you want to tell me." His flirtation was so straightforward and friendly it was nearly wholesome.

Laughing, I recited the chef's latest breakfast creations, but the guy ordered something basic, scrambled eggs with wheat toast and fruit. We chatted lightly whenever I stopped by his table to check on him, and he wished me a good day when he left.

At lunchtime, I was surprised to see him back again, sitting in the same spot.

"Hello again," I said. "Can't get enough of the Cliffhouse's fabulous cuisine?"

He grinned. "Or its beautiful employees."

When I gave him a chiding glance, he said, "Seriously. Have you seen the woman at the front desk? Stunning."

I laughed, thinking of Patricia, who *was* quite attractive... for a seventy-nine-year-old. "I'm sorry to disappoint you, but Patricia is taken. She and her husband just celebrated their fiftieth."

The guy snapped his fingers and screwed up his face in mock disappointment. Then he gave me an appraising glance.

"Maybe *you'd* be free later then? After your shift. I mean, you're no Patricia, but I'm in town for a couple of days, and I'd love to see the sights with a local."

Instead of answering his question, I responded with one of my own. "You look very familiar. Has anyone ever told you that you look like someone famous?"

"I have one of those faces," he said casually as if he heard it all the time. "So what do you say? If you're worried about going off alone with a stranger, the manager of this place knows my parents. They own one of the houses along Oceanview Avenue. He can vouch for me."

I narrowed my glance. "I thought you said you wanted to sightsee."

"I do. My parents may own a house here, but that doesn't mean they're in town. It's one of their properties, and I'm visiting it for them to make sure it's being taken care of and run well. I'll be happy to show it to you... but I'd prefer to see *your* favorite Eastport Bay venues. Shall I come back and pick you up when you get off work?"

I *would* check with my boss to verify the guy's story, but I got a good feeling from him.

"Sure. I'd love to. It's been a while since I played tour guide. And you won't have to come back. I'm off in a half hour. We can just leave together."

"Great." He beamed at me. "I look forward to it."

The guy had paid for breakfast in cash, but he gave me a credit card for lunch. When I took it to the register to ring it through and saw the name on the card, I realized why he looked familiar. I'd seen his face on the nightly news.

Before I could take his slip back out to him, Jana came charging into the back office.

"Did you *see* who's out there? Larson Overstreet from WNN. He's so much taller than he looks on TV. And hotter."

"Really?" I said blandly. "I hadn't noticed."

When my shift ended, Larson and I walked out of the inn together. A familiar black Bentley was parked in front. Hunter got out, wearing a determined look.

"You're a little late for lunch," I joked to cover the instant attack of nerves brought on by his unexpected appearance. "Robbie might get you a to-go box since you're his *favorite* customer."

Hunter came right to me, appearing not to even notice Larson's presence or famous face.

"I'm not here for lunch. I came to give you a ride home. It's too cold out today for your bike, and there's ice on the roads. It's not safe."

"Which is why Tucker gave me a ride to work," I said sensibly. "But I'm not going home now. I have plans."

Turning to gesture toward Larson, I said, "Hunter Bestia, this is Larson Overstreet. His family has a house here in Eastport Bay. Have you two met?"

Hunter's gaze strayed from my face to take in Larson's svelte six-foot-something frame, well-tailored clothing, and perfectly in-place hair. He frowned but grasped Larson's hand in a firm handshake.

"No. Good to meet you. Visiting your folks?"

Larson smiled. "Just their beach house. I'm in from New York for the weekend. I recognize you—congratulations on the success of Chipp. So you're a friend of Kristal's?"

The frown deepened as Hunter ascertained Larson and I were on a first name basis. He flicked his eyes to me before staring directly into Larson's.

"We live together," he said bluntly.

A yelp of a laugh escaped my throat. "Along with six other people," I clarified quickly. "We're housemates. We're actually filming a reality show pilot—I'll tell you all about it in the car."

Larson arched a tawny brow. "Really? That should be an

interesting story. I look forward to hearing it almost as much as I look forward to your tour of Eastport Bay's finest highlights."

Hunter's frown morphed into a full-on scowl. "Could I speak to you for a moment, Kristal—*privately*?"

Touching Larson's arm, I asked, "Would you mind? I'll just be a minute."

He smiled. "Sure. I'll get the valet to pull the car around. Hunter—good to have met you."

Hunter gave him a curt nod then pulled me to one side of the inn's covered porch.

"What is this… a date?" He spat out the last word like it was a bite of rancid meat.

"No. He just asked me to show him around town."

My answer sounded more defensive than I'd intended. I had every right to spend time with Larson Overstreet or any other man I wanted to see.

And yes, to *date* if I wanted to. Hunter had certainly made no claim on me.

"He was one of my customers today, and we struck up a conversation. He's very nice."

"You *just* met him?" Hunter said. "So then you have no idea if he's really nice or not. He could be a serial killer for all you know."

"He's a national news anchor. I highly doubt he's a serial killer. And if I do go missing, at least you'll know where to find him."

"That isn't funny," Hunter hissed under his breath, darting his eyes toward Larson then back to me. "You can't go."

"What?"

I blinked a couple of times, taking a beat to make sure I'd actually heard him right. *Can't?*

"Of course I can, and I will. I'll see you later at home."

I turned to go, but Hunter caught the sleeve of my coat. "Wait—I think we're supposed to do some extra shooting for the show today."

His gruff tone made it sound like he was accusing me of playing hooky on a test day.

Giving him a patient smile, I said, "And I'm sure Hap will be in raptures when I show up with a nationally known TV star. It'll put the pilot, as he would say, 'Over the top.' Goodbye, Hunter. I'm going on my 'date' now, and I will see you *later*."

Turning away from his scowl, I walked toward the passenger side of Larson's luxury rental car, where he stood holding the door open for me.

He wore a quizzical smile. "Everything okay?"

"Sure. Just fine. You're not a serial killer, are you?"

Larson barked a laugh. "No."

"Good. Then we're fine."

He hesitated, shooting a quick glance to where Hunter stood glowering down at us from the porch.

"It's just that your… friend doesn't seem too happy."

"Hunter's fine," I assured him before slipping into the warm car. "He and I are like siblings. Sometimes brothers and sisters bicker."

Clearly having overheard my intentionally loud remark, Hunter scowled and kept his eyes locked on the car until it rounded the bend out of sight.

FOURTEEN
Missing Lipstick

Hunter

Siblings? Had Kristal really said that? Did she really see me as a brother?

Because I did *not* see her as a sister. Never had, never would.

Watching her drive away with Larson, I took off my coat, suddenly blazing hot though the day was frigid.

Maybe it was the acid boiling in my veins.

I hadn't met Larson Overstreet before, but of course I'd recognized him—and not just from TV.

Larson's father was the president and CEO of one of the oldest and largest asset management firms in the country.

His mother was Corina Videau, the famous clothing designer and heir to the Vivienne Videau cosmetics fortune.

He was the heir to a double-fortune, not to mention the hefty salary he must have pulled down from his gig on national television.

No wonder his family had a "beach house" in Eastport Bay. While I'd always been level-jumping with Kristal, this guy was firmly in her league.

She belonged with somebody like Larson—which meant I couldn't *stand* the idea of her spending time with the sonofabitch.

It took all my strength not to tail them in my own car. Instead, I forced myself to go home and get some work done.

As the hours ticked on, that became more and more difficult to do. By the time darkness fell, I had determined to make some changes. This intolerable situation couldn't go on.

Pretending I didn't want Kristal was just lunacy at this point.

Giving up on work, I started pacing the front of the house, keeping an eye on the windows to check for headlights pulling into the drive.

"What's with you tonight?" Josh asked. "You're jumpy as a jackrabbit."

"Nothing. I'm just thinking."

I checked my phone for the umpteenth time. It was after nine p.m. They'd been together for nearly seven hours now. How many sights was she going to show him anyway?

And then I thought about what *kind* of sights she might be showing Larson Overstreet and nearly threw the phone against the wall.

Finally, a car pulled into the driveway and stopped in front of the house. My shoulders sagged in relief.

But Kristal didn't get out of the car right away. Instead, it sat running, the headlights on, but the passenger cabin remaining dark.

What was going on? Were they making plans for another date?

Was he kissing her?

I went to the front door, intending to fling it open and charge outside like a shotgun-wielding father, but I stopped with my hand on the doorknob.

What am I doing?

I *wasn't* her father. I wasn't her boyfriend. I sure as fuck wasn't her "brother." I had no right to question her relationships with other guys.

Turning back around, I resumed my pacing, grabbing handfuls of my hair in frustration and impatience.

"What the hell are you doing?" asked Hap.

"Kristal's home."

"So?" He gave me a puzzled look. "Where was she?"

"She went out—with a guy."

Hap nodded in understanding, staying silent, but Reid must have picked up on the vibe of the exchange.

"What do you care?" he asked. "It's not like you're dating her… are you?"

Paul's head popped up. "We had a pact. None of us is going to date her. Right?" He looked around the room for support. "Right?"

At that moment, the door opened, and Kristal breezed in. "Hello everyone," she sang out.

As the others returned her too-cheerful greeting, I studied her face. She was smiling and looked… *glowy*? I wasn't sure that was a word, but whatever you called it, I didn't like the expression of elation she wore.

And her lipstick was gone.

Incendiary jealousy exploded inside me as if the room had been filled with invisible, scent-less gas and someone had lit a match.

I rushed to her, getting too close, invading her personal space.

"How was your *date*?" I snarled. "Did you have a nice time?"

Kristal's happy expression dropped, and her chin lifted in defiance. "As a matter of fact, we had a *fantastic* time."

I hadn't missed the pronoun change from singular to

plural. So Larson Overstreet had had a good time as well. No, not good—*fantastic*.

Which meant that *he* was the cause of the missing lipstick. My brain and body jolted into Mayday mode.

"Why were you gone for so long? Where did you go? What did you do with him?" The questions came out in rapid fire succession.

"Not that it's any of your business, but I showed him around Eastport Bay—the Bluff Walk, Brady's Wharf. We did a mansion tour," she said. "Afterward we had dinner at Nookie's Diner since it's a local institution."

That was it? Sightseeing and dinner wasn't so bad. Larson may have given her a goodnight kiss in the car, but he hadn't gotten any further.

Maybe I'd let him live.

"And then we went back to his beach house."

Nope. He was a dead man.

"... because he needed to get his bags. He was going straight to the airport after dropping me off."

And once again, Larson Overstreet had a future.

This woman was giving me whiplash. I'd never experienced higher highs and lower lows than I felt when I was with her.

"Well, good riddance," I muttered. "Did you ever notice how big his head looks on TV? I mean, it's like he's got a watermelon sitting on his shoulders or something."

Kristal rolled her eyes and headed for the stairs. "Suddenly, I have a headache. I'm going to bed. Goodnight everyone."

As she stomped up the staircase, I spun away, clenching my fists and letting out an exasperated "*Fuuuuuuuuuuck.*"

Reid held up his hands. "Don't look at me. Who knows why they do what they do?"

Coming into the room and scrubbing one hand through

his bed-head hair, Tucker looked around, blinking. "What's going on?"

"Hunter has his panties in a wad because Kristal went on a date," Hap explained.

"With who? Is he a bad guy or something?" Tuck asked.

"That remains to be seen," I muttered. "Hap—can you get in touch with that security expert friend of yours? That massive, ripped football player who became a Navy Seal?"

"Wilder Lowe? Sure. Why?"

"I want to hire him to look into someone."

"A client?" Hap asked.

"Kristal's new boyfriend," Josh offered helpfully.

"He's *not* her boyfriend," I fired back a little too harshly.

And if I can find one speck of dirt on the guy, he never will be.

Every fiber of my being screamed the title of "boyfriend" should be mine and mine alone, but at the moment that possibility seemed farther out of reach than it ever had been.

Ever since she'd moved in, I'd been watching and waiting for signs Kristal might be interested in more than a friendship with me.

After today's events, one thing was for sure—I couldn't sit back and wait any longer.

I had to take action.

FIFTEEN
I Want You

Kristal

I lied. Not about the sightseeing and dinner part, but about the day being "fantastic."

It hadn't been *bad*. Not at all. In fact, Larson was quite entertaining, much more laid back than he seemed on the nightly news. He'd been funny, sweet, and of course he was very nice-looking.

But he wasn't Hunter.

Fool that I was, the only blue eyes I wanted to spend the evening gazing into were those amazing, turquoise-shaded ones unique to the Bestia brothers.

The only voice I wanted to listen to for hours on end was Hunter's raspy, deep scrape of masculine sound.

All day I'd thought about how sore and possessive it had sounded out on the porch of the Cliffhouse as he'd forbidden me to leave and spend the day with Larson.

And the way he'd acted moments ago downstairs.

Could he be jealous?

Even daring to entertain the thought made my belly swoop like the seagulls soaring and diving outside.

More likely he'd just been looking out for me the same way he fussed over all the guys in the house. They didn't call him "Doc" for nothing.

Based on the way he'd behaved around me the past few weeks, he saw me no differently than he saw them.

But what about the hungry way he'd looked at me that day when he'd accidentally walked in on me in the shower? (Not to mention that *memorable* wood he was sporting)

And the way I'd sometimes look up and catch him staring at me when we were in the house together?

Plus, I could have *sworn* he was milliseconds away from kissing me on the beach before Romeo showed up.

Thinking about his confusing hot-and-cold behavior twisted me into complicated braids of confusion, anger, and longing.

I showered and put on my pj's and curled up in bed with a novel, which I was failing miserably to read. Distracted by my whirling thoughts, I skimmed the same page at least three times.

What I'd told Larson about my relationship with Hunter was so far from the truth it was laughable. I didn't regard him as a brother.

At all.

But today, he'd behaved exactly like the annoying "big brother" I'd accused him of being. In fact, Hunter had treated me like a *child*.

Of course, when I thought about it, how could I really blame him?

Ugh. I'd done it again. I'd made myself dependent on someone, let him take care of me, and now he thought he could control my life.

As much as I hated to admit it, it was time to go—not just away from this house but away from Rhode Island.

My phone rang. I picked it up from the bedside table and

checked the screen. It was Cinda—our friendship ESP must have pinged her.

She was exactly the person I needed to talk to right now.

"Hey, what are you doing?"

"Honestly? AJ's down for the night, and I'm sucking down a glass of chardonnay like it's my *job*," she drawled. "Because of my actual job. Is it frowned on to *fire* family members, by the way?"

I chuckled in spite of my own misery. "Why did you hire your lazy step-sisters in the first place?"

"Because they begged, and I'm a complete sucker? I don't know—I guess I felt bad for them and somewhere deep down inside I'm probably still trying to recreate my dad's dream of a 'family business.' Of course it helps if the family members in question actually show up for work every once in a while." She blew out a long breath. "Okay, rant over. What are you doing? Did I wake you?"

"No. I can't sleep. I've actually been doing a lot of thinking."

"About..." she prodded.

"Pulling the plug on my job search in Rhode Island. I've been trying, but all my efforts are coming up empty."

"I'm sorry. You know I'd hire you in a heartbeat, but I can't afford to pay you what you're worth. Besides, I know you want something in the art field, and I don't think dust doodles count. Where are you thinking of expanding your search to?"

"New York."

"Oh." She sounded surprised, but then she said, "Yeah, actually that makes sense. There have got to be so many more opportunities there with all the galleries and museums in the city."

"Exactly. When I told Larson about my degree—oh, wait —I didn't have a chance to even tell you because everything happened so fast. I went out with Larson Overstreet today."

"What? Larson Overstreet as in the guy whose gorgeous face is on my TV screen every weeknight at six-thirty?"

"That's the one."

"Oh wow. How did that even come about? Do you know him from like, college or rich-kid-summer-camp or something?"

I laughed. "No, I met him at the Cliffhouse this morning. And there's no such thing as rich-kid-summer-camp... I don't think."

"There totally is," she said. "I've heard my clients talking about it. I've never seen people so eager to ship off their kids for months at a time—and this is when their kids aren't away at boarding school. I can't imagine doing that with AJ."

"I know. I can't see you doing that, even if you *were* rich. No offense," I added hastily.

"None taken. So anyway, what did Larson say?"

"About what?"

"You were saying when you told Larson about your degree..."

"Oh right. When I told him what my degree was and about my unpaid directorship at the local Art Preservation Guild, he had all kinds of leads for me. He knew of several job openings right off hand in Manhattan. The rents there wouldn't be any more affordable there than they are here, but I could get a roommate—or two—or three."

The thought of leaving pinched my heart, but I kept my tone upbeat. "At least I'd be using my degree and building a future. Alone." So much for being upbeat. "Ugh. It's so depressing, but what am I going to do? I have to face reality."

"And where does Hunter Bestia fit into this reality?"

My sigh was audible. "Nowhere, I guess. You know I've always liked him, but either he's not interested, or he *is* interested but not enough to actually do anything about it. I'm at the point now where I'm kind of making a fool of myself over him. Even if he returned my interest, that still doesn't solve my employment issue. I've made up my mind—tomorrow I'm going to start looking into the New York City job market and check on those openings Larson mentioned."

"I get it. I hate to think about you being so far away though," Cinda said.

There was that pinch again. "Me too. But you and AJ can come visit me in the city. I bet he'd love riding the train there."

Dropping the cheerful façade, I admitted. "I'm going to miss you so much."

I'd also miss the Dwarves terribly. I'd miss the town itself. And of course I'd miss *Hunter* beyond bearing.

But I couldn't stay here any longer. Not with the way I was feeling about him.

Pretending I didn't care was an exercise in self-torture and becoming harder every day.

A knock at my bedroom door startled me so much I dropped the phone.

"Hello? Kristal?" Cinda's far away voice called from the bedspread.

I snatched the phone back up. "Hey Cin—can I call you tomorrow? Someone just knocked on my door."

"Oooh," she said in an excited voice. "You'd *better* call."

"I will. Love you—bye."

Nerves rattling, I crept to the door on bare feet and opened it a crack.

Hunter stood on the other side.

Judging from his expression, his mood had mellowed considerably from earlier. "Can we talk?" he asked softly.

The rattling was now a full-blown drumbeat. I wouldn't have been surprised if he could hear it. "It's late. I'm already in my pajamas."

"Please, Kristal. I won't keep you long. I'm not going to be able to sleep unless I talk to you."

"Okay." *Interesting.*

I opened the door wider and stepped back. "Come in."

He entered the room, looking around warily, as if checking to see if perhaps I'd snuck in some gang members, and they might be waiting to jump him from the shadows.

"Want to sit over there?" I pointed to the two overstuffed chairs near the large picture window.

Hunter nodded and walked that way. I noticed his fingers tensing and flexing, as if he was filled with barely suppressed energy. He sat in one of the chairs, and I took the one opposite him, folding my legs to one side and beneath me.

Then I waited.

"You look pretty," was the first thing he said. *Not* what I was expecting.

"Um... thank you? I took off all my makeup, though, and I didn't feel like messing with the hairdryer tonight, so I'm sure my hair looks like an unruly mop."

"No. It's beautiful." In contrast to the sweet words, his voice was gruff, almost unwilling. "You're always beautiful."

All the air suddenly left my chest. Hunter seemed different. And he was telling me I looked pretty. I was fairly sure he hadn't come here just to compliment my bedtime look, though I had no idea what he *did* want.

Whatever it was, he certainly was serious about it.

"What's going on, Hunter?"

He folded his lips in, rolled them out, took a breath, then locked gazes with me. "I'm sorry for the way I acted tonight—and earlier today. I was a jerk, and I apologize."

My breathing resumed. "Okay... I appreciate you saying that." After a hesitation, I asked, "Why *were* you acting like that? You've been strange the past few days, actually."

His focus didn't waver but stayed locked on me. "You don't know?"

I shook my head. When he maintained his silence, I

decided to be brave and hazard a guess. "Were you... jealous? Of Larson?"

His answer was little more than a grunt. "Maybe."

Still, warmth spread through my chest and belly, making me feel like I'd just consumed a cup of decadent hot chocolate. "I see."

"As for acting weird the past few days... I didn't realize I was. I'm sorry about that. I was *trying* to be normal."

Hope formed in my heart like the bud of a new rose. But I didn't want to jump to any conclusions. I'd taken Harry's feelings for granted and had been horribly wrong about him.

"Why did you... have to 'try?' Why don't you feel completely comfortable with me?"

Hunter didn't answer, just sat there looking at me with a tortured expression on his face, so I decided to give him a little encouragement.

"There was no reason to be jealous today, you know—*if* that's how you felt. Larson and I had a nice time, but nothing happened beyond talking. There's nothing there between us. Not like there is with... other people."

At his sudden intense stare, I clarified. "*One* other person, I should say."

Hunter's body relaxed, and the barest hint of a smile played at the edges of his lips. "Would I happen to know this lucky guy?"

I chuckled softly. Apparently he was going to make me do all the heavy lifting here. Well, I was going to make him work for it.

"Yes. It's Tuck."

His eyes popped wide, and he leaned forward in his chair. "What?"

I laughed. "Just kidding. You *know* who I mean."

Taking in Hunter's relieved exhale and growing smile, I went on. "I was honestly surprised at your reaction to Larson today. I really didn't think you'd care if I went out with someone."

"I cared," he said simply.

A sense of wonderment filled me. Was it possible Hunter and I had been living together these past few weeks, right under each other's noses, and we'd each been feeling the same way but hiding it from the other?

"Why did you pretend not to?" I managed to whisper.

He shifted in his seat, glancing away at the dark window. "I didn't think you'd want me to care. We're... different."

"We're not so different. Unless you mean that you're a smashing success, and I'm basically a homeless failure."

Instead of laughing at my joke, Hunter frowned. "You're not a failure. Why would you say that?"

I counted off the evidence on my fingers. "Underemployed, bumming rides, oh, and sponging off my high school buddies for a place to stay. I promise I'm working on that. I'll be out of your hair soon."

Hunter's face went through a series of expressions, landing on irritation. He stood abruptly. "I should go. Like you said, it's late. I wanted to apologize, and I did, so I should let my *buddy* get some sleep."

I stood as well. "Wait a minute—that's it?"

"Yeah. I can apologize again if that's what you want."

"No, Hunter."

I moved around the low coffee table and went to stand directly in front of him. We were so close now I had to tilt my head back to see his face.

"That is *not* what I want. And I don't believe that's why you knocked on my door tonight. What I want is for you to tell me what you're thinking. You would never talk to me back in high school, but we're adults now, and I think we can manage to discuss our feelings like adults."

He stared down at me, his gaze shifting from my eyes to my mouth and back again. But he said nothing.

I'm an idiot. What was I doing?

Not fifteen minutes ago, I'd made up my mind to move out of state, to go wherever I had to go, do whatever I had to do to take care of myself and stand on my own two feet.

Now here I was, essentially begging Hunter for crumbs of hope and affection—something he was either unable or unwilling to give.

Frustrated, I threw my hands out to the sides. "Fine. You're right. It's late. And I need to get some sleep because I'll have a busy day tomorrow applying for jobs in New York City."

That snapped him out of his mute spell. His dark brows drew together. "I thought you said there was nothing going on between you and that Overstreet guy. Now you're moving to New York for him after one date?"

"I'm not moving to New York for *him*, idiot. I need a job —a career—and there are more opportunities there. Apparently, there's nothing to keep me here."

Hunter's hands shot out to grab my arms. His warm fingers wrapped around my biceps, holding me in place. "You can't go."

"Why not?"

"I want... you. I mean, I want you to stay."

He took a deeper breath, let it out on a shudder, swallowed hard. "And I also want *you.* I always have."

Oh thank God. Finally.

No longer struggling to get away, I met his pleading look with a challenging one of my own.

"I'm listening."

SIXTEEN
Worthy of You

Hunter

It took all the nerve I had, but I willed myself to stay and look at her. And be honest at long last.

I was fucking terrified, but it was now or never if I ever wanted a chance with Kristal. I couldn't let her run off to New York without knowing the truth.

"In spite of the fact that you see me as a... 'buddy'..." I scowled around the word. "... or a *'brother,'* I've always wanted you. You were all I could think about in high school. And then... after that night at the Charity Ball..."

"...when you kissed me by accident," she prodded.

"Yeah, well, it might have been accidental on your part... but not on mine. I knew it was you. Which I know was messed up because you were with Harry at the time. I was just... caught off guard... and overwhelmed by what was happening."

"I wasn't really with Harry. Or rather, he wasn't with *me*," she clarified. "We broke up for good about five minutes after you left the room."

"Because of me?"

"Because he'd moved on with another woman without

bothering to mention it to me until that night. And for the record… I don't see you as a brother. *Or* a buddy. I never have." She gave me a dazzling smile. "I can't believe you felt that way about me in high school."

I huffed a short breath. "I can't believe you didn't *know.*"

"How would I have known? You were so quiet. I *wanted* to get to know you. I tried. I gave you signals, but you would never even talk to me, much less ask me out."

"You gave me signals? You…" My shock was so great it was hard to form words. "*You* wanted *me* to ask you out?"

She nodded, smiling shyly. "I liked you. And I was always attracted to you."

My mouth fell open. "How is that possible?"

Kristal laughed. "Um, let's see… smart, funny, good looking. What's so hard to understand?"

"But we were from totally different classes. My family was poor. My father was… well, we were poor."

She acted insulted. "I don't care about that. I never did. Why should that have mattered?"

Yeah right. Everybody cares about that.

"It mattered to me. It's part of what drove me—to get a college scholarship, bust my butt in school, and then afterward, create the software, start my company, to work out and dress well and change my image from that skinny math geek I used to be. I wanted to be…"

I took a breath before admitting the truth. "… worthy of you."

"Hunter," Kristal whispered, stepping closer and slipping her small, soft hand into mine. "You're giving me way too much credit. I was just as geeky as you were as a kid. I was just as insecure as you were—if I hadn't been, I would have asked *you* out."

I made a disbelieving *pshaw* noise, shaking my head. "You

were the prettiest girl in school. You could have said the word and had a date anytime with any guy you wanted."

She shook her head, looking mystified. "That's not true, but it's beside the point. The point is we're *not* those insecure kids anymore, but we've been acting like them. Have you really been wanting to ask me out since we've been living together?"

"Longer. Since that night at the charity ball. But I thought you were still with Harry. Then your father passed away. Then we were housemates... and I *couldn't* date you."

"Why not?"

"First of all, I didn't want you to feel like it was some kind of 'requirement' for living here. I didn't want you to be uncomfortable. Second... honestly? I was chickenshit. I wasn't sure how you felt, and I didn't want to keep being a fool pursuing a girl who only wanted to be friends. And third..."

I offered a sheepish grin. "We all kind of made a pact that none of us would date you."

Kristal blinked hard, obviously stunned. "You did?" She shook her head in amazement. "I had no idea any of this was going on."

After a few seconds of silence, she said, "Hunter... it might have been an accident that I kissed you at the charity ball... but I don't regret it."

My eyes lasered to hers, my mind and heart spellbound by her words.

"You don't?"

She shook her head slowly, never breaking eye contact with me. "No. I've... I've thought about it. A lot."

My heart leapt up to my throat then fell back into place, battering my chest wall. I moved toward Kristal cautiously, afraid the extraordinary moment would disappear like a shiny soap bubble—sparkling with iridescent beauty one moment and popping out of existence the next.

Reaching her, I slid my arms around her, and when she showed no sign of objection, drew her close.

And she felt fucking *incredible*.

Her body, so lush and feminine was *right there*, and those heart-shaped lips, soft pink and perfectly defined even without a drop of makeup, beckoned to me.

"So have I," I murmured. "A lot."

My fingers slipped beneath her hair, going to the nape of her neck and base of her skull, massaging the delicate, tense muscles I found there, holding her securely in place.

Now that I finally had this chance with her, I was *taking* it and not letting it get away.

"I'd like to give you a little more to think about," I whispered close to her cheek, hunching over to accommodate our height difference.

Before I could make the move to close the last torturous inch between us, Kristal stood on her toes and pressed her mouth to mine.

The kiss affected me like an electrical charge. I was paralyzed from a jolt of pleasure. My muscles braced, and it became a second-by-second battle to manage the torrent of sensation that threatened to overpower me.

I fought for self-control—I didn't want to scare her with my intensity, but it wasn't easy to contain my enthusiasm.

After so many years, so much longing, so many daydreams and nighttime visions, it was finally happening, and the reality of holding this woman and kissing her was so far beyond my imaginings I was literally awed by it.

As the kiss went on, I deepened it, cradling her face then letting my hands move to her neck and shoulders, down to her waist, shaping it, loving the feel of her curves, pulling her closer, closer.

She made a little whimpering noise that absolutely lit me

up. Encouraged and unable to contain my greed for her, I slid a hand up her ribcage toward her breast.

"Hunter, wait." Kristal worked her hands between our bodies, pushing gently. Her breathing was fractured. "We should probably stop… before this turns into something we *do* regret."

"That's not even possible for me," I said honestly, speaking against her lips, still drugged by their sweetness.

She giggled, sounding shaken and a little nervous. Her hands exerted more pressure, and I managed to take a half-step back, though everything in me objected.

"Well, you know, I don't sleep with someone on a first date—and definitely not *before* the first date," she said.

"Right. Of course." I breathed like I'd just finished a five-mile sprint, struggling to rein in my charging desire for her.

"Kristal?"

"Yeah?" she answered, still sounding breathless herself.

"Would you like to go out with me?"

She laughed and slapped at my chest. "You're bad."

Grinning I said, "I'm serious. I do want to take you out. Tomorrow night if you're not working then."

"What about the pact?"

The phone in my pocket rang, and I pulled it out, silencing the device before slipping it into my back pocket again.

It was my brother Jack. If it was important, he'd leave me a message. In any case, I'd get back to him later.

There was no conversation in the world more important than this one. After years of longing, I was on the verge of getting what I'd always wanted.

"I'll talk to the guys," I said with a shrug. "We'll work it out. They'll just have to understand. I mean, they won't *like* it… they all have crushes on you—"

"Really?" Kristal interrupted, sounding incredulous. "Is that really true?"

I nodded. "Pretty much. Everyone except for Reid. But I have dibs. I saw you first."

Her head tipped to the side. "At the charity ball?"

"In seventh grade. Mr. Allen's language arts class. Third row, second desk, red dress. You should wear red more often, by the way. It looks amazing on you."

A pretty blush spread across her face, followed by a smile. "Yes."

"Yes what? You'll wear more red?"

"Yes, I'll go out with you. Tomorrow night. It's a date."

I couldn't help myself—I did a fist pump. "Finally. It only took, what, seventeen years?"

She laughed. "Yeah, but who's counting?"

I was.

Kissing her lips softly once more, I left the room, already planning for tomorrow night.

I wasn't quite sure what our first date would look like yet, but I did know one thing.

Whatever it took, I'd make it worth the wait.

SEVENTEEN
Out to Dinner

Kristal

I was still tingling when I woke the next morning, smiling dreamily in the bathroom vanity mirror as I applied my makeup and got ready for work.

Last night had been... remarkable.

The things Hunter had said. And the way he'd *kissed* me.

It had been every bit as good as our first kisses at the Charity Relief Foundation fundraiser, except this time there had been no mistaken identity, no need to hide or hurry. There was just Hunter and me and chemistry as powerful as a hurricane.

No one—*no one*—had ever kissed me like that before. Like it was the only thing in the world he cared about, the only thing he wanted to do.

It was like I'd been able to *feel* his emotion through the contact, feel the years of longing and pent-up attraction.

And it had felt so, so good.

He'd probably been able to sense my potent feelings for him as well, but I didn't care anymore. I was ready to put it all on the line for him, to be out and open about my feelings concerning Hunter.

He was an amazing person—brilliant and hard-working but also sweet and charming. An *incredible* kisser.

And tonight, we'd have our first date. Butterflies hatched and wriggled in my belly, spreading their new wings for a test flight. I could hardly wait to be alone with him.

Eager to see him, I practically skipped down the staircase to the first floor and went directly to the kitchen, expecting to find him there making a healthful breakfast for all the guys as usual.

He wasn't there.

And by the looks of things, he hadn't been there this morning at all.

I found Josh digging into a bag of donuts and Aiden shaking a box of sugary cereal over a bowl. Reid was pouring himself the world's tallest glass of iced coffee and making a toaster waffle.

Had Hunter slept in? That wasn't like him.

"Good morning," Reid said, looking abashed when he spotted me. "Listen, I, uh… I want to apologize again for what I said last night. I was totally out of line, and—"

I interrupted. "Don't worry about it. It's over. I'm fine. Really. So… looks like everyone's fending for themselves this morning. Where's Hunter? Still asleep?"

"Tuck saw him leave the house last night," Aiden informed me. "Said he had to deal with some kind of family issue. He hasn't been back since."

Alarm seized my breath. "I hope everything's okay. No one's heard from him today at all?"

Hap came into the kitchen and apparently picked up the end of my question. "I wouldn't worry. He texted me about the filming schedule for today. He stayed over at Jack's house last night."

I nodded but didn't feel very reassured. Were Jack and Bonnie okay? Had something happened to Hunter's father?

Leaving the kitchen, I pulled out my phone and tapped Hunter's number. The call went to voicemail. Then I texted.

Kristal: Everything okay? Can I do anything to help?

After a few minutes there was a terse response.

Hunter: I'm fine. Be back soon.

Breakfast had ended and it was nearly time for me to leave for work by the time he returned to the mansion.

At this point, I was thoroughly twisted up with anxiety and concern, trying to imagine what kind of family matter he'd been dealing with. It must have been pretty serious for him to leave in the middle of the night and stay away.

Hunter looked exhausted. Dark smudges underlined his eyes, and his shoulders sagged as if under a heavy weight.

"Sorry guys," he announced to the room. "Give me a few minutes to grab a bite and clean up, and I'll be ready to go."

"No problem," Hap said. "I went ahead and gave the film crew the day off. We could all use one."

I followed Hunter into the kitchen, where he stood with his back to me, peering into the coffee pot, apparently checking to see if there was any left.

Sliding my arms around his lean waist, I pressed a kiss to the center of his back, seeking to comfort him.

Hunter went rigid. Then his body relaxed, and he turned around, meeting my questioning gaze. Wow, did he look tired.

"Are you okay?" I asked softly.

He nodded. "Yeah. Just a little beat. I didn't sleep well. Crashed at my brother's place, but we stayed up pretty late."

"What were you doing?"

Again, Hunter's posture stiffened. "Just had some things to discuss. Everything's fine."

Okay then.

He obviously didn't want to talk about it. "All right.

Listen, if you want to postpone our date tonight, I totally understand."

His arms around me tightened. "No. I've waited decades for this. I'll be fine. I just need to catch up on some work first. How's four o'clock for you? An hour before sunset?"

It sounded a little early for dinner, but I smiled. "Sounds perfect. That'll give me just enough time to shower after work and get ready."

"Great. Can't wait."

In spite of his enthusiastic words, Hunter didn't sound or look excited about the evening to come.

Something was wrong—I felt it. I wanted desperately to help him the way he'd helped me so many times recently. I just didn't know how.

He released his grip on me, as if to move away, but I wasn't quite finished with him. Pulling him closer, I rose to my tiptoes and kissed him.

At first he didn't respond, remaining passive and simply allowing the intimate contact. But then some sort of switch was flipped.

Hunter tightened his hold on me, nearly crushing me, and he kissed me back with all the passion and intensity I could ever hope for, plus some.

He was so big, so powerful, but I felt the trembling in his body and hands.

What had happened last night? Why did his kiss, as pleasurable as it was, feel tinged with desperation?

Loud laughter from the other room seemed to awaken Hunter from a spell, and he broke the kiss. "I should... let you go. Don't want to make you late for work."

"Hap's giving me a ride on his way into town, but you're right. I should get going." I studied his tired eyes. "Hey... if there's anything I can do to help... I hope you know you can tell me anything."

For a moment Hunter froze, the connection between our eyes so intense it was almost ferocious.

Then his flickered away. "Everything's fine," he repeated. "Have a good day at work. I'll see you later this afternoon."

I worried about him all day, but at four o'clock, he knocked on the door of my room, and I opened it to see a bright smile that stole my breath.

The rest of him wasn't too shabby either. He'd told me in a text to dress casually for the outing, and he'd done the same, wearing a nice pair of jeans with a light blue cashmere sweater and deck shoes.

Eyeing my outfit, a red sweater paired with off-white corduroys and boots, he said, "You look amazing," and leaned in to kiss my cheek, adding, "And you smell great. Ready? Bring your coat. Oh, and you might want to grab your camera —it *is* the golden hour, you know."

"You remembered."

Feeling like I'd just swallowed a lump of sunshine, I went back for my camera bag and coat. We left the house with Hunter giving vague and evasive answers to the other guys' questions about where we were going.

"Kristal needs to grab some more shots," he said to Paul before shutting the door and escorting me to his Bentley.

When he got in behind the wheel, I turned to him. "I'm guessing you haven't told them yet?"

He shook his head. "No time today. Maybe I'll talk to them tomorrow. So… you hungry?"

It felt like Hunter was trying to change the subject, but I answered, "Yes, so I hope we're going out to dinner."

"Oh, we're going out all right," he answered with a grin.

He drove to Eastport Bay's historic harbor area, parking near Brady's Wharf, a popular dining and shopping destination that boasted some of my favorite local restaurants.

"Are we going to Nooky's Diner?" I asked as he pulled into a spot. "I love that place."

"We are not," he said with a cryptic half-smile. "The place I'm taking you is a bit more... exclusive."

We walked together, passing by the tourist spots and entering the Eastport Bay Yachting Center Marina.

"Oh my gosh," I squealed. "We're going on one of those dinner cruises, aren't we? I've never done one of those. I've never even taken a sunset champagne cruise, though I've always wanted to. Either way, I'm so excited."

Hunter held his tongue, sliding me a knowing grin.

Contrary to my expectations, we didn't proceed to the end of the dock where a tall, white-sailed schooner was waiting, or to the right where one of the double-decker tour boats was moored. Instead, he directed me to a private slip where a huge, white yacht was docked.

"Here we are." He motioned toward the ramp to its deck, indicating that I should go first.

"Whose is this?" I asked as I climbed the ramp's slight incline.

"A friend's. Reid's actually," Hunter said from behind me. "He's lending it to us, along with his captain."

"Oh. I didn't know he had a boat. Or a captain."

Of all the guys in the house, Reid Mancini had been the most difficult to get to know. As attractive as he was, he put out an emotional deflector shield that kept others at a distance. Or maybe it was just me.

Hunter nodded. "He loves fishing. He hasn't used the yacht much lately because he's been basically doing double duty with my company and his own. He's stretched pretty thin. I don't know how much longer I'll be able to keep him. StillYours-dot-com is really blowing up. Eventually he's going to have to devote his full-time attention to it."

I chuckled. "It's still hard to believe someone as cynical as he is created one of the world's most popular social media sites —and it's all about *love.* I read it's on the verge of eclipsing Facebook."

"Pretty crazy, huh? There's definitely a story behind it, but I doubt he'd want me discussing his personal business."

When we stepped onto the deck, I forgot all about Reid's business, personal and professional. I was too overwhelmed by his floating mansion.

"Watch your step," Hunter warned. "The area near the pool might be slippery."

It wasn't, but I wouldn't have minded falling in. The cozy soaking pool glowed with underwater lights, and it was obviously heated—shimmers of inviting steam hovered above the blue water, beckoning me to step in and submerge myself.

The ship's interior was spectacular as well. I'd been a guest in many glamorous homes, and none was any more impressive than this.

With dramatic skylights and ocean views from every room, the yacht was the picture of understated elegance.

There was luxury everywhere I looked, from the white wool and silk carpet in the sunken living area and media room, to the marble bathrooms, custom made lintels and columns of natural wood, and fully equipped gym.

In the dining room, the soft glow of recessed ceiling lights glanced off the gleaming burled wood tabletop and sparkling crystal and silverware.

"Mmmm. It smells amazing in here," I said. "So we're having dinner onboard?"

"Yes, in a little while. I thought you might like to be out on deck as we leave the harbor and go out into the bay. I asked the captain to keep it close to the shore for a while in case you wanted to get some shots of the mansions and lighthouses, or maybe the Eastport Bridge at sunset."

I beamed at him. "You know I do."

"Okay, let's go."

Though it was winter, the day was unseasonably mild. I was comfortable in my down jacket as I snapped shots of a Revolutionary War fortress, the Cliffhouse, and Clingstone, Eastport Bay's famous House on the Rock.

The three-story, twenty-three room, ten thousand square foot home had been built in 1905 atop a small rocky island and was beautiful in its rustic solitude.

The captain also sailed us past the childhood home of Jacqueline Kennedy Onassis. President John F. Kennedy spent so much time at the seaside estate it had been nicknamed the "Summer White House." The owner of the Fruit of the Loom company had since bought the place.

After giving me a perfect vantage point for photographing some of Eastport Bay's other well-known mansions, the captain turned the yacht out to sea. The chef texted Hunter to tell him dinner was ready to be served.

"Thank you," I said as we went back indoors and into the beautiful and delicious-smelling dining room. "That was worth the trip even without dinner—though I am starved."

"Me too. Not sure if the food can live up to the view though."

Hunter needn't have worried. The chef he'd purloined from one of the area's top restaurants for the evening had prepared a sumptuous feast.

The appetizer course consisted of tiny crab cakes served atop mixed baby greens, fresh asparagus, and edible flowers, and drizzled with the most delicious sauce.

Next the chef brought out bowls of lobster bisque with espresso cream.

The main course was lobster flown in from Kennebunkport, Maine and prepared with a champagne glace, caulilini, gnocchi, fennel, and morel mushrooms.

For dessert, blueberry pie soufflé with Vanilla Crème Anglaise.

"Oh my gosh—blueberries are my all-time favorite," I exclaimed, my mouth watering at the sight of the gorgeous dessert in spite of all the delicious food I'd already consumed.

"I know." Hunter looked quite pleased with himself.

"You do? How?"

He shrugged. "I *might* have done a little recon. I called Cinda today."

"You did?" I shook my head, amazed and feeling a little light-headed that he'd gone to so much effort for my sake. And then I lifted the first bite of the sweet souffle to my mouth.

All conversation ceased.

When I finally came up for air, I laughed at my empty plate. "I think I might have just embarrassed myself there. I've never eaten so much so fast in my life."

"I have to admit... that *was* pretty impressive," Hunter joked. "And I live with six large men."

I gave him a chiding glance but laughed again.

The sound of his rich laughter joined mine, and for a moment, I was suspended in time, as if watching the two of us together from outside my own body.

Hunter had removed his sweater and now wore just his dress shirt. The top two buttons were undone, giving me a glimpse of his throat and the beginning of his muscled chest.

The sleeves were rolled up to his forearms, and the interplay of muscles and tendons beneath the masculine skin of his arms and hands was nothing short of fascinating.

There was no getting around it—Hunter was devastatingly handsome.

But more than how he looked, it was the way he was acting tonight that was a revelation. He'd smiled more, laughed more, and talked more than I'd ever seen him.

Relaxation looked *good* on him.

After dinner, we went back out on deck to take in the 360-degree water view and starry skies. The yacht moved at a leisurely pace, stirring a light breeze that ruffled Hunter's dark hair.

I longed to reach up and touch it, to stroke his clean-shaven jaw and run my fingertips over the plush lips that had drawn my eyes like a magnet all evening long. It had been hard not to stare at them.

I wanted to take pictures of *him* to keep and enjoy, to look at as long as I wanted to when he wasn't around.

Well that wouldn't be weird at all now, would it?

The wind kicked up, and I shivered.

"You cold?" Hunter asked. "Come here."

He drew me close, and now the scent of him was all around me, fresh and intoxicating and warm, like him.

"Better?" he murmured, his breath tickling my cheek.

I nodded, feeling a bit like I was in a dream. As we pulled apart slightly, our gazes connected.

Hunter's was filled with fiery intensity, tiny rushlights springing to life behind the extraordinary blue irises. My breath caught then picked up pace, moving in and out of my lungs in shallow streams.

And then he kissed me, and there was no dream that could match it.

Hunter's hands slid from my back to my sides, clenching the heavy fabric of my sweater desperately as his lips moved over mine in ways that had my mind racing and my body pulsing with an energy I'd never felt before.

From the way he was breathing and the tension in his hands and body, I could tell he felt it too.

Nothing had ever been better than this, being wanted by Hunter Bestia.

"Do you want to go in?" he murmured against my lips.

"In the ocean?" I asked through a fog of lust. At this point if he'd suggested wading into a swamp teeming with starving gators, I'd have probably gone for it.

"No." A chuckle from Hunter. "In the hot tub. It's a balmy hundred and two degrees as opposed to the ocean, which is about thirty-nine right now."

Bathing in a hot tub on a luxury yacht under the stars—with Hunter—sounded amazing. But I wasn't sure I was *quite* ready to go au natural al fresco with him yet.

"Are you suggesting we... skinny dip?"

He grinned widely. "Hey, if you're up for it, you won't hear any argument from me. But... there *are* some brand new swimsuits in the cabana."

He nodded toward the enclosure off to one side of the pool deck. "I think they'll fit you."

Letting out a sigh of relief, I practically skipped over to the cabana, pulled back the curtain, and peered in. A sizable shopping bag with a familiar logo sat on the teak bench inside.

I looked back at him. "Hunter? What did you do? You went shopping at Saltwater Style? That's my favorite shop."

Grinning, he lifted his shoulders and let them fall in a *no big deal* shrug. "I ordered over the phone, and the owner Chelle delivered the stuff here. Jack actually suggested the shop for me—said he ordered a bunch of stuff for Bonnie from there when she became his 'unexpected houseguest' and had nothing to wear. Go ahead, try them on. I'll meet you in the water."

He started unbuttoning his shirt, which gave me all the motivation I needed to hurry.

That body? In a hot tub? Yes ma'am, thank you please.

Closing the cabana curtain behind me, I reached into the bag and pulled out an array of swimwear. All of it red.

Though the tags said they were my size, none of the suits seemed to consist of much fabric.

I peeked through the curtain opening. Hunter was in a pair of trunks, stepping into the bubbling water.

"What kind of swimsuits did you tell Chelle to send over?" I asked suspiciously.

"Nice ones," he said. "And I told her you look incredible in red."

Okay then. I could do this. One of these was bound to fit and not be completely embarrassing to wear.

As I tried them on, each one seemed skimpier than the last. Finally, I settled on an apple-red bikini. Evaluating the fit in the mirror, I decided it offered the most coverage of the lot —which wasn't saying much.

The triangle top adequately covered the centers of my breasts, though it left plenty of side cleavage exposed—on both sides. The bottom half of the suit consisted of a tiny panel of red fabric that barely covered my bikini zone in the front.

When I turned around to check the back view, I literally gasped.

Oh dear God.

It was worse than I'd expected. I looked basically naked from behind.

I can't do it. I can't go out there in this.

But then I thought about it. These were not "just friends" swimsuits. Hunter had picked this out for me. He *wanted* to see me in something sexy.

Buoyed by the thought and gathering every shred of courage I possessed, I took a deep breath and threw open the curtain.

Hunter was already in the pool, submerged to his upper abdomen. He must have dipped the rest under before I came out because his chest, shoulders and upper arms glistened in the moonlight and the subtle glow of the underwater lights.

Steam rose around him, making him look like some sort of

underworld god rising from the depths to capture innocent maidens and pull them under.

There may have never been a more willing victim.

I walked toward him on shaking legs, trying my best to focus on him and not on holding in my stomach.

He watched me approach with a look on his face I could only describe as *hungry*. His gaze roamed over me, lingering on the parts he seemed to find most interesting before it met mine.

"That looks great on you." His voice was raspy. "It fits… perfectly."

"Thanks. How's the water?"

"Lonely."

Holding the handrail, I stepped down into the hot, bubbling pool. "I think you need some company."

"I think you're right."

Hunter stretched out his arm. When I placed my hand in his, he pulled me close with one strong tug. I ended up seated sideways on his lap with my chest pressed against his.

The feel of his bare skin next to mine coupled with the hot, frothy water tickling my legs and feet was incredibly erotic.

Apparently it was having a similar effect on Hunter. In our current positions it was impossible to mistake his arousal. A thick erection pressed against my hip.

"Hi," I said, suddenly breathless.

"Hi." He stared at my face, a look of wonder in his eyes. "You are beautiful," he whispered.

I smiled. "You too."

The rearing pressure beneath me grew even more conspicuous. Raising my brows, I cast a pointed glance downward, and my smile widened.

Hunter huffed a laugh, licking his lips and looking away in apparent embarrassment. "Ignore it. It's been happening around you my entire life. At this point my dick is accustomed to having high hopes that go nowhere."

I leaned in and kissed him then pulled back enough to murmur against his mouth. "There's a lot to be said for high hopes. I've always had a thing for optimists."

There was a pronounced movement against my hip as his body reacted to my flirtatious tone and words, and a ripple of excitement went through me.

"And *you* apparently have a thing for tiny swimsuits," I added.

He laughed. "Only when it comes to you. I knew there was no chance of getting you naked tonight, so I was going for the next best thing. Wish I could say I was sorry…" He glanced down at my cleavage. "…but I'm not."

"No chance?" I lifted one brow and ran my fingers down his chest to the fascinating terrain of his firm, segmented abdomen. "What happened to the optimism?"

Both his eyebrows went up, and he tipped his head to one side. "Last night you said you never have sex on a first date."

"I've never had a first date with *you* before," I clarified. Then I let my hand continue on its downward path.

The skin of his stomach was taut and silky smooth, except for a dusting of hair forming an intriguing path from his navel to the top of his trunks.

Hunter sucked an audible breath through his teeth when my fingertips slipped beneath the waistband. My own breaths were coming harder and faster.

Touching him like this after all the days and weeks of fantasizing about it was almost an otherworldly experience.

With a groan, he clamped his arms around me and dragged me to face him so that my legs straddled his lap, and that glorious hard-on was snug against the center of my meager bikini bottoms.

Seizing my mouth in an open, searching kiss, Hunter let his hands roam ravenously.

It seemed like each time he touched a new part of me his excitement reached a new level.

He moaned into my mouth, and his tongue plunged deeper, coaxing out more and more pleasure as his hands explored and branded and claimed.

I welcomed it all, melting under his touch, pressing my breasts further into his hands when he cupped them, urging my lower half against the ridge of his arousal with increasingly rhythmic motions.

Breaking contact with my mouth, Hunter stared at me with such an absorption he appeared dazed.

Wearing a drunken looking smile, he said, "I can't believe this is happening. It's like I'm dreaming... but I'm also hyper-alert, like I have super-powered senses or something."

I raked thick, dark hair back from his face and leaned forward to pepper feathery kisses over his forehead, the bridge of his nose, and the tops of his cheekbones, working my way toward his ear.

"Well... you *are* Ant Man," I said in a teasing whisper.

He laughed and took my face between his hands, kissing me with a growl. "You make me feel like the Hulk—only I want to rip *your* clothes off instead of mine."

"No ripping required." Reaching behind my neck, I tugged at one of the strings supporting my bikini top.

The knot loosened, and the twin triangles collapsed, baring my aching breasts to the night air and to Hunter's gaze. Which looked gratifyingly enraptured.

"My god..." he whispered. And then he didn't speak for a while.

Moving his tongue in lazy strokes, he teased the tip of one breast then the other before focusing his attention on one side, licking and tugging fixedly, layering sensation on top of sensation.

Tingling excitement combined with near-hypnotic pleasure, and my head dropped back on my shoulders. The inky blue sky was dotted with stars, faraway globes of fire standing witness to the single best night of my life.

Closer to home, the fire inside of me billowed, growing and gathering in every limb and nerve ending and setting off an insistent throbbing between my thighs.

Only one thing—and one man—could satisfy it. I rose slightly onto my knees, rubbing my core against that tantalizing hard length.

Hunter gripped my hips, stilling me as his chin dropped to his chest. "Hold on, I've gotta... I need a little break here. You are too... I'm sorry. I've wanted this for too long."

Sliding my fingers under each side of his jaw, I lifted his face so our eyes made searing contact. "I want it, too," I whispered.

"Are you sure?"

Hunter's singular blue eyes were bright with passion. So I knew what it cost him to say, "We don't have to do this."

We didn't *have* to. But I definitely wanted to.

"You don't want to?" I teased.

Hunter choked over a laugh. "Me? *Of course* I want to. I've been waiting for this moment since I was twelve. There's a legit chance I'll die of lust overdose if we stop. But I'll do it—if you're not ready."

Running my hands down the sides of his strong neck, over his wide shoulders and muscled chest, I looked him straight in the eye.

"I'm *so* ready."

"Oh, thank God."

Gripping my head, he slanted his mouth over mine and

kissed me again and again while I rose and worked my bikini bottoms down.

Hunter shifted to help me then kept his hands on my waist as I lowered onto him.

When the tip of his cock made contact with my entrance, his grip tightened, stopping my momentum. "Oh shit. I didn't bring any condoms. I told you I didn't expect this tonight."

"I didn't either. I'm on the pill," I offered. "And I haven't been with anyone in months—not since Harry. I got tested as soon as we broke up because he was, you know..."

"Cheating on you," Hunter finished for me. "Right. Same here. I mean, not about the cheating—I've been tested too. All good. And I haven't been with anyone since... how long ago was the charity ball?"

My head jerked back in shock. "You haven't been with a woman since that night?"

He smiled. "See what you did to me with your magic kiss? You ruined me for life. I only want *you*."

My heart swelled almost painfully at his sweet words. I shook my head. "Remind me why we didn't get together in high school and live happily ever after?"

"Because I was a fucking idiot."

"A genius-idiot," I corrected.

"That's right. But I'm a smarter genius-idiot now. I've wised up. And I plan to make up for lost time."

Sinking a hand into my hair, he held my nape and guided my mouth to his, not just kissing me but possessing me with his lips, teeth, and tongue.

As I began to move against him and rise to my knees once more, Hunter broke the kiss. "I just thought of something else. Don't we need some sort of, you know, lubricant or something? I know the water's not exactly—"

His words broke off mid-question as I slid onto him. "Not

a problem," I sighed with a saucy grin. "*You* are lubrication enough."

"And you are the sexiest fucking woman on Earth. God, I could eat you alive." Hunter thrust upward, caressing my breasts and lowering his head to take one erect nipple into the wet heat of his mouth.

As his tongue stroked me on the outside, his thick length stroked me inside. Gripping his shoulder with one hand and the back of his neck with the other, I bore down and undulated my hips, relishing in the masculine impalement and setting a rhythm that seemed to feel good to him.

It sure as hell felt good to me. In fact, this wasn't going to last long.

Between the months of celibacy and Hunter's sweetness and his absolutely *incredible* body, I could already feel a climax creeping up on me.

Hunter ensured it when he slid one of his hands around to clench my bottom, helping to drive me harder and faster on his solid shaft. His tongue worked faster, too, swirling and sucking the sensitive tip of my breast until I was on desire overload.

Turning to rest his cheek against the slope of my breast, he gritted out a warning. "Kristal... I'm sorry... I'm not going to be able to hold onto this..."

And then my screams drowned out his voice. I bucked against him, clenching his hair, twisting and groaning as a kaleidoscope of sensation rolled through me.

The voluptuous feeling was so acute I was gasping for breath.

"Yes," Hunter yelled, as his hoarse cries joined mine. "Come for me Kristal. Fuck, you're so good. Better than anything."

And it was. Making love with Hunter was like a whole

new thing... better than every other sexual experience of my lifetime combined.

As wracking aftershocks of pleasure eased into afterglow, he held me close and cuddled me against his warm, wet, bare skin. It felt almost as good as the sex.

I nuzzled into him, breathing deeply of his unique masculine scent and running my free hand over the scruff on his jaw and neck, down to the light fur of hair on his chest and abdomen.

When my body finally stopped throbbing with sensation, Hunter gently lifted me and moved me to the side, pulling my shoulders toward him and tucking my head against his chest. He kissed the top of my undoubtedly disheveled hair several times then let out a long exhale.

"That was..." He didn't finish the sentence, just dropped his head back to rest on the edge of the pool, biting his lower lip and shaking his head as if in disbelief.

After a moment he turned slightly to slide a heated glance at me. "*What* are you doing to me?"

Blushing from embarrassment and pleasure, I searched for a response. All I really wanted to do was kiss him again.

"I don't know. What are you doing to *me*? This is amazing, this whole night."

I lifted a hand toward the starry night sky then swept it down to indicate the luxurious yacht deck and then toward his magnificent physique.

"I've never been on a date that's come even close to this. I mean, if *this* is how you wine and dine all your dates, it's a miracle you've stayed single this long."

Hunter's expression soured, as if he found the thought distasteful. "I've never done anything like this for anyone before."

"Oh." My heart contracted in a sharp, sweet pang. "Well, *no one* has ever done anything like this for me. Honestly, no one I know would ever have planned an evening so special, so… perfect for me. Thank you."

"I would have thought Harry spoiled you every chance he got."

"Not really. I mean, yes, we went out to some nice places, but he was like my dad, busy all the time, working. Even when it was just the two of us, he was distracted."

In contrast, Hunter seemed completely focused on me. It was flattering to have the full attention of a man like him—brilliant, successful, charming, and so handsome he took my breath away.

At the moment, that handsome face was wearing a frown I couldn't account for. "I would have loved to take you on a date like this in high school," he said. "I didn't even have a car most of the time, much less the money to plan a sunset dinner cruise."

Climbing back onto his lap, I wrapped my arms around his neck and pressed a soft kiss to the straight, sullen line of his mouth.

"I wouldn't have needed anything like that. We could have gone to the movies, or on a picnic, or even for a beach walk. I would have just loved spending time with you. If you'd invited me to go bowling tonight, I'd have been just as excited to go."

"Yeah, right." He sounded cynical enough to give Reid, Mr. Grumpy himself, a run for his money. "You wouldn't even be here if I didn't live in a mansion and have access to a yacht."

"Hunter… it's true. I mean, this is nice…" I gestured at the incredible view. "But money *isn't* everything."

"Maybe not, but it does matter. I mean, there was a reason you chose to go out with Larson Overstreet, a reason you were dating Harry McAllen of the Oceanview Avenue McAllens instead of, say, the guy who caught the lobster we ate tonight… or grew the vegetables."

"I'd have no problem dating a lobsterman or a farmer," I insisted, feeling a little insulted.

"Money can come in handy, for sure. But it's just a means to an end, a tool. If you let it rule you, then you wind up like Margot, who's one of the unhappiest human beings I've ever known. Even Harry. I'm fairly sure the reason he dumped me right after my dad's stroke is he knew of our precarious financial situation. He started dating the daughter of one of the firm's other founding partners, whose parents own half the prime waterfront property in the state. Trust me, money doesn't make someone a good person."

At Hunter's unconvinced expression and *hmmph* noise, I went on.

"Once when we were in high school, I think we were seniors, I saw you buy lunch for that kid Elliott who used to eat just one sad little peanut butter and jelly sandwich every day for months. I didn't realize it until later that day when I asked someone, but that's what they gave the students who weren't paid up on their lunch accounts."

"Yeah. I knew what it meant."

"Well, I was aware at the time that your family didn't have much money..."

Hunter's eyes darted away toward the pool deck. Clearly, I'd made him uncomfortable, but I persisted. What I had to say was important for him to hear.

"I watched you deliver a full hot lunch tray to that kid, and you told him you had to go and didn't have time to eat it. You walked out without eating at all that day."

I shook my head, reliving the admiration I'd felt for him in that moment.

"You made *me* want to do something. I went home and talked to my dad about what could be done to stop the lunch-shaming situation, and he got involved. Hunter... *that's* the reason I liked you... because of your heart."

Resting my hand on his pec, I rubbed a gentle circle over his heart. "You were always looking out for other people, doing kind things. I'm here tonight because you're still that same guy. You may have more money now than you could ever spend, but you're still the same person inside. You're still that sweet, skinny, big-hearted kid. At our core, we never really change who we are."

Instead of making Hunter happy, my words seemed to bother him. With a hand on each of my hips he lifted me and set me aside, then stood and moved toward the steps to get out of the water.

"What's the matter?" I asked.

"Nothing. We should go ahead and get inside. It's getting late, and the captain's going to want to increase speed to get us back to harbor."

When his feet were firmly planted on the deck, he turned back and offered me a stiff smile as well as a hand out of the pool. I took it and climbed the short set of steps to the deck.

Though Hunter immediately wrapped a large, fluffy towel around me, I shivered, feeling extra cold.

And it wasn't just the chilly night air that was responsible.

EIGHTEEN

Bad Timing

Kristal

Inside, Hunter busied himself with getting me a robe and showing me to a cabin where I could shower and change.

"The bathroom's fully stocked with toiletries—all the brands you have at home. Take your time. I'll meet you back in the living room."

He gave me a brief, tight-lipped nod and continued down the corridor toward another cabin. Something had changed, but I couldn't put my finger on it.

"Okay. See you in a few minutes," I said to his back.

I rinsed off then dressed in the clothes I'd worn onboard—someone had placed them on the bed while I showered in the adjoining bathroom.

Then I went back into the bathroom to brush my teeth. By the time I finished, the mirror had de-fogged enough for me to see my reflection.

Good Lord. I was a disaster. No wonder Hunter had run away.

He probably thought he was in a fairytale reversal where

the princess turned into a frog instead of the other way around.

I finger combed my hair and rubbed at the mascara smudges under my eyes, but there was no hope of restoring my makeup to its former glory. My lips looked swollen, and there was a whisker burn on one side of my neck.

That part of my reflection, at least, made me smile. I'd had fun getting that whisker burn. I wanted a *lot* more of them.

Whatever was bothering Hunter, we'd talk about it, get it straightened out, and get back to the good stuff. Because things had been very, *very* good tonight.

"Everything's fine," I told my frowzy doppleganger. "Everything's going to be okay."

When I returned to the living room, Hunter was already there, dried off and dressed and once again looking ready for Town and Country magazine to drop by for a photo shoot.

It wasn't fair that he could look so effortlessly dashing while I looked *exactly* like I'd just been banged in a hot tub.

He offered me a glass of wine and gestured to a buttery soft white leather sofa. "Want to have a seat here until we dock?"

"Sure."

But he didn't sit next to me as I would have expected. Instead, he took the matching sofa opposite mine.

"You warm enough?" he asked in a polite, almost businesslike tone, as if I were a plane passenger and he was offering me a complimentary blanket for the flight.

I nodded, studying his impassive expression. "I'm fine."

A low cocktail table separated the two couches where we sat, but it wasn't the only obstacle between us. Some sort of invisible wall had dropped around him.

What had happened? Over the course of a few minutes his demeanor had shifted from relaxed and happy to quiet and tense.

A sense of foreboding grew inside me like the fog beginning to build on the water outside.

"Hey—you okay? Did I say something wrong?" I asked.

Hunter smiled, but it didn't reach his eyes. He looked... haunted.

"Of course not. Last night's lack of sleep is catching up with me is all." He stood abruptly. "Why don't you gather your things and get ready to disembark? I'm going to check in with the captain."

Hunter left the room, and I didn't see him again until the yacht had docked. He returned and led me down the gangway to the dock and toward the parking area.

A strong odor of low tide permeated the chilly air.

"We're going to have a hard time hiding where we've been tonight, reeking like fish," I quipped, trying to break the new, uncomfortable silence. "Might as well just go ahead and confess to the guys when we get back, although I assume Reid already knows what's going on with us."

Hunter stiffened beside me. "Listen... about that. I've thought about it, and maybe it's not the best idea to talk to them just yet."

"You mean you want to keep us a secret?"

I didn't like the idea of hiding our relationship from our housemates. It felt too much like lying. "Why? Are you ashamed of me?"

"Of course not." He sounded fierce. "I could never be ashamed of *you*. It's just not a good time to rock the boat. We've got to finish up the show. Work on Chipp is crazy busy."

A cold sensation washed through me and remained even after we'd gotten into Hunter's pre-heated car where I turned his words over in my head.

"Are you saying you don't think we should date?"

From his answering expression I realized that was exactly what he'd been getting at.

Wow. One minute he was full-speed ahead, and now he was slamming on the brakes.

"What happened Hunter? What changed between last night, when you told me you wanted me, that you always had, and right now?" I paused, blushing. "I mean other than you giving me the best orgasm of my life. *Talk* to me. Where did you go during the night? What did you do?"

He shook his head, wearing a frown. "Nothing. It doesn't matter. It's just... I don't think we should say anything to the guys. They're not just my friends. They're my co-workers. They're my housemates. We all have to work together every day. Live together. And this company we've built... it means everything to me. I can't let a rift with them slow it down. I've clawed and scraped and sacrificed to get where I am—I can't go back."

His voice increased in intensity as he white-knuckled the steering wheel. "I can't risk losing it all when I've finally made it. Can you understand that?"

I nodded, feeling numb. "Yes," I whispered, but it was a lie.

I *didn't* understand. Not the part about why he'd pursued me so avidly if he was worried having a relationship with me would destroy his friendships and his company. I *did* understand the part about his company meaning everything to him. About putting work first.

It sounded just like my father.

Suddenly I was ten years old and hearing my dad's voice as he explained why he couldn't make it to my soccer game... my spelling bee... my school arts night.

"I wish I could be there, sweetheart," he'd said. "But this case is very important. My clients are counting on me. I can't let them down. There will be other events."

There had been, and he'd made it to precious few of them.

Harry had been on the same track, one paved with good intentions and excuses and ending in lonely nights for me and a pervasive feeling that I was an afterthought—or a bother—for having any needs that went beyond what money could buy.

He'd made work his priority, which left me begging for scraps of his time. It was one reason I'd been slow to pick up on the clues he was seeing another woman.

I was *used* to him not being around.

What was wrong with me? Why did I keep falling for unavailable, career-obsessed workaholic men?

I'd thought Hunter was different. He'd claimed to have always wanted me, to have been pining for me since high school.

Yet now that we had a chance to finally be together, he refused to open up to me and really *be* there.

Even Larson Overstreet, the only other man I'd gone out with since Harry, had a demanding career and said his work hours were ridiculous.

Apparently, I had a type. And it was time to break the pattern.

"I understand," I said as Hunter made the short drive from the marina to Oceanview Avenue.

"Your company is your priority, and that's fine. You need to keep your focus on it. You also made a promise to your friends and partners, and you should keep it. I'm moving out soon anyway, possibly out of state, so it doesn't make sense to start anything. Chalk it up to bad timing."

"Wait, Kristal..." he protested weakly.

"No, let me finish. It's fine, Hunter. We've been friends for a long time—let's just keep it that way. We're better as friends."

His grip on the steering wheel didn't loosen, but he

uttered a tight response. “If that’s what you want.”

Though my suggestion had made sense to me when I’d said it, my heart shriveled at his easy acceptance. It wasn’t what I wanted at all.

“Yes,” I managed to whisper. “I think it’s for the best.”

Tucker was the only one awake when we made it back to the mansion. He was sprawled out on the couch with his laptop, snack wrappers piled on the table beside him.

“Hey guys. Where ya been?” he asked in a friendly tone.

Hunter grunted a one-word answer. “Out.”

“We went out on Reid’s boat,” I said, forcing a brightness I didn’t feel. “I needed to get some shots of the mansions from the water and the Eastport Bridge lights at night. It was beautiful.”

“Sweet,” Tucker said. “So, you two staying up for a while?”

“Oh, not me. I’m exhausted. I’m gonna head up to bed,” I said.

I needed this night to end, and I prayed Hunter wouldn’t feel compelled to walk me to the door of my suite.

Standing there with him and *not* kissing him goodnight after this incredible “date” would be too heartbreaking.

Hunter scrubbed a hand through his short hair. “I should probably get some work done. I was gone a long time. I’ll hang with you for a while, Tuck.”

“Look at Doc—burning the midnight oil,” Tuck said with a laugh. “Settle in bro. Plenty of junk food to share and a fresh pot of coffee in the kitchen.”

“Thanks.” Hunter nodded, but his gaze wasn’t on Tucker. Instead, his sad eyes locked with mine just before I turned to head up the stairs alone.

“Good night guys,” I called back over my shoulder.

“Night, Kristal,” Tucker replied.

Hunter said nothing, and I purposely didn't look back to see if he watched me go.

It didn't matter. As promising as our relationship had looked this morning, it was clearly over now.

And Snow White was done with waiting for Prince Charming's kiss.

I was wide awake—and on my own.

NINETEEN
Just Friends

Hunter- One week later

The great room had never felt so small.

Hot, bright lights blazed from every corner, and no less than twenty crew members were crowded into every available space.

Guys in sneakers and backward caps held huge cameras on their shoulders and awaited instruction from Hap while two women with cosmetics cases moved from Aiden to Paul to Kristal to me, making sure the "talent" was ready to begin shooting for the day.

Reid, who was still not thrilled with the whole thing, complained as he swatted away one of them, "I thought this was Tech House, not a makeover show."

Hap had sent some dailies to the network he'd been talking to, and they were interested. Very interested.

They wanted to fast-track the pilot and have the shooting wrap up in a couple of weeks, which meant all hands on deck.

Even Tuck, who'd needed more undereye concealer than the rest of us, was there, though his mouth had been stretched in a semi-permanent yawn for the past half hour.

Following the loose script Hap had given us, we went through the motions of working, discussed the "software" we'd allegedly designed for the show's competition and argued a bit.

Hap said some conflict was important to keep things interesting and maintain the tension of the episode, even if we had to manufacture it.

When it came to Kristal and me, the tension was a hundred percent legitimate.

We weren't fighting. No, it was far worse than that. She'd been nothing but pleasant and polite for the past week since our ill-fated date.

But she was distant. She rarely spoke to me directly and avoided eye contact.

When I'd asked how her job search was going, she'd given me a breezy one-word answer, "Fine," and found some reason to leave the room.

When I asked how her photos from the sunset cruise had turned out, she'd told me she hadn't had a chance to look through them yet.

We'd agreed to keep our relationship limited to friendship, but honestly, it didn't feel like we were even friends anymore.

Even the other guys had noticed.

"Okay, cut. Let's take a break everyone. Back in thirty minutes, okay?" Hap said.

Tuck, Aiden, Josh, and Paul dashed for the kitchen where craft services had laid out a spread. Several crew members filed out the back door to smoke on the terrace, and Kristal headed for the stairs as usual.

When she wasn't at work, shooting photos, or filming the show, she was in her room these days.

Once she was out of earshot, Hap turned to me. "What is *up* with you two?"

"What do you mean?"

"You're moping around, and Kristal's like a phantom. Neither one of you has said more than a few words the past few days. Did you have a fight or something? Did she shoot you down?"

"I hope it's not my fault," Reid interjected, walking over to join us. "I didn't mean to mess up your game, man. I hoped the thing with the yacht would help make up for the way I acted before, but I guess it didn't work."

I shook my head, my eyes downcast. "No. It wasn't you. It was me. The yacht was great. The whole night was great."

There was a pause before I said, "But I told her we should be friends."

"Excuse me, *what*?"

Hap's arms flailed, and his eyes bugged out. "You've gotta be kidding me. This whole thing was because you wanted *out* of the friend zone. Although I'm not complaining about doing the show now that it's about to be picked up by the network. But I don't get it."

"Why would you say you wanted to be just friends?" Reid asked, looking truly dumbfounded. "You've been drooling over that girl since the second she moved in. What—she's not as great as you thought she was?"

I gave him a sharp glance. "No. She's incredible. It's just... we're not right for each other."

"Does this have something to do with your dad being in jail?" Hap asked.

"Keep your voice down," I hissed. "I don't want her to know about that."

Just then the sound guy called out to Hap to come over and listen to something, holding out a pair of headphones for him to put on.

"Be right back," Hap said.

Reid laid a hand on my shoulder. "You love her, huh?" he asked in a low voice. At my continued silence, he said, "Look, if there's one thing I know… it's unrequited love. It sucks, man."

"Is that why you started StillYours-dot-com?"

Reid shot me a forbidding glance. "We're talking about you and Kristal, not me and Mara. So… do you love her or not?"

What was the point in lying? The answer was already obvious to Reid and probably anyone else who had eyes.

"Yeah. I do. Always have. And I'm not even sure it was unrequited. But I blew it. Things were going great the other night… and then I freaked."

"The famous Hunter Bestia lost his ice-man control? Hey, I'm just kidding. The right woman can do that to you, and a little polar-cap-melting passion's not a bad thing."

I shook my head. "Some of the things she was saying about me… she thinks she knows me, but she doesn't. She's got me built up to be some kind of hero. I don't want her to find out about my past… about my dad. And it's inevitable. When she finds out, she's going to be sorry she said those things to a white-trash nobody, a convict's son, a—"

"Hold on there," Reid interrupted. "You are *not* trash. And you're not your dad."

"I could be—easily. It doesn't matter how much money I make, how much power I gain. I'm still his son. When I saw him that night he got arrested, he said…"

My voice broke, and I stopped, shaking off the thought. "It doesn't matter. Kristal was right—you don't really ever change who you are at your core. You're always essentially the same person."

Reid's hand on my shoulder clamped down harder.

"That's right. And you're one of the best people I've ever known, now *and* back then. When Mara split, you were there for me—you've always been there for me and everyone else. You're good to everyone—except yourself. And that needs to change. You need to let other people do things for *you* for a change. I'm going to start by helping you fix things with Kristal."

"How? She'll barely even look at me, much less talk to me. She said we were 'better as friends.' It's too late."

"Don't worry," Reid said. "I have a plan. First... we need to talk to Hap."

TWENTY
Good at Pretending

Kristal- Later that night

My gaze bounced from Hunter to Hap to Reid then made the rounds again.

"You want me to what?" I could hardly believe what I'd heard coming out of the director's mouth.

"It's just for the cameras," Hap assured me. "The network looked at the dailies, and they like the show, but they want to see it 'spiced up' a little. They want an in-house romance. It happened naturally at the Boston Tech House, and they loved it."

He'd been traveling back and forth between the houses, shooting in both locations to give the network an idea of how the competitive teams would look pitted against each other in separate houses.

Now we were all gathered in the great room of the Eastport Bay house.

"If we had another girl on the show, I'd ask her to do it, but you're all we've got. And I'm afraid everyone here is firmly hetero, so there are no other possibilities. Come on—it's all fake. It'll be funny."

I shook my head. “I said from the start I wasn’t doing this if it was going to turn into some sort of dating show.”

“It’s not a dating show. It’ll be just a few scenes here and there. We’ve come this far—might as well finish strong. And it’s just for a couple more weeks.”

I eyed him suspiciously. “Who would I be ‘involved’ with?”

“Well, I’m the director, so I’m out. No one would buy that you’d be involved with Josh or a grumpy SOB like Reid.”

“Hey,” Reid protested.

“Seriously dude, you’re about as charming as a hemorrhoid these days—no offense.”

Reid squinted and gave him a syrupy grin. “How could I possibly take offense at being compared to a swollen rectal vein?”

“Paul is out because of the allergy issue,” Hap continued. “No fun kissing a guy who’s got to stop and blow his nose every few seconds. Tuck’s barely around, and when he is, he’s yawning the whole time. Aiden’s so shy he can barely look at you, so it won’t make sense if he suddenly turns into some kind of lothario. I mean, everyone knows reality shows are fake, but we can only strain believability so much.”

He paused. “That leaves Hunter.”

My reply was instantaneous. “No. It’ll never work. We have zero chemistry.”

Hunter narrowed those spectacular turquoise eyes at me, and my stupid heart responded, revealing my lie by flip-flopping vigorously.

The area between my legs flooded with heat, reminding me, as if I could ever forget, exactly how good our chemistry was.

“Come on,” Hap cajoled. “All you have to do is flirt a little bit—some witty banter here and there. I’ll write it for you if you want. Maybe let us catch *one little* 'forbidden' kiss on camera."

He held up his hands at my obvious bristling. "It's all pretend. We're really close with the network, and I know this will put us over the top. It would be a huge favor. I'll owe you. Please Kristal... I'm literally begging."

My gaze slid from one pleading expression to the next, landing on Hunter's unreadable one.

"Fine," I deadpanned. "I guess I can force myself to seem interested in him—*if* he can do the same."

He smirked at my insult. "That should be no problem. I'm good at pretending."

Getting a job out of state was starting to sound more appealing all the time.

"When do we start?" I asked.

Hap checked his phone planner app.

"The crew will be back tomorrow at one. You'll go on your first 'date' then. We want it to be unique and picturesque for the cameras—one of our selling points is the beauty of Eastport Bay. Thankfully the Winter Festival is going on, so we're sending you guys to First Beach."

I balked. "The beach? I'm not one of those Polar Plunge people, so if your idea of picturesque was my pale winter legs shivering in a swimsuit and my lips turning blue, you're out of luck. This girl is keeping her clothes *on*."

This time.

* * *

As it turned out, Hap hadn't planned for us to swim but to attend a beach polo match.

Normally Eastport Bay Polo matches took place on the grassy playing fields of the nearby equestrian center and polo club —and in much warmer weather.

But as a special exhibition for the Winter Festival, it was being played today on the sand at low tide.

Hunter and I stood side-by-side with about a thousand other spectators lining the playing field, which had been carved out of the intertidal area of one of Newport's most picturesque beaches.

The sandy stretch was cradled in a cove between the famous Bluff Walk and the mansions on one side and, on the other, a public pavilion complete with a snack bar and a 1950's carousel.

As opposed to how it had been on our real first—and only—date, the conversation between us was stilted.

We both wore microphones tucked into the necklines of our clothing. The wiring of mine snaked down through my bra and around my waist to a battery pack at my lower back.

Every time I moved, I felt it, and it made me extra-conscious of the fact I was being listened to—and watched. Which made it difficult to even think of things to say.

I should have let Hap write that dialogue for me after all.

Hunter was apparently handling it better. He leaned down to me, his breath fogging the cold marine air as he spoke close to my ear.

"I read that the thoroughbreds are accustomed to the sandy footing—it's like their natural habitats. They play on similar footing materials in arena polo. But you probably already knew that. I'll bet you've been to lots of polo matches, huh?"

"Actually no," I replied, feeling contrary. His nearness was as unsettling as ever. "My family never went. I always wanted to go myself but never made the time."

He gave me a charming smile, just perfect for the camera trained on us.

"I'm glad you made the time today. It's nice to be with you—just the two of us."

I had to refrain from rolling my eyes. If I did, Hunter would have to repeat the cheesy line for take two, and I was eager to get this whole ridiculous experience over with.

It didn't help that he was, as he'd said, "really good at pretending." My heart was apparently too stupid to know the difference.

When he smiled over at me, took my cold hand inside his impossibly warm one, murmured comments on the match and the view in my ear, it tripped all over itself, stumbling and rolling in my chest.

It all felt so *real.*

After the second chukker, or period of play, we walked over to warm ourselves by the fire pit. Hunter bought two hot chocolates from the cash bar and handed one to me. I gripped it gratefully, lifting the cup to my chin to warm my face.

"Maybe we should watch the rest of the match from up there," he suggested, pointing at the rocky cliff overlooking the beach.

Atop it, just on the other side of the famous Bluff Walk, sat the gracious Astor Hotel. Housed in a twenty-room Gilded Age mansion, the Forbes Four Star hotel offered a birds-eye view of First Beach and luxury accommodations fit for royalty.

I'd never stayed there, but I'd eaten at its elegant signature restaurant, Madeleine, several times. I could see people watching the match from its outdoor terrace café, which glowed with the flickering light of towering patio heaters.

They looked… warm.

"That would be great."

"Great," Hunter said. Together we strolled up the hill on the beachside sidewalk. I shuddered from the cold, and he slipped an arm around my shoulders.

"For the cameras," he whispered when I stiffened in response.

I allowed the contact but remained quiet for most of the

walk. It took some self-talk to remind myself the warmth and solid feel of his tall frame were simply part of the show and not something to be enjoyed.

Or craved, as I'd been doing since our date night on the yacht.

Memories of the more pleasant parts of that evening continued to plague me, stubbornly intruding on my thoughts despite my best efforts to control them.

It just didn't make sense.

Why had Hunter so carefully planned out the perfect evening—the sunset photography opportunity, my favorite foods, the sweltering kisses on the deck—the hot tub—then shut me out?

I'd probably never know, which was tragic considering the happy times I'd spent with him were among the very best moments of my life.

My plan was to make a beeline for those heaters I'd spotted in the Astor's open-air café and bar area, but when Hunter and I reached the hotel, my plans changed abruptly.

A large, fragrant bonfire roared in the firepit at the center of the beautifully manicured lawn.

It drew me like the proverbial moth, especially since a hotel employee was handing out s'mores kits. I was starving, and s'mores happened to be a particular favorite of mine.

"Oh, this is good," the cameraman said as he followed us to the blazing firepit. "Make sure you toast some marsh-mallows."

"Way ahead of you," I assured him.

Five minutes later, I was warm and had a mouthful of chocolate, graham cracker, and marshmallow—the combination of which was proof that God loved humanity and wanted His children to be happy.

And I *was* happy. For the first time since the ridiculous faux-dating idea had been proposed, I actually felt relaxed.

Hunter had enjoyed a couple of s'mores as well, though perhaps not as much as I had enjoyed them. My gaze flickered to his face.

His very, very handsome face—the eyes that threatened to drown me in their blue depths every time they met mine and lips so sensuous, I could barely stand to watch him eat, much less keep from imagining kissing him again.

Which I'd been doing far too often. Relaxation—gone.

Licking those lips to remove a remnant of marshmallow, Hunter looked over at me and chuckled.

"You've got a little chocolate..."

He pointed at the left corner of my mouth, and I probed it with the tip of my tongue, understanding that I'd made a mess in my hurry to consume my own tasty treats.

Biting his lower lip and squinting in amusement, he reached for me. "Come here."

He used his thumb to swipe at the offending splotch.

As he did so, his knuckles grazed my chin, eliciting full body shivers that had nothing to do with the cold.

Then he did the most astounding thing.

He popped the tip of his thumb into his mouth and sucked it to remove the chocolate, holding steady eye contact with me the entire time.

In an instant, my skin was blazing like the fire pit beside us, and my heart was racing crazy circles around my chest.

Honestly, I felt like I needed to remove my coat, but I didn't because the ever-present camera was watching. I didn't want whoever edited the video to wonder why I'd felt the need to shuck layers in thirty-degree weather.

Why *did* Hunter's touch affect me like this when no one else's ever had? When I *knew* a relationship between us was impossible?

It was sheer stupidity, but I couldn't seem to help myself.

Show or no show, I wasn't sure how much more I could

take. Being so close to him all the time without truly being *with* him was becoming painful.

Hunter had wanted to discuss the idea of a "fresh start" once or twice in the past week, but there was no point to it. Living with him had given me an up close and personal view of his life.

And I'd seen enough to know Hunter and I didn't have a real future together. He was too much like my father.

As much as I'd adored Richard Bianco, I didn't want to marry a man like him.

The prospect of creating a life with Hunter, falling deeper and deeper in love with him, perhaps having children with him... and then losing him to an early stress-related death was too agonizing to contemplate.

Even if he remained healthy, I wouldn't be happy married to an ambitious, driven man who was never around.

Maybe one of the jobs I'd applied for in New York would pan out soon. I'd finish up the filming for Hap's sake, pack my things, and make my fresh new start in a brand-new place.

Maybe if I didn't have to see Hunter and talk to him every day, I could move on with my life.

TWENTY-ONE

The Kiss

Hunter

The plan wasn't working.

Over the past couple of weeks, I'd taken Kristal on several more "dates," none of which had resulted in a kiss at the end or even a single instance of legitimate hand-holding.

Instead of warming to me, she'd grown even more distant, if that was possible.

On camera, she was sweet and flirty, playing her part perfectly. When the cameras stopped rolling though, she reverted to her cool, unflappable self.

I could almost feel my dreams slipping through my fingers.

"What am I gonna do?" I asked Hap as we waited for Kristal to come downstairs for the day's filming. "She's combing the internet for jobs every day. Eventually she's going to find one and move out. We've gotta kick this thing up a notch."

Hap seemed to consider it for a moment. Then he nodded rapidly, slapping my back in reassurance.

"Okay, I know what to do. Leave it to your director."

Kristal came into the great room, wearing a red turtleneck and winter white pants.

My eyes nearly popped out of their sockets. The woman was born to wear red. The hair stylist and one of the makeup artists had been upstairs with her, and she was camera-ready perfection.

"Hey," she said to the assembled "dwarves" and the film crew. "What's on tap today? I promised Cinda I'd stop by for a visit. I haven't seen her in weeks, and it's my day off from the restaurant, so I was hoping maybe we could film my parts early?"

"No problem," Hap said. "We just need to get a few quick pick-ups today—you know, scenes we're missing to sort of fill in the blanks and round out the show for the editors."

He grabbed his clipboard and did a quick perusal of the shot sheet attached to it.

"Right. Okay... so the only thing we'll need you and Hunter for, Kristal... is the kiss."

His tone was matter-of-fact, so blasé, I almost believed I hadn't heard it right. But Kristal had heard the same thing because she repeated the words immediately.

And her tone was the farthest thing from blasé.

"The kiss? What kiss?" she yelped.

"What are you talking about, Hap?" I demanded, playing along, while gratitude and anticipation grabbed each other and did a little whirling jig inside my chest.

Our director friend elaborated. "Well, we need one. I mean, more than one would be great, if you two are willing, but we've got to have at least one. Otherwise, the dating storyline just isn't gonna fly. The viewers will be pulling for it. We gotta deliver."

"What do you mean 'we?'" Kristal snapped. "It's not you and Hunter kissing. You're asking *me* to do it."

Hap pressed his hands together in front of him, forming

the prayer position. "No, I'm *begging* you. Come on, Kris, he's not *that* ugly."

She smirked, but there was panic in her pretty green eyes.

My gaze traveled from them down her petal-soft cheeks to that heart-shaped mouth. A mouth I'd literally been dreaming about.

It was torture to be given something you'd spent decades longing for only to have it snatched away again after a tiny taste.

The past few weeks had felt like withdrawal. But the addict was on the verge of another addictive hit—I would *finally* be allowed to kiss Kristal again.

And it was going to happen in front of a roomful of people.

I'd have to maintain absolute mastery over my emotions, clamping down on every last nerve ending to keep from responding to her kiss the way I had in the past and embarrassing us both.

How would she react? Judging from the outward signs, kissing me would be like pulling teeth for Kristal.

But as our gazes locked, there was something intriguing in her eyes, an intensity I hadn't seen in weeks.

Hope surged inside me, battling with a desperate fear that she'd refuse altogether.

Slowly, she nodded to accede to Hap's request, and my pulse leapt in a primal victory dance.

Hap slapped his hands together and whooped. "All right! That's what I'm talking about. We're gonna shoot a love scene today."

* * *

For a "love scene" it felt awfully technical.

Forty minutes after Hap's announcement, Kristal and I

were wearing microphones and positioned in the walk-in pantry, which had been perfectly lit.

Hap, wearing a set of headphones, stood just outside it along with a cameraman and the sound guy, Ethan.

"Okay, so you two have snuck away for a little privacy," Hap directed. "It starts as a conversation, and then you're gonna kiss."

"What are we supposed to talk about?" Kristal asked.

"I don't know—your plans for the day. Talk about going to visit Cinda and ask for a ride or something. It'll be very damsel-in-distress."

Kristal scowled. "I don't want to be a damsel. I never asked any of you to save me—Hunter asked me to move in and be in the show as a favor."

Hap's hands went up in front of him in a defensive gesture. "Whoa whoa. Okay. Okay."

Wanting to appease her, I interceded. "I'll ask her to come with me to my brother's house today. They're having a dinner thing, and I'll say I want my brother and his wife to meet her. Then she can pretend she thinks that's sweet, and we'll kiss. How does that sound?"

Hap answered, "Great," though the question had been intended for Kristal.

She visibly relaxed. "Okay. I guess that'll work."

As the lighting guy made some last-minute adjustments and the cameraman focused his shot, Kristal spoke to me in a low voice.

"I hope you *don't* see me as a damsel-in-distress. I never wanted anything from you. I never expected you to take care of me."

I lowered my own voice, speaking close to her ear in a soothing tone. "I know that. You've never done anything to make me think you wanted or needed me."

Pausing, I wondered if I had enough courage to say the next words screaming in my brain.

"Although... I wouldn't have minded if you had," I whispered.

"Oh nice," Hap said. "We're definitely keeping that line."

"You were rolling?" I yelped. "No—you are definitely *not* using that line—or anything she just said. Cut it, Hap—I'm serious." I pointed to the cameraman. "Roll it back and record over it."

"Fine." Hap blew out an exaggerated breath. "You two are touchier than a pair of Pomeranians today."

He turned to the camera operator. "Okay, roll it back and let's record."

To Kristal and me he said, "We're about to film, so don't anybody whisper any sweet nothings they don't want the world to hear."

The warning was full of sarcasm. Then he raised his voice, addressing the whole crew. "Okay... speed... and rolling."

Getting into character, I smiled down at Kristal's somber face.

"So... Jack's having a little dinner party at his place today, and his wife Bonnie wants to meet you. They've been hearing good things."

Kristal's wide green eyes stayed serious, but she faked a small smile in response. "Oh really? And where would they have heard these things?"

"Oh, I don't know," I said. "I might have mentioned you a few hundred times. But who's counting? So... will you go with me?"

"I'm not sure I should," she hemmed. "Would it be just the two of them and us?"

"Nah, it's a family thing. Her sister Rachel will be there too. Come on, it'll be fun. And I want to show off my girl."

If only she *was* my girl, I'd love to show her off. I'd brag to anyone and everyone who'd listen. I'd put her on a float and drive her around town with a bullhorn blasting the news while I threw beads and candy to the onlookers.

Tears filled Kristal's eyes. *Wow.* She was quite an actress.

Either that, or my invitation had made her sad. I was shocked by the vulnerability in her expression, but I wasn't sure what was behind it.

When she finally answered, it was in a whisper. "Okay, I'll go."

"Good, now kiss her," coached Hap.

Behind my back I flipped him off, then I turned my focus exclusively back to Kristal.

Dropping my head so our noses were only an inch apart, I took her face between my palms and brought my lips to hers.

I wanted to remind her of our first kiss, when she'd let go and melted in my arms, when I'd thought there might be the barest hope of a chance for us.

But as *this* kiss went on, I forgot about my agenda entirely, forgot about the people watching, and lost myself in the moment, in her.

My senses were assaulted by the sweet taste of her lips, the soft scent of her shampoo, the sound of her rapid breaths.

Moving us both so her back was pressed against the pantry's back wall, I yanked her tighter, deepened the kiss.

More. I wanted more. I would never get enough of this woman.

And she seemed to be feeling the same way. Kristal's hands found their way into my hair, and she hummed a little, a happy, hungry sound that sent my heart soaring and my cock priming the rockets as well—because it meant she was just as into this as I was.

And then it was over.

Kristal abruptly pulled away, breathless and blinking rapidly.

Lurching toward the pantry door, she wheezed, "I've gotta go. I'll... see you later."

The cameraman turned and followed Kristal as she speed-walked to the mansion's front door and left it with a shuddering slam.

"Cut," Hap called out. Then he looked around. "What the hell was that?"

Hurrying after Kristal, I answered. "If I'm lucky? A step in the right direction. See you guys later."

As I reached the door, I heard Paul say, "No one's ever going to buy those two being in a relationship."

Kristal was already climbing onto her bicycle in the driveway when I caught up to her. She was talking on her phone with her back to me.

"...so embarrassing. I can't wait till this is over," she was saying to whomever was on the other end.

I stopped in my tracks. Was she talking about our kiss?

My still-speeding heart crashed into a barricade and dropped to the driveaway.

Apparently, she'd been wholly unaffected by what had just taken place inside while it had struck me like a lightning bolt.

Working hard to keep my manner pleasant, I resumed walking, approaching Kristal from behind as she ended her call and hung up.

"Where are you going?"

She jumped, clearly surprised by the sound of my voice. She twisted to face me before dropping her gaze to the paving stones. "I told you... I'm going to Cinda's house today."

"Let me drive you. She lives clear on the other side of town. It's cold. And it's *not* a damsel rescue. I'm going out anyway. I need to pick up some things to take over to Jack's later."

She appeared to consider my offer for a few minutes. "Okay, thanks. That would be nice."

Once we were on the way, I said, "I'll swing by and pick you up later, and we'll head over to Jack's house together."

Kristal's head whipped toward me. "I thought that was just for the cameras. You don't *really* want me to go."

"I really do."

"I'm not sure that's such a good idea."

"Well, if you don't want to, no pressure," I said. "But we're supposed to stay away from the house for the rest of the day so they can wrap up filming anyway. We're *supposed* to be out on another date. And I'd feel a lot more comfortable if you'd come. You know how I mentioned Bonnie's sister would be there? I got the impression Bonnie's a little over-eager for me to meet Rachel—she's trying to convince her to move to Eastport Bay. If you're there, it won't feel so much like a blind date."

TWENTY-TWO

Second Thoughts

Kristal

A blind date? I wasn't sure why that notion hit me like a sledgehammer to the chest.

I knew there was no future for Hunter and me. *Of course* he would date other women.

But Bonnie was beautiful—I'd seen her pictures many times. Her sister was probably gorgeous too.

And Rachel was a successful private chef. Hunter had been talking about wanting to hire a chef for the billionaire bachelor house.

I should be happy for him. I was leaving. We weren't going to be a couple. I should want him to find a nice woman and be happy. But sometimes "should" and reality weren't the same things.

Tamping down the ridiculously inappropriate surge of jealousy, I forced a smile. "I'll think about it. I'm not sure if Cinda had plans for us tonight."

Cool relief settled over me as the car pulled up to the curb in front of Cinda's small cottage.

My friend was out in the front yard, supervising her son

AJ as he rode his tricycle in the short driveway. It had seen better days.

Tufts of grass grew up through the numerous cracks, though that didn't seem to deter the toddler, who pedaled vigorously, wearing a puffy coat and a large helmet that made him resemble a tiny astronaut.

Spotting us, Cinda smiled and jogged over to the car.

Clearly the mother and son had been outdoors for a while because her cheeks and nose were pink, which did nothing to dull her blonde beauty.

She made a hand motion encouraging me to roll down my window. When I did, Cinda leaned into it, beaming.

"Hey Hunter. It's been a long time. How are you?"

Acting completely unaffected by our sizzling kiss only twenty minutes ago, Hunter smiled back. "Great. Couldn't be better. It's great to see you. I guess that's your little man?"

"It is. That's AJ. Come on. I'll introduced you."

Hunter shot a questioning glance at me, obviously seeking permission.

Reluctantly, I gave him a tight smile. "Sure. That's a great idea."

Both of us got out of the car and walked up the drive. AJ stopped his trike and looked up. "Kristhal!" he shouted in his babyish lisp.

I dropped to my knees. "Hi buddy. How are you today? You're getting pretty good on that thing."

He nodded vigorously. "I am. And Mommy says I can ride it on the bike path in the spring."

"Wow. That sounds great."

Cinda spoke up. "AJ, I want you to meet someone. This is an old friend of Mommy's and Kristal's. We went to school together. This is Mr. Bestia."

Hunter squatted to put himself on AJ's level and stuck out his hand. "You can call me Hunter. I really like your bike. I noticed the flames on the wheels. Do they make it faster?"

AJ pumped Hunter's hand up and down in a floppy handshake and nodded his pudgy, dimpled chin, showing a full set of tiny white teeth.

"Uh huh. I'm a astronaut." He made a roaring rocket engine noise and jumped toward the sky.

"Wow. I've always wanted to meet an astronaut," Hunter said, clearly charmed by the boy.

Cinda laughed. "He's obsessed with anything that flies. Always has been. Sometimes we go to the airport just to watch the planes take off and land."

"I was like that as a kid," Hunter confessed. "Although, I think it had more to do with wanting to get away than a love of aviation." Turning his attention back to AJ, he asked. "Do you have any toy spaceships?"

AJ's wide brown eyes grew even wider. "Yes, and planes, and helicopters, and rockets too. Want to see them?"

He grabbed Hunter's large hand and started tugging him toward the house. "Mommy, can I show Mr. Hunter my toys and my room?"

"It's up to Mr. Hunter," Cinda said. "But he's certainly welcome."

Hunter looked for all the world like he actually wanted to accept the child's offer, but he glanced up at me with an expression of uncertainty.

"I wouldn't want to horn in on your plans for the day," he said.

The last thing I wanted after that disconcerting on-camera kiss was to spend several hours sitting and chatting with Hunter a few feet away. I'd been so flustered by the powerful sensations it had awakened I'd literally had to run from the mansion.

Before I could respond, Cinda did. "Nonsense. In fact, I

made enough chili and cornbread to feed an army, so we're going to need some help. AJ eats like a horse, but Kristal here barely makes a dent."

Looping her arm through Hunter's, she ignored the visual daggers I was throwing at her and started guiding him toward the front door.

AJ ran ahead of them, literally hopping with excitement when he reached the doorway and turned back to make sure his new best friend was coming.

Great. What was I going to do? Tell AJ no?

My best friend would be getting an earful the minute the two of us spoke privately. I had *just* gotten off the phone with her, telling her how horribly awkward the forced kiss had been.

While Hunter had faked his way through it, my body had taken it a hundred percent seriously and assumed full alert status.

Nipples tightening and drawing as much attention as possible? Check.

Panties damp and making me squirm? Check.

Face flushed and breathing accelerated and audible? Check and check.

Cinda knew good and well I *wouldn't* want Hunter there for lunch.

Fuming quietly, I followed the merry assembly into the tiny house and shut the door behind me, soaking in the warmth and delicious smells of Cinda's small, functional kitchen.

The single mother ran a home-cleaning business, the Fairy Godmother Cleaning Agency, and worked long hours but somehow managed to keep her own home spotless and welcoming, with AJ's framed drawings and preschool art projects proudly displayed. And there was always something good to eat whenever I visited.

It was such a contrast to the massive and sterilely beautiful home where I'd grown up. Well, it hadn't always been that way. Once upon a time, my mother had cooked—I had fond memories of baking cookies together.

But Margot literally forbade anyone to use the kitchen for its intended purpose because she didn't like the smell and she wanted the kitchen to stay "sanitary" and sparkling for guests.

Under her rules, it had been more of a showroom for expensive chef's grade appliances than a place for food preparation.

Oh well, no doubt the new owners would appreciate the low mileage on them.

Needless to say, I'd never learned to cook, though I certainly would need to pick up some skills very soon. Maybe Cinda could give me a few lessons.

She and I followed AJ and Hunter back to the little boy's bedroom. It had blue-painted walls with murals of animated airplanes from a popular kids' show.

A set of shelves and cubbies housed his toy collection. He eagerly led Hunter to it, and Hunter sank to the floor, sitting cross-legged and listening intently to AJ's enthusiastic description of each item.

As he responded in a warm tone I'd never heard him use before, I felt an odd, squeezing sensation in my chest.

Cinda leaned over and spoke close to my ear. "He's a sweetie—gonna make a great daddy someday."

Louder, she said, "Okay guys—lunch is in ten minutes. Be sure to wash your hands before you come to the table."

"Come on." She pulled me with her into the hallway and started toward the kitchen.

I frowned as I followed, considering Cinda's observation. "I don't think you're right. Hunter is too obsessed with work."

"Of course he is—right now. He's single. What else is he

going to focus on? My father says he was the same way until he met my mom. Men need a *reason* to relax and start appreciating the simple pleasures of life."

"Not all men. Not my dad. Having me didn't change his ambitious nature at all. He still worked himself into an early grave."

"I knew your dad," Cinda said. "Hunter is *not* your dad. Nothing like him. I think Hunter could be very easily persuaded to stop and smell the roses." She winked. "*And* the homemade chili."

"Maybe *you* should date him," I muttered, shocking myself with the bitter tone of my words.

The notion of my best friend marrying Hunter turned my insides into a toxic waste disposal site.

Cinda laughed out loud. "Nope—for one thing, I don't date. For another... *that* one's off the market—tagged and bagged."

That got my full attention. "Why do you say that?"

"Oh honey..." Cinda placed a motherly hand over mine on the counter. "...the way he looks at you. He's a smitten kitten."

I was about to argue, but Hunter and AJ appeared from the hallway.

Hunter had the child riding on his shoulders, and AJ was making airplane noises with both arms held out to the sides like wings.

"Look Mommy! I'm flying. I'm a pilot."

Cinda grinned up at him. "Yes, you are. And I hope you're a pilot with shiny clean hands. Let me see."

AJ held his palms out for his mother to inspect. When she pronounced them clean, Hunter swung the child off his shoulders and deposited him in his booster seat at the table.

"You need a whole house full of those," Cinda told Hunter, nodding toward AJ.

The big smile he'd been wearing vanished. He looked almost frightened.

"I don't know about that. I didn't have too good of an example. I'd probably make a big mess of the whole dad thing."

He kept his eyes down, making a project of placing his napkin onto his lap just right.

"Nonsense. You're a natural. As long as you love them—and their mom..." Here Cinda shot a quick glance at me which earned her a wide-eyed glare in return. "...you'll be great. You'll see. Having a family is the best. I'd have ten more if I could."

"Speaking of... anyone special in your life these days? Other than the Rocketman here." Hunter grinned at AJ.

"Goodness no," Cinda said. "Who has the time? My work hours are insane. The only man I have time for is the one currently decorating his shirt with chili."

She leaned over and dabbed the front of AJ's clothes with her napkin then kissed the boy's cheek and threw her hands up in a what-are-you-gonna-do gesture, laughing.

"We keep the makers of OxyClean in business around here."

"How's *your* business going?" I asked.

"Not bad. It's growing. I got another mansion added to the weekly schedule. We could use more though. Hunter, if you hear of anyone who needs housekeeping, keep us in mind. The Oceanview Avenue types like referrals."

"I'll absolutely do that. In fact, our place might provide you a few new customers in and of itself. My condo's pretty decent because I'm used to cleaning house. I never go into the other guy's units, so I don't know what kind of shape they're in, but I can find out if there's any interest."

"Josh and Tuck definitely need your help." I laughed.

Hunter blinked in surprise. "You've been in their place?"

"Of course. They've got a pool table. We play sometimes."

"When was this?" He sounded perturbed.

I shrugged. "A few times when you were out."

If I didn't know any better, I'd swear Hunter was jealous.

Which was ridiculous. I had zero interest in Tuck or Josh or any of the other guys in the house. And did he really care?

After what he'd said about not wanting to mess up his company and the relationships with his friends, he had a lot of nerve acting jealous. The man was truly a mystery.

As hard to read as he was with me, Hunter couldn't have been any more open and charming and sweet with AJ. The two of them chatted throughout the meal.

Afterward when AJ invited him to do a puzzle, Hunter sprawled on the living room floor with him, searching for pieces, seeming captivated by the boy's every comment.

Captivated. That was a good word for *me*, I thought as I watched the two of them together.

As hard as I'd been fighting it, I had to admit it, at least to myself. I was totally infatuated with Hunter. And Cinda was right—he *would* make an amazing father someday.

Unfortunately, I wouldn't be there to see it. Some other woman would have his children, share his life, grow old with him.

For the first time since getting the news about my brand new job, I had second thoughts about leaving.

TWENTY-THREE
Fifth Wheel

Kristal

Of course I *had* to take the offer. There was no choice.

If the past two weeks had shown me anything, it was that I needed to get away, have a fresh start, and stand on my own two feet.

I needed to love myself enough to break my old patterns, to find out what I was capable of achieving all on my own.

And that was why accepting the position in New York had been the right thing to do. I was too susceptible to Hunter.

If I stayed in Eastport Bay, I'd constantly be tempted to go against all my newly learned life lessons and just be with him, no matter the cost.

That was ultimately what was behind my decision to go with Hunter to Jack and Bonnie's house. I didn't have much time left with him, and every moment in his presence was becoming more precious to me.

It had also been the reason I said "yes" to Hap earlier about doing the on-screen kiss.

All I would ever have of Hunter was memories, and God

help me, I wanted just a few more of them before I packed my things and moved to New York.

As we were leaving, Hunter invited Cinda and her son to come along.

"Oh, I couldn't impose," Cinda said.

"I promise you wouldn't be imposing. Their chef, Monsieur Laplume, would be thrilled out of his brilliant French mind. He loves nothing better than to cook for a crowd. And it's a family thing—Bonnie's sister will be there. You two are Kristal's family, so it's perfect."

Cinda stood on tiptoe, kissing his cheek. "You're just as sweet as ever. But AJ needs his nap, and I've got to go over this week's schedules for the business. We'd love to do it another time though. You two go on and have fun."

We said our goodbyes, and Hunter and I departed for Jack's house on Oceanview Avenue, not far from the Billionaire Bachelor House. As we pulled into the drive, my stomach churned with nerves.

"Are you sure it's okay I'm coming along?"

"Of course. They'll be thrilled," Hunter assured. "The more the merrier. My recluse brother has blossomed into the consummate social host since getting married."

"Okay, I just don't want to be a fifth wheel or something."

"Don't worry about it. It's a casual thing. I think Jack mentioned some neighbors might drop in as well."

* * *

No neighbors dropped in.

In fact, when we arrived and I met Bonnie's sister Rachel, it was apparent the dinner party had been intended as a setup for her and Hunter.

Bonnie was more than gracious about it though.

"We're so happy you could come tonight," she said when the two of us were alone in the kitchen after the meal. "The way Hunter's been talking, I didn't think there was any chance for you two. He's been pretty down about it, actually. But he's a different man tonight. He's on cloud nine."

"Really?" I asked, surprised.

"Absolutely. Since I met him, he's always been so serious, all about work, driving himself into the ground. But with you around, he relaxes. He's smiled and laughed more tonight than he has in all the time I've known him. You make a great couple."

"Oh, we're not a couple," I corrected her misunderstanding.

"No?" Bonnie looked confused. "It's just... well, Jack said Hunter's been into you since middle school. And when you came with him tonight..."

I hadn't even told Hunter yet about my new job, but I blurted the news out to Bonnie.

"I'm moving to New York. I got a job there. It's in my field, so I'll finally be putting my degree to use. I found a nice apartment to rent too, and with the new salary I can actually afford it."

For the life of me, I couldn't understand why I sounded so defensive.

Bonnie's brows pulled together. "I see. I'm sorry. I completely misread the situation."

"No. It's understandable. We've been pretending to date for the Tech House show, but the filming is almost done, and it's past time I stood on my own two feet and made a plan for the rest of my life."

Bonnie still looked concerned, but she gave me a smile and a supportive hug.

"Congratulations. I hope the new job and new city are everything you want them to be." As she pulled away, she added, "Just so you know... Hunter wasn't pretending."

A little shell-shocked from Bonnie's words, I followed her back into the incredible library where Jack was showing off his extensive novel collection to Rachel and Hunter.

"I'm working my way through them now," Jack said, throwing a warm smile and a wink in his wife's direction. "When we met, Bonnie shamed me because I'd hardly read any of the classics. I had to get busy or be read under the table by my wife—a *newbie* author, at that."

Rachel and Hunter both laughed loudly, clearly familiar with the story already.

Obviously Bonnie and Jack had each confided in their siblings about the rocky beginning of their relationship.

Resentment swept through me like a tidal wave, and I suddenly felt like an outsider at this family event.

Bonnie approached Jack, giving him a chiding glance over his teasing remarks, but sliding her arms around his waist.

"I don't think 'shamed' is exactly the right word, honey."

"You're right. In reality, you raked me over the coals, called me an entitled jerk, and stormed out of the room." He laughed.

"Oh my goodness, Jack," she scolded. "What are they going to think of us?" Turning to the assembly, she explained. "I promise we actually do get along—we just got off to a bit of a rough start."

He planted a kiss on the top of her head, drawing her closer to his side. "A *bit*. Of course, she *was* dealing with 'Bestia the Beast.'"

"Former beast," she corrected, gazing directly into his turquoise eyes, so like his younger brother's. "He's completely tame now."

"Yes, I am," he growled and whispered something in her ear that made her turn scarlet from the chest up.

"Whew," Rachel said, fanning herself. "Is that fireplace throwing a lot of heat, or is it just me?"

Hunter laughed at her obvious reference to the chemistry between the newlyweds. Speaking of well-matched couples, Hunter and Rachel both sat on the leather sofa in front of the fireplace.

They weren't sitting close, but still, it was hard to miss what a pretty pair they made. Her fair skin and copper hair were a lovely contrast to his raven-dark hair and olive complexion.

They'd been getting along swimmingly all night.

Teamed up during a game of Articulate, they'd wiped the floor with the rest of us, quickly guessing the correct answers and finishing each other's sentences as if they'd been friends their whole lives.

Though I knew I should encourage the friendship, all I could think was that my body would barely be cold, so to speak, when I was neatly replaced in the Billionaire Bachelor House.

And Rachel offered something I did not—she was an award-winning, highly experienced personal chef.

I dreaded the inevitable moment when Hunter put two and two together and offered her the job.

About an hour later, the moment of truth arrived.

"So... how's Colorado treating you?" Hunter asked Rachel. "Eager to get back to work?"

She rolled her eyes. "If only there was a job to go back to."

His brows shot up. "You quit? Or were you let go?"

"Um... I guess you could say it was a mutual decision. Either way, the end result is the same. I am officially unemployed."

She had Hunter's full attention now. I could almost see the wheels spinning in his head. "Are you looking for a new position in Colorado... or would you consider making a move to the East Coast?"

"Why? Do you know of an opportunity? Someone looking for a personal chef?"

"As a matter of fact, I know seven someones—my housemates and me. I've been thinking about the idea for weeks. I just hadn't gotten around to launching a search yet because I have so much else on my plate."

Rachel's eager expression cooled. "I wouldn't be able to offer a reference from my last job. Things didn't exactly... end well with my former 'employer.'"

"That wouldn't bother me," Hunter said. "I like to think I'm pretty good at reading people... besides, you've got some stellar character references."

Bonnie leaned forward from the chair she'd taken near the sofa. "Oh Rache—it would be *amazing* to have you living here in Eastport Bay."

Hunter sweetened the pot. "The position comes with room and board, so you wouldn't even have to find a place to live."

"It's a live-in job?" Rachel asked, her tone souring. "I don't know about that."

"Well you wouldn't have to, of course, but since you'd be cooking for so many people—one of whom is nocturnal—it would make sense. If you're worried about privacy, don't be. The mansion is seventeen thousand square feet and divided into five separate units. We've got plenty of extra space."

He threw a quick glance at me as if to say, *And we're about to have a vacancy.*

Jealousy lit a fast-moving brush fire in my soul. I fought to stamp it out.

This was ridiculous. I was leaving. I had no right to feel jealous. I was making the *choice* to move out.

The guys needed a full-time chef desperately. Rachel needed a job and apparently a fresh start in life. Having her move into the house and take the job would be the best thing for everyone.

Maybe she'd even star in Hap's new show. He could simply recast the role of Snow White. Within a short while the guys—Hunter included—would forget all about me.

I squirmed as the flames of envy burned even brighter.

Get it together, girl. This is what you wanted, right?

"I'll give you a fifty percent raise over whatever your last employer was paying you," Hunter said, throwing one final enticement at the personal chef.

Rachel's eyes bulged. "You don't even know what he was paying me."

Hunter smiled, clearly confident he was about to close the deal. "Doesn't matter. What do you say?"

"I'd say I'm very tempted—especially for that kind of a bump in salary. Together with the included room and board, it would give me a great start on opening up my own café, which I've been wanting to do forever. But..."

"But what?"

His eyes shone with the thrill of the hunt. This must be what Hunter was like when dealing with potential investors and clients—smart, persuasive, absolutely irresistible.

No wonder he'd gone from Eastport Bay's poorest neighborhood to an Oceanview Avenue mansion on nothing but intelligence and sheer determination.

"Well, I'd want it to be spelled out in my contract... there'd be no possibility of personal involvement with any of the guys I'd be working for. I've been burned plenty of times as a chef—but I'm still smoking from this last job. There is no *way* I would *ever* get involved with someone I work for ever again."

"Absolutely," Hunter assured her. "We'd be completely

agreeable to that sort of stipulation. In fact… we already have a little experience with it."

His eyes slid over to land on me, while I blushed hotly. Because I knew better than anyone that an agreement like *that* one could be changed.

And once Rachel got to know Hunter better, she'd be all for taking a red marker to her contract and striking through that particular clause.

Would he move her into my room in his condo—right down the hall from his own suite?

I stood. "You know… I am actually getting a little overheated. I believe I'll step out onto the terrace for some fresh air."

Turning, I strode out of the room without waiting for a response. Hopefully my hosts weren't insulted, but I couldn't stay in the room a second longer, watching as Bonnie's sister took over the life I wanted.

But you chose to leave, I reminded myself.

It didn't matter how sensible the decision had seemed at the time, at this moment, the prospect of walking away and leaving Hunter was ripping my heart out.

"It's nice out here."

The deep male voice behind me made me jump and whirl around.

Hunter had apparently followed me from the house onto the moonlit back terrace—also he had amazing potential as a ninja.

When I didn't respond, he said, "Having a good time? Or are you on Bestia overload? If you've had enough, I'm ready to go whenever you are."

"No, no, I'm fine. Your brother and Bonnie are wonderful. And Rachel is lovely."

"She's great," he agreed. "She took the job."

It wasn't a surprise, but still, my heart flopped out of my chest and splatted on the cold terrace stones.

"Of course she did. That's awesome," I managed to say, forcing a smile so fake it hurt my face. "When is she moving in?"

I hadn't found the right moment yet to tell him about my own new job and plans to move to New York, but perhaps now was the perfect time. I'd give him some notice so he could have the room cleaned.

That way it would be ready and waiting for the new "lady of the house."

"Next week," he said. "She's going to take my suite."

I blinked in surprise. "*Your* suite?"

Hunter nodded. "Yes. We haven't had any time alone to talk about it, but I'm moving out. The pilot's almost finished, our software is launched, our lease is nearly up. You can absolutely keep living there as long as you'd like to—I'm sure several of the guys will stay on. But Reid's going to get his own place in Eastport Bay, and I am too. I'm sure Rachel would be thrilled to have you sharing my unit with her as long as you want to stay."

I couldn't answer—just nodded tightly, searching for the right words.

"Hey, you sure you're okay?" he asked. "You've seemed a little off all night."

Drawing in a deep breath and releasing it, I dug deep into my well of common sense, determined to actually use it for once.

"I'm just... listen, Hunter... I've been meaning to talk to you too."

I shivered, and he stepped closer, removing his jacket and sliding it around my shoulders.

No. No no no, don't do that. Don't be sweet. Don't be a gentleman. Not now.

His jacket was so warm, and it held the scent that always made me want to lean closer to him, to feel his arms wrapped around me.

How was I supposed to do this, tell him I was leaving?

"Yeah, we're a little overdue for a heart to heart," Hunter said. "I've got a lot of things to say that really, I should have said earlier. Mind if I go first?"

TWENTY-FOUR

Slipping Away

Hunter

Looking down into Kristal's upturned face, I was overwhelmed with emotion. Things were working out so perfectly.

The launch of Chipp had surpassed even my most optimistic predictions. And over the past few weeks I'd been taking a hard look at my life, realizing I didn't necessarily have to be on call twenty-four-seven, that I didn't *have* to work ridiculously long hours every single day to keep the company running strong.

Things were at the point where I could downshift a bit, take a step back and focus on other things—namely my personal life, and specifically, Kristal.

Now that I'd found a personal chef to take care of the guys, I wouldn't feel so bad about moving out and getting my own place, about moving forward with her.

Once my friends and I weren't all living together, it would be much easier to tell all of them about my feelings for Kristal —that I loved her.

And I had a very special house in mind to purchase. I

could hardly wait to see Kristal's reaction when I told her I planned to buy her parents' home back from the bank.

I almost wished the cameras *were* around for this moment, to capture the happiness shining in her eyes.

"Actually," she said. "I think I should go first."

"Oh. Sure."

I tapped the emotional brakes, which wasn't easy when I was so excited about my plans for Our future. But the look on Kristal's face told me she was determined to speak first.

"Okay, go ahead."

"I'm moving, Hunter."

"I know. Moving out. Me too. That's sort of what I wanted to talk to you about."

"No, you don't understand. I'm moving... to New York. Next week. I got a job."

"What?" My heart sputtered to a stop. I couldn't believe my ears.

My tongue had stopped functioning, though my mind raced with questions.

When had *this* happened?

How could it be happening—now—when things were about to work out the way I'd always dreamed they would?

"You've already accepted it?" I asked.

She nodded. "It's a good position—at a museum in Manhattan. I'll be using my degree. I found an apartment in a safe building."

She gave a weak laugh. "No more sponging off the Chipp Charity Fund."

That earned a frown from me. "You weren't sponging—you were never a charity case. I wanted you there—*want* you there."

"I know you *said* that. And believe me, I appreciate your kindness more than I can say—"

I cut her off, my voice coming out harsher than I'd

intended. "It wasn't kindness. It was *selfishness*. I asked you to move in because I wanted to spend time with you."

"What? But... the show."

"I made that up," I confessed—a little too late, apparently. "The whole thing. I mean, it turned into something real, but in the beginning, I concocted the whole idea because I wanted us to finally have the chance to get to know each other."

Struggling and uncomfortable, I fought to control my emotions, feeling like the needy little kid I used to be.

"I don't want you to go," I finally blurted.

Kristal looked as if she was fighting back tears. Her voice sounded thick. "I don't want to, either. I'll miss... everyone here. But it's the right thing—for all of us. I'll finally be independent, the guys' lives can go back to normal, and you'll truly be able to focus on your work again."

"Screw that," I said. "The guys' lives were *better* with you there—mine too."

"I'm confused. What about not wanting to cause a rift in the house? What about doing what's best for your company? Not losing everything you've worked so hard to build?"

"The company's fine. In fact, I'm thinking of taking a step back, slowing down and letting the other guys handle more of the responsibility."

She smiled sadly. "You say that, but you won't. You'll never slow down or step back."

"How do *you* know?"

"I know because I've been living with you the past few weeks. It's not just your job. It's who you *are*. The big deals, the money—it's where you get your sense of self-worth. I'm different. I can do anything for a living, really, and be happy as long as it pays the bills. And it's time."

Though she stood right in front of me, I felt Kristal slipping away. I gripped her arms as my heart thrashed in my chest like an escapee trying to avoid going back to prison.

It had been over twenty years since I'd lost my mother, but I was right back in that hospital room, clinging to her fragile body, begging her not to leave me, begging her not to go.

I *hated* this feeling, this weakness in myself, but I could *not* let Kristal move away without taking my best shot at keeping her.

Speaking rapid-fire, I began throwing out arguments one by one, hoping one of them would stick and convince her.

"You don't need that job. You don't *have* to work for a living. I'll pay the bills. I'll take care of you—anything you need, I'll buy it. I was planning to buy your parents' old house from the bank. If you don't want that one, pick another. If you don't like any of the houses on the market right now, I'll build you a new one. Pick any car you want—or several if you can't decide. You can go back to your old life, the one Margot stole from you. You can work at the art guild, throw big society parties. We'll join Kingsley Beach, that ridiculously overpriced beach club that all the Eastport Bay snooty toots like for some reason. I'll give you anything you want. I'd do anything for you. I love you, Kristal. I always have."

Out of breath, shaking, and having left it all on the table, I waited, watching Kristal's expression move through an array of emotions before she responded.

She reached for my hand, slipping her small, cool one inside it.

"I love you too."

My heart soared but then plummeted mid-flight when I spotted the tears in her eyes. They weren't the happy kind.

I took both her hands in mine. "What is it? What's wrong?"

"Hunter..." She swallowed hard. "I still have to go."

TWENTY-FIVE

One Last Chance

Kristal

Hunter's face contorted in a mask of confusion and hurt.

"What? Why? Why do you have to go? I don't understand."

"I know you don't. I'll try to explain. Your offer *is* very tempting."

I faltered, swallowing hard again. "Too tempting, because I *do* love you. I do want to be with you. But it doesn't matter what kind of house I live in or what you could buy for me or give to me. I'd never be happy with just material things. I want real closeness. I want to build a *life* with someone."

"That's what I'm offering." Hunter's tone was scarred, sullen. "In case I didn't make myself clear, I want you to marry me."

If the situation hadn't been so sad, I might have been amused at the angry, unromantic nature of his proposal.

Still, my heart ached with longing at those words. Being his wife, being able to see him every day, have his children, grow old with him here in Eastport Bay—the temptation was almost too much to bear.

Could he really change?

Would he ever be the sort of man who could truly relax and enjoy what he'd achieved and acquired?

Or would he always be striving for more? He'd invented an entire TV show to get my attention for goodness sake. Would he ever trust that he was enough—had always been enough?

Would he ever open up and let me see the real him, flaws and all?

I wanted to believe he could more than I'd ever wanted anything in my life.

It shouldn't matter. I *should* still leave, to prove to myself I could make it on my own, that I was more than just the pampered daughter of a rich man.

Still… I had to ask.

Hope bubbled up inside me as I took one last chance.

"Hunter… tell me where you went that night… after that kiss in my room. What happened? Why did you shut me out afterward? If putting a wedge between you and the other guys wasn't the real issue… what was?"

Wariness filled the spectacular turquoise eyes that had always fascinated me.

Before he even opened his mouth, I knew Hunter was going to deny me the truth I wanted. The truth I *needed*. The bubbles popped, leaving me deflated.

"It doesn't matter. That's the past. I want to leave it in the past. You're my future. Isn't it enough that I love you—that I've loved you my whole life?"

His words tore my heart into a million pieces. But I'd learned words were *not* enough. It was actions that counted.

I'd spent too many years of my childhood and youth hearing the empty ring of "I love you," longing for the man I loved to spend time with me while he chased money and success.

I wouldn't—would *not*—replay the same heartbreak in my adult life. Or do that to my future children.

Tears stung my eyes. I had to blink them away before responding in a choked voice.

"Thank you. Thank you for saying that. I'm honored, truly. But I have to go. It's for the best—for both of us. One day you'll meet someone you can truly give yourself to, and you'll understand."

Hunter's dark brows lowered.

"Oh, I understand. I understand that I love you, and you're leaving anyway. Because I'm not good enough for you. No matter how many billions I make, how many titans of industry I have kissing up to me, I'm not in your class. I thought if I worked hard and long enough and made something of my life, I'd finally be worthy of you, but it was all pointless. I was born into the wrong family, to the wrong man. There's nothing I can do to change that. So you're right, you *should* go."

My throat closed, and I choked on sobs.

"It's not about social class or money. I never cared about who your family was. I never cared where you lived or what you drove. Don't you see? All I've ever cared about is the person you are inside, the *real* you."

"All I see is that you're forcing me to live the rest of my life without you. I see that you're giving me no choice in the matter. So go on, go be happy with Larson Overstreet of the 'Manhattan Overstreets.' I wouldn't want you to lower yourself by slumming with me anyway. And don't worry. I won't be bothering you anymore."

He turned to stalk back into the house. As he reached the door, Bonnie opened it, wearing a big smile.

"Who's up for a game of Scrabble?"

"I'm through with games," Hunter growled. "Ask Kristal—she loves them."

At Bonnie's astonished look, I said, "I told him I'm leaving. Would you mind giving me a ride to my friend Cinda's house?"

TWENTY-SIX

Just Like My Father

Hunter—two months later

Hap entered the darkened and mostly deserted home theater of the Billionaire Bachelor House, holding a plate full of appetizers and wearing a huge smile.

"There you are, man," he said, locating me in a seat near the back of the room and taking the plush chair next to me.

"Have you tasted these yet?"

He held the plate out, displaying an array of savory smelling finger foods. "You are a genius for hiring Rachel. I swear, she's got some kind of magical abilities when it comes to food. Not bad looking, either."

"I'm not hungry."

Once again I directed my gaze toward the enormous video screen where footage from the pilot of Tech House played for any wrap party guests who wanted to watch.

At the moment, Hap and I were the only ones in the theater.

The show had been officially picked up by a network and was scheduled to start filming—for real this time and with a whole new cast—within the next few weeks. Thus, tonight's party.

Hap was obviously in a celebratory mood, and for good reason.

As the show's "creator" and director, he'd gotten a sweet contract and was already fielding a slew of other directing offers. It appeared his Hollywood comeback was a success.

My role in the project, thankfully, was now reduced to simply being listed as an executive producer. In fact, I was moving out of the house altogether in two days.

Since Kristal had left a couple months ago, it had been decided that my unit would be used for filming as soon as the new Tech House cast was selected.

Rachel had moved into an empty suite in Hap's unit. Everyone seemed happy with the arrangement so far, especially Hap.

"Sure you don't want any food?" he asked.

I shook my head. I didn't feel like eating.

I *definitely* didn't feel like socializing with the crowd I could hear talking and laughing downstairs. I didn't even feel like working, which was a first.

It was a good thing my company had already successfully launched, and I had partners and co-workers to pick up the slack because I hadn't exactly been pulling my weight lately.

I just couldn't seem to drum up any interest in anything—except for maybe the drink in my hand.

Lifting it to my mouth, I took another swallow, feeling the mellow burn on my tongue and anticipating the blessed numbness that was coming.

Hap put a hand on my shoulder.

"You know, I've been meaning to mention that 'liquid diet' you've been following the past few weeks is probably not the healthiest. And what are you doing up here all alone? You're turning into a bigger recluse than your brother ever was. It's a party, man. Half of Eastport Bay is downstairs. You're the producer—this is your victory lap too. You should be down there having a good time."

"I'm *having* a good time," I deadpanned.

My eyes went back to the screen, which now featured a scene with all the "dwarves" and Kristal piled up together in this very room watching a sappy animated film.

It shifted to a tight shot of Kristal. The tip of her nose was red, and her beautiful green eyes glistened with unshed tears.

Noticing it, Josh and Tuck teased her for crying at a "kiddie movie," and she laughed, dabbing at her eyes in embarrassment before laughing again when she realized she wasn't the only one sniffling. Reid had teared up at the emotional scene as well.

Hap sighed, and the tone of his voice softened.

"You gotta move past it, man. I know it sucks. You loved her, and she left. I'm sure I'd be miserable if I—God forbid—ever actually fell in love with someone, and she took off for another state. But what are you gonna do? Hide away up here for the rest of your life?"

"I'm not hiding."

"You kinda are. And not just tonight. You don't go anywhere or do anything. You don't run or work out anymore. I'd say you're gonna get fat, but you barely eat. We're all worried about you, man."

Now I took my eyes from the screen and looked at Hap.

"Don't be. Okay? I'm fine. I'm just going through... a rough patch, that's all."

Hap studied my face. "Okay. I'll let you work through it at your own pace." He leaned forward in his chair and started to rise, but then fell back into it. "No. I gotta say it..."

"What?"

"You're not your dad."

I snorted and started to take another swallow from my

glass, which just so happened to contain my father's poison of choice.

Little do you know, friend.

"I know that," I said aloud.

Hap gripped my wrist, preventing the glass from reaching its intended destination. "You. Are. Not. Your. Father," he repeated more deliberately.

Now I turned to glare at my friend, who clearly thought he was helping somehow but *really* needed to mind his own business.

Hap had some idea of the things that had transpired in my childhood, but only my brother Jack understood the full truth.

And well-meaning though he was, Hap hadn't lost his mother as a child, dealt with a neglectful, alcoholic father, experienced childhood poverty—or watched the only woman he'd ever loved slip through his fingers.

Fully annoyed now, I extracted my drink with my other hand then yanked my wrist forcefully from Hap's grip.

"I *know* that," I growled. "You don't need to say it."

"I think I do," Hap argued. "I've been wracking my brain trying to figure out why things fell apart with you and Kristal—and why you haven't gotten in your car, driven to New York, and brought her back when it's so obvious you two are meant to be together. She was in love with you, man. We could all see it. And *everyone* knows you're in love with her. You've been walking around like a zombie since the day she left. The only thing I can come up with is that you *pushed* her away. On purpose."

"That's not true. I told her I wanted her to stay. I offered her anything and everything she wanted."

"Everything? Really?"

"Yeah. You know I'd do anything for her."

Hap hesitated. "From the time I spent with Kristal, I'd say

she's about as real and transparent as it gets. She told me the reason she liked me—as a friend of course—was that I wasn't afraid to be transparent too. I talked to her about my past, about growing up with Jessica and the messed-up Hollywood stuff we both went through. I told her about my regrets, the mistakes I made. She did the same. We got to be really good friends."

"Good for you. What's your point?"

"You've gone after her with the same determination and work ethic that helped you build Chipp from the ground up. But she's not a tech company. She's not a tricky piece of code. She doesn't need your drive to succeed... she just wants your heart." He paused. "Did you *tell* her about your dad? About what happened at the jail that night?"

My eyes narrowed. Hap was treading dangerous ground here.

"I saw you back way off after that night," he said. "And it was pretty clear Kristal was confused about the change. I'm just saying... you're not your dad... but it sure as hell looks like you're trying to be."

I bolted from my chair, gesturing angrily at my friend.

"You have no idea what you're talking about. Go back to the party, Hap. If I want a psychologist, I'll hire one—not some 'actor' who plays one on TV."

"Fine." With a weary sigh, Hap stood and walked to the doorway, turning back just before leaving.

"By the way, your brother and his wife just got here. And that guy from high school... Harry McAllen. I didn't think you two were friends. I know I couldn't stand him."

That got my attention. "Harry is here?"

"Yeah, came in about half an hour ago with some smokin' hot cougar. He's down there hitting up the open bar and talking shit to the L.A. people about wanting to be a TV producer. I guess the law practice is going well if he's got that kind of money to invest." Hap left.

Feeling the first spark of life I'd felt in weeks, I rose from my chair and headed for the theater room exit and the staircase beyond it.

Though I was a little dizzy and somewhat numb, I was pretty sure the spark was anger. What on earth would Harry McAllen be doing here?

From the top of the grand staircase, I surveyed the great room below, taking in the smiling faces, the sparkling glasses, the laughter.

Hap must have selected a lights, camera, action theme for the party because set lights glowed from each corner and there were cameramen roaming the room, interviewing people. A red carpet runner stretched from the foyer to the great room entrance.

None of it interested me. And I didn't see Harry McAllen anywhere.

But I *did* see Margot Bianco.

She stood near the bar, dressed to the nines in a low-cut dress and sky-high heels, chatting up a network executive. As she reached over to play flirtatiously with the man's tie, a wave of nausea swamped me.

I turned and stumbled to my suite, not eager to encounter Kristal's vile stepmother up close.

She and Harry McAllen and the rest of their elite society crowd were welcome to stay and party all night if they wanted.

It was no longer my business, and in two days this would no longer be my home.

I'd be on my own—just like I wanted it.

Just like my father.

TWENTY-SEVEN
Cold Turkey

Hunter

Staggering downstairs the next morning, I went directly to the kitchen and searched for the ingredients of the hangover cure recipe I'd just looked up on my phone.

"Hey, Doc. Want me to get you something? Make you some toast and coffee?" Aidan's sympathetic voice offered.

"I don't need any help," I grunted.

I was the caretaker of the house. I didn't need anyone to take care of me. I didn't need anything from anyone.

"Okay, boss. Those bloodshot eyeballs beg to differ though." At my baleful glare, Aidan raised both hands to the sides, yielding. "I'll get out of your way."

Once I'd made the drink—nasty tasting stuff—I left the kitchen as well, encountering a few stray members of the film crew packing up their equipment cases and chatting over pastries.

"Hey, Hunter," one of the cameramen, Pete, said. "Didn't see you around last night. I would've gotten a sound bite for the entertainment shows."

I shook my head then groaned at the resulting pain, shuffling past the guy toward the stairs. "Let Hap do all the talking. It's his show."

Hap had certainly done a lot of talking last night. And I should probably have been a little nicer about it.

From my friend's perspective, it probably *did* look like I was determined to disappear into a bottle. But Hap was wrong if he thought I was an alcoholic.

And he was wrong about me and Kristal being made for each other.

I hadn't heard from her, but I assumed she was happy in her new life.

She was certainly better off there than she would be with me. I wasn't worthy of her.

What my father had said to me that night at the jail was right—I was needy, always had been.

Kristal could have anyone, and she didn't need someone like me dragging her down. I'd never be able to love her in a normal way.

I already needed her so much it was physically painful to be without her, and that was after only a few weeks of having her in my life.

What kind of voracious attention vacuum would I become after a few years with her? A few decades? I was probably better off without her too.

At least now I wouldn't turn into a walking, talking black hole of need. I'd be self-sufficient and strong and—

"Hoo boy, get a load of these two. *Somebody* enjoyed the party a little *too* much."

I turned at the audio technician's raucous laughter. The tech stood in front of a tabletop monitor, wearing headphones and watching the screen with a couple of grips.

Gesturing to Aidan and me, he said, "Come here, come here. You guys have gotta see this."

When I waved one hand in a dismissive way, Aidan pulled

me along until both of us stood facing the screen. It showed a scene from last night's party.

A man and woman, who most likely didn't realize they were being filmed, were entangled with each other, enthusiastically making out in the meager shelter of a tall houseplant.

Rolling my eyes, I started to walk away from the distasteful PDA, but the sound guy said, "Wait! This isn't even the good part. Wait for it..."

Within a few seconds, the woman extracted herself from the lip-lock and whispered something to the man. And I got a look at their faces.

It was Margot Bianco and Harry McAllen.

Were they *involved*? Or was it just a case of being tipsy and desperate at a party? In any case, things had apparently not worked out for Margot with the tie-wearing network executive.

"Here it comes." The sound tech cranked the monitor's speaker volume, removing his headphones.

"You greedy bitch," Harry said, his voice coming through loud and clear. It must have been picked up by the camera's expensive boom mic.

There was a loud crack as Margot slapped Harry across the face.

"It should *all* have been mine anyway," she informed him haughtily. "He left her a ridiculous amount. She doesn't even like shopping. And *you* wouldn't have gotten a dime if I hadn't given you the security code and password. So when I say I want a bigger cut, the only thing I want to hear from you is 'how much?' That's *if* you know what's good for you. The fraud investigators are still sniffing around, you know."

"If you think you're going to blackmail me, I warn you, I won't be going down alone," Harry promised.

"Hey Hap," one of the grips called out when Hap came in through the front door. "I think we've found your next project for you. Real Housewives of Rhode Island. *Lots* of drama."

"I wonder what fraud they're talking about?" the sound guy asked.

I didn't wonder. I already knew. There was no doubt in my mind the two of them were referencing the money drained from Kristal's trust fund.

The authorities needed to know about this. Kristal needed to know.

My heart raced at the thought of calling her. Someone had to, and this was *not* an instance where she'd be better off without me.

She needed that money.

She needed my help.

Unless she really was involved with Larson Overstreet.

Dousing the burning ball of fury that idea produced, I tried to think logically through my next steps. I didn't even have Kristal's new number. I'd have to get it from Cinda. But first... I turned to Hap.

"How can I get a copy of this?"

My friend gave me a strange look, as if I might want to save it for my own personal video collection.

"The video of Harry McAllen and his date? Uh, I can ask Greg to make you a copy and email you the file, I guess."

"That would be great."

I headed upstairs to shower and dress, powered by a burst of energy that cleared my head and settled my stomach. "I'd like that within the hour if you can manage it. And Aidan?"

My housemate gave me a baffled glance. "Yeah?"

"I'll take that toast and coffee if the offer's still good. I've got a lot to do today."

* * *

After a quick breakfast, I drove to Cinda's business, The Fairy Godmother Cleaning Agency.

It was located on the second floor of a modest two-story office complex in Eastport Bay's business district.

Just inside the front entrance, her stepsister Olivia greeted me warmly from the receptionist's desk.

A little *too* warmly, in fact.

"Hunter Bestia, it's been too long," she drawled. "We should have a drink sometime and catch up."

I gave her a curt response. "I don't drink." *As of today.* "Is Cinda in?"

With a pout, Olivia reached for the phone on her desk. "I'll see if she's available."

After a brief conversation, Olivia hung up the phone and directed me to the closed office door behind her. "She said to go right in."

Cinda stood from her desk chair as I entered. "Hunter. This is a surprise. Are the guys happy with our service? Is there some kind of problem?"

"No, everything's fine. That's not why I'm here."

"Oh. How are you? Please, sit down."

"Thanks, but I can't stay. I just need to get Kristal's new number from you."

Cinda's open expression shuttered. "I'm not sure I should give it to you. She changed it for a reason, you know. What's this regarding? Can I maybe give her a message or something?"

"I just need to speak with her briefly. Something important has come up. I think I'd better explain it to her directly."

Cinda sat back down and nodded toward the chair in front of her desk, indicating that I should sit as well. Her face was sympathetic.

"Hunter... you had months to explain. And you didn't. Now I'm not sure if it's the best thing for Kristal to hear from you. She's finally getting to the point where she can function normally again. She needs a clean break from you—it's the only way she'll ever be able to move on and find some happiness."

The unexpected words thrilled me while simultaneously kicking me in the gut.

"Did she say that? Did she really care that much for me?"

Cinda rolled her eyes. "She was in love with you, you big dope. Believe me, you don't just move on from that right away."

I shook my head, fighting a sense of dizziness that had nothing to do with my lingering hangover. "It's still hard for me to believe, I guess. But that's not what I'm here about. I've got some news about her trust fund."

"The one someone emptied out?"

"That's the one. And I have a pretty good idea who that someone is. Her dad's law firm is already looking into it, and so are the police."

"Wow. That's great. Of course she'll want to know about that."

Cinda picked up a pen and dragged a notepad toward her but stopped mid-motion.

"I'm still not sure if I should give you her number. She might be furious with me. She said she needed to go cold turkey."

Cold turkey. As in one method of breaking an addiction.

My belly simmered with excitement, but I kept it out of my tone. "I understand. I wouldn't ask if it wasn't important."

After another moment's hesitation, Cinda printed some numbers on the pad and ripped the top sheet off, handing it to me.

"It's her work number."

Practically leaping out of my chair, I took the paper and strode quickly to the office door. "Thanks. I really appreciate it."

"Hunter."

I stopped and turned back to face Cinda.

"I miss her too," she said. "I'd love nothing more than for her to come home. But just know... even if she recovers that trust fund money... it might be too late. She's been trying really hard to get over you."

There was a sinking sensation inside my chest, but I pasted on a smile.

"Yeah. It's okay. I'll just tell her about the developments and... let her get on with her life. I'd never do anything to hurt her again. I only want what's best for Kristal."

Even if that meant living without her.

TWENTY-EIGHT
Voice from the Past

Kristal

Locking the door of my apartment, I took the elevator to the lobby.

"Good morning," the doorman, said. "Pretty nice out today—no rain."

I smiled at him. "That's what I like to hear. Have a good day John."

Joining the stream of humanity on the sidewalk, I was grateful for the pleasant weather—I had a twenty-minute walk to the museum, and it was no fun in the rain. I'd finally figured out how to hail a taxi, but I avoided them if I could. They were pricey, and it felt like I was taking my life into my hands each time I rode in one.

Still, it was better than driving in from one of the suburbs or even across the city. That kind of daily commute in the crazy Manhattan traffic would have driven me mad.

The city was busy and loud and moving at top speed today. It was like that *every* day. It seemed like everyone was late—*all* the time.

Even a couple months into my new life here, I hadn't acclimated to the change of pace or the sheer size of the city. The population of the New York City metro area was almost nineteen million compared to Rhode Island's one million people in the entire state.

I missed it sometimes. Well, more than sometimes. I missed it all the time, especially Eastport Bay.

My life here in Manhattan was definitely not *bad.* I enjoyed my job. I'd made some friends through work and in my building. I loved my cozy little apartment and the tiny galley kitchen I'd actually learned to cook in.

The dating pool here was certainly larger—not that I'd taken advantage of it. A few guys had asked me out, but I'd declined.

I wasn't ready yet.

Larson Overstreet had been one of those guys, but as nice as he was, I couldn't look at him without thinking of Hunter, and it was imperative to do everything possible to avoid thoughts of him.

Even speaking to Cinda had become difficult.

I missed her and AJ so much. And talking to my lifelong best friend on the phone gave me the false sensation that I could step outside and breathe in the crisp New England air, that I could ride my bike to the waterfront on my lunch break and listen to waves crashing against the rocks and the cries of seagulls and inhale the briny scent of the ocean.

The longing for home had only gotten worse since I'd been contacted by the Eastport Bay Art Preservation Guild's interim director.

The woman had informed me the Guild's board had voted unanimously to attach a salary to the director position and had tried to persuade me to return to Eastport Bay and take the job, which she didn't want. She said the board members had all agreed I was the perfect person to carry on my mother's legacy, especially as I held a masters of fine arts degree and already had experience with the Guild.

Where was this *three months ago?* I'd wondered and regretfully turned down the offer.

I had a new life now, hundreds of miles from Eastport Bay. And even that distance wasn't enough to keep me from thinking of Hunter constantly.

I simply couldn't live in the same town with him, where we might run into each other and I'd find it impossible to avoid mentions of his name and possibly whatever woman he might be spending time with.

Reaching the museum, I stepped out of the muggy, superheated city air into its air-conditioned interior.

Pulling my blouse away from my body, which was coated in a fine sheen of sweat, I hurried past the giant sculptures of fruit flanking the museum entrance and across the glossy floor of the soaring ultra-modern lobby. Taylor was working the front desk.

"Good morning," the young receptionist said. "You had a call from a guy just a few minutes ago. I sent him to your voicemail. He sounded cute," she added with an eyebrow waggle.

"Thanks." I headed back to my office, stopping by the small employee break room to fill my coffee cup first.

Putting down my bag and settling in at my desk, I lifted the phone receiver and pressed the button to listen to my messages.

There was only one, and when I heard the recorded voice, I nearly spit out the sip of coffee in my mouth.

"Kristal. It's me..."

Hunter. The sound of his voice sent literal pain spiraling through my chest.

"I know you probably don't want to hear from me," he said, "but there's something important going on here..."

My heart hammered with a blend of excitement and fear.

My first thought was that something must have happened to Cinda or one of the dwarves for Hunter to be calling me and speaking in such an ominous tone.

"Everyone's okay, so don't panic," he continued, and my pulse dropped to a more normal level.

"It's good news, actually. Well, good news/bad news. There's a new lead on your trust fund. You might be able to recover the money. The bad news is who the suspects are. Well... I don't want to leave any more of this on a recording. Just call me back when you get a chance, okay?"

I replayed the message once more then got up and crossed my office on shaky legs to shut the door.

Then I went back to my desk, pulled out my cell phone, and dialed the number Hunter left at the end of his message.

He answered on the first ring. "Hello? Kristal?"

For a moment I couldn't answer. It seemed all the oxygen had evaporated from the room, and there was apparently a large moth trapped in my chest, frantic to escape.

Oh god, do I miss him.

The two months apart had done exactly nothing to dull the longing I felt for Hunter.

I swallowed and managed to take a breath. "Yes. It's me. Hi Hunter."

"Hi." He sounded nervous too. "How are you?"

"I'm... okay. I got your message."

"Yeah. I'm sorry to bother you. I know you're at work, and I know the last time we talked, I wasn't exactly my 'best self.'"

"It's okay," I assured him. "It sounded like you had a good reason to call."

Unfortunately, the reason had something to do with my trust fund instead of oh, him calling to say he loved me and desperately wanted me to come back.

Not that I'd pull up my shallow roots here, quit my new job, and high-tail it back to Eastport Bay if he asked.

Would I?

"Yeah, like I said, there's been a development in the trust fund case. I'm not really sure how to say this, so I'm just gonna say it... it looks like it was Harry and Margot."

"Harry and Margot what?" My heart raced so hard it was making my head spin.

Had Harry and Margot somehow gained some new information that had broken the case?

"They did it. They were caught on video talking about draining the trust fund and splitting it." There was a long pause. "I'm so sorry, Kristal. I know this has to hurt."

"Hurt" wasn't the word I would have chosen. "Hurt" was a stubbed toe or burning your ear with a straightening iron. This was more on the scale of falling face-first into lava.

I felt like I was broiling all over. I stripped off the sweater I always wore at work due to the frigid air conditioning.

"Kristal? You still there? You okay?"

I nodded rapidly, then realizing Hunter couldn't hear me, croaked, "Yes. I'm here."

"I'm sorry," he repeated. "I'm sure you'll be hearing from the investigator soon. He called this morning, looking for a phone number or forwarding address for you. I didn't have an address, but I did give him your work number. Hope that's okay."

"Sure. Yes. Of course."

My insta-fever had cooled a little, but in its wake, a sense of numbness was rising.

"Well... thanks for letting me know. That was... nice of you. I guess I'll let you go—"

"Wait," Hunter interrupted. "How are you doing? How are things going there? I mean, other than the bombshell I just dropped on you."

"Oh. Good. Yeah, everything's good. The city's interesting. I like my job—most days. The people are nice. How are you?"

"You'd be proud of me." He gave a snarky laugh. "I've been taking some time away from work, and guess what? Things run just fine without me there fourteen hours a day. Hey, I was down at Brady's Wharf and saw some of your photographs in the front window of the Sandcastle Gallery. Looks like your asking price has gone way up—they must be selling well."

"Yes. They are—thanks." I wasn't quite sure what I was thanking him for, but now that my shock was dissipating, my nerves were coming back.

"I uh... one of my shots placed in that photography contest. I didn't win the grand prize, but I took first in the landscape division. It did wonders to raise my profile in the photography world. Toni said people have actually been coming into the shop asking for my work."

"Wow. That's amazing. Congratulations. You deserve it. Now that the demand is there, you should really think about setting up a website and selling your work online. I know someone who can help you with online payment processing," Hunter quipped, obviously referring to his own company, Chipp.

"I'll think about it. I haven't really had any time to go out and take any new photographs lately though. Even if I did, I'm kind of at a loss for subject matter here in the city. Urban scenes aren't my area of expertise."

"You could come home," Hunter said softly, then, as if catching himself, he added, "I mean... maybe when you come home to deal with the trust fund issue, you'll get a chance to get out and take some new shots."

"That would be nice. Yeah, I guess the investigation *does* give me a reason to come back and visit."

My heart was screaming, begging him to give me a *better* reason, to tell me he missed me and still loved and wanted me.

In spite of what I'd vowed before, I found myself sorely tempted to beg *him* for a second chance, to take whatever scraps of time he could afford to give me and just let it be enough. Anything to be with him.

There was a prolonged silence on the line before Hunter spoke again. "I wouldn't ask you to come back for me."

"You wouldn't?" I blurted, in shock that he'd actually addressed the elephant in the room head on.

"No. You've made a nice life for yourself there. You're happy now, and I'm really happy for you."

"Well..." I started to argue, but he continued.

"You deserve better than anything I could offer you. I'm sorry I kept trying to throw money and 'things' at you. It's not that I was trying to buy you—I know you can't be bought. It's just... I knew that *I* didn't deserve *you*. No matter what I did, what I had, what I earned, I could never deserve you. I tried so hard to prove otherwise, but I knew it. It killed me because you were always what I wanted most in life. Not just 'want'—I *needed* you—too much."

"Hunter," I whispered, unable to say more with my throat constricted as it was.

Tears ran down my cheeks as he continued pouring his heart out.

"But I wouldn't ask you to come back, to be with me. Because I'm no good for you. That's the thing I never wanted you to figure out. That's what I was hiding from you. I'm like that poisoned apple in the fairy tale that looks shiny and delicious on the outside, but inside, it's all rotten."

"Why would you ever say such a thing?"

"That night... after that kiss in your room... when I was out all night... I was with my brother. And my father."

He paused to draw a ragged breath.

"Dad had gotten into a traffic accident. He was drunk. He was always drunk. Back in high school there wasn't a day he wasn't wasted by noon. Jack and I covered for him. We lied when his boss would call—back when he still had a job. We forged signatures on each other's report cards. We took care of the house, the yard. Jack started driving without a license at fourteen so he could be sure I got home safely from sports practices and games. When he went off to college, I had to quit all my teams and extracurriculars so I could work. Otherwise, Dad and I would have been living in a house with no heat or power. We would have literally had nothing to eat."

Shock competed with overpowering sympathy for him—for that innocent child he'd been, for the brave teenager who took on the role of caretaker and breadwinner while his friends and classmates went about their lives in carefree ignorance of his horrible circumstances.

"Hunter, I'm so sorry. I didn't know. How terrible for you."

"It's fine. I'm fine. I'm just trying to explain to you the kind of stock I come from."

"No—that's not true—"

"Please. Just let me finish, okay?"

His voice was ragged, like an aluminum road sign peppered with buckshot. The tormented sound of it made me want to climb through the phone connection to get to him.

"I thought when I went away to school, I'd left him and all his issues behind," he said. "Other than paying his bills and occasionally dropping in to make sure he was eating, Jack and I basically have had nothing to do with Dad for years. But that night... I realized we can't leave it all behind. It's part of us. He's *in* us both. Our father is a drunk and a convict. He *hurt* someone in that accident. We took care of the family, but the thing is, they can't keep Dad locked up forever. He'll get out, and he'll do it again. It haunts me. Jack's doing all right. But he's different from me. He always was better at handling the whole thing. He's not as... *needy* as I am."

"Hunter, you are *not* needy," I argued. "You're the most accomplished, self-starting, capable man I've ever met in my life."

"You don't know me."

"I *do* know you. And your father getting into a DUI accident has nothing to do with you."

"It wasn't just the accident," he said quietly. "It was what he said to me at the jail after Jack and I refused to bail him out."

My heart sank, imagining what kind of toxins the angry alcoholic might have spewed at his son as they stood there in the middle of the night separated by iron bars.

"He said..."

Hunter's voice failed, and I almost said something, but then he spoke again. His tone was flat now, devoid of any emotion.

"He called me a needy little parasite, a tapeworm, a bedbug. Said I always had been that way, that when my mom was weak from cancer, I was always hanging around, wanting her attention, asking her to read me a story, color with me, to look at something I'd made... to give me what *I* needed. He said I exhausted her when she should have been saving her energy to fight the disease."

My breath caught at the mean-spirited lies, and an unpleasant chill trailed down my spine.

It sounded to me like Hunter had been a normal child, terrified to see his mother growing frailer by the day and slipping away from him, devastated to lose her love in his young life.

Of course he'd needed her—he'd been an eight-year-old boy. Children were supposed to need their parents—not be vilified for it.

His father, in his own grief over his wife's death, had lashed out at his heartbroken child. I'd never heard of a worse parent.

"Hunter, that was a horrible thing for him to say, and it's not true. Do you hear me? It's not. Your mom would have *wanted* to spend time with you and Jack when she knew she was running short on it. That's how mothers are. It's how mine was. And I see it with Cinda—nothing is more important to her than AJ. I'm sure your mother felt the same. And you can't *kill* someone by needing them. Cancer killed your mother. Not you. Not your love."

"You weren't there," he said in that dead-sounding voice. "And you shouldn't be in my life now. I've loved you as long as I can remember, and I always will... but I won't do the same thing to you. Anyway, I didn't mean to dump all over you. I just wanted you to understand. It's not that I wanted to keep things from you. I just... I was ashamed. I didn't want you to know what I'm really like. I wanted you to love me. I wanted to be with you. But now I see it's impossible."

The pace of his words increased, coming out rapid-fire.

"Anyway, I'm glad you're doing well there—I really am. Good luck with the trust fund thing. I hope that works out too. Okay well, I have to get off the phone. Take care."

And the line went dead.

I sat in place, phone in hand, for a long time as I grappled with shock and empathy and heartbreak. No productivity awards would be won at work today for sure.

Hunter had finally given me what I'd wanted. He'd opened up and showed me his truth, his badly damaged heart, his real self.

And I was stricken—by the bare-bones vulnerability—by the utter *wrongness* of the beliefs he held.

I was also stricken by a new realization about myself.

Though I hadn't been utilizing my degree and hadn't had

a real "career" back in Rhode Island, I'd been *happier* there as a picture-taking waitress than I was here in New York as an associate curator with an office and a secretary.

I loved my hometown—and especially the people in it. I missed it—and them—to a painful degree, and that wasn't something that was going to get better with time.

Yes, I'd created a new life here, but it wasn't anything that couldn't be undone. There had been a great deal of competition for this job. If I left it, the museum director could likely fill the opening within days.

My co-workers and neighbors here were nice, but I wasn't an important part of their lives.

For me, New York City was just a place. Eastport Bay... was *home.*

My heart began to flutter with anticipation as my mind continued down this new path I'd inadvertently turned onto.

I could call the Art Guild and see if they'd found someone for the director position yet. Maybe Bonnie's sister Rachel and all the guys wouldn't mind me rooming in at the Billionaire Bachelor House again.

Or if that wasn't a possibility, I'd find a little one-bedroom apartment somewhere in town.

If my photographs continued to sell—or the trust fund thing panned out—perhaps I'd do as Cinda had done and buy a small cottage in town.

Or not. It didn't really matter. The luxury of the place I went home to at night meant nothing compared to *whom* I shared my life with on a daily basis.

And I knew exactly who I wanted that to be.

Hunter thought he was scaring me away by telling me how much he needed me. He couldn't have been more wrong.

I *wanted* to be needed by him. I wanted *him*—and whatever baggage might come along with the deal.

It would likely take some work to convince him of that, but I'd gotten used to hard work.

And Hunter was worth it.

There was only one problem. He was in Eastport Bay, and I was in Manhattan.

Stepping around my desk, I headed for my office door and then down the hallway to the director's office.

I knocked and, at my boss's invitation, stepped inside.

"Hi. Could we talk for a minute? I have some news."

TWENTY-NINE
Favorite Season

Hunter

I stared out the window of the Cliffhouse's small dining room at the sun setting behind the Eastport Bay Bridge.

The food had been phenomenal as usual, and now that it was spring, the view of the lush green lawn and the deep blue ocean beyond it truly couldn't be beat.

But I was ready to leave. This was the first time I'd been here since Kristal had left town, and I was considering never coming back again. This place was now inextricably tied to memories of her—and I was better off avoiding those.

Right, like that's even possible.

The entire city was one big parade of Kristal-memories. Maybe I'd buy a penthouse apartment in Providence like Reid had done and just leave Eastport Bay behind completely.

Speaking to her on the phone three weeks ago had reopened wounds that had barely even begun to heal. Now I walked around nearly anemic from the internal emotional bleeding.

In my peripheral vision, I saw someone approaching, most

likely my waiter—Kristal's old fanboy Robbie—returning with my credit card.

But instead of the sullen male voice I'd expected, I heard a woman say, "No six-thousand-dollar bottle of wine this evening? You're not getting cheap on me now, are you?"

I sucked in a sharp lungful of air as Kristal slid into the chair across from me.

"Hi," she said with a mischievous smile.

Somehow managing to choke on nothing but air, I coughed a couple of times and finally responded with a gravelly, "Kristal. What a surprise."

She smiled and nodded to my empty dinner plate. "How was it? Let me guess, you got the... brisket burger."

"Yes. It was... good... good."

My brain unfroze and began to wrap itself around the fact that Kristal was actually *here*, in person, talking to me and not a hallucination conjured by the sheer force of my need for her.

Why wasn't she in New York? What was she doing in Eastport Bay? Belatedly, I realized what was going on.

"You must be in town to resolve the trust fund situation. I heard you were getting most of the money back. Congratulations. I'm glad it worked out."

"Thanks." She shrugged. "Margot is down a yacht, and Harry won't be practicing law again anytime soon, but I'm glad that Mom and Dad's hard-earned money is back in the bank where it belongs."

"You won't be using the fund to live on?"

Kristal grinned, and my heart tore in half from the utter beauty of that smile. I'd missed seeing it more than I'd even thought possible. And she was wearing red lipstick to match her red sundress.

Somebody just shoot me. Please.

"I don't need to. I have a job now. I *will* use some of it

when I find the right house to buy. I'm thinking of a cottage—nothing fancy. I don't need much."

I nodded, not surprised at all to hear that she didn't plan on buying a mansion. She'd always told me she didn't need all the trappings of wealth to be happy. I'd been such an idiot to try to impress her with mine.

But did they even have cottages in New York City? She must have been planning to move out to the suburbs of Connecticut or New Jersey.

"How's living in New York? Must be pretty exciting."

"It's great—for some people," she said. "I've discovered I'm more of a New England girl though."

My heart gave a hard thump. "Really? You're not going to stay in New York?"

"Actually, I've already left. The city and the people are awesome, and there *is* a lot to see and do. But I gave notice at my job weeks ago. All my stuff is in storage. I just got back to Eastport Bay today. I'm staying with Cinda again until I can find the right place to buy."

The hard thump was followed by another then a smattering of frantic beats. I fought to keep my voice sounding normal, though I was struggling for breath.

"You're... moving back to Eastport Bay?"

Another breathtaking smile. "Yeah, you know, I don't want to miss my favorite season."

"But... winter is months away."

"I'm not talking about winter—I'm talking about wedding season."

Kristal gave me a significant look.

What was going on here? My mind buzzed with confusion. Maybe Robbie had poisoned my burger, and I really *was* imagining this whole encounter.

"You're going to be a wedding photographer?" I asked, struggling to make sense of the absurd.

"No silly." She laughed. "I'm talking about *our* wedding."

"Our wedding?" *Yep. Definitely hallucinating.*

I took in a deep breath, looked around, and spotted Robbie walking toward us with the leather folder containing my card and receipt.

"Kristal!" Robbie exclaimed when he saw her and rushed over to give her a hug. "It's great to see you. You coming back? I need someone to cover my shifts this weekend," he teased.

She laughed. "Afraid not. I'm going to be working at the Art Guild again. I took a job as the director—this time *with* pay."

"That's great. I'm so happy you'll be back in Eastport Bay. We'll have to get together and catch up. *Soon.*"

To me, he said, "Thanks for dining at Cliffhouse. Will there be *anything else*?"

If I hadn't been so discombobulated, I might have laughed at the obvious disdain in the other man's voice. As it was, I could barely manage a quiet, "No, thank you."

After the waiter left, Kristal sat back down. "Maybe I should have thought out my proposal location a little better. I just wanted to see you the minute I got back into town, and Hap told me you were here."

She looked down at her dress. "Also, this outfit isn't exactly suited to get down on one knee... but I'll do it if that's what it takes."

Proposal? So, I hadn't misheard her *or* hallucinated. What was she doing?

Hadn't she understood a word of what I'd been trying to tell her over the phone last month?

Confusion mixed with unwilling excitement inside me. I wanted to grab her and pull her close—I also wanted to get up from the table and run out the door in a last-ditch effort to save us both.

"Kristal... I told you... I can't be with you. I'm no good for you."

"You're wrong," she said pertly. "You see, when you were telling me about your supposed neediness and how it made you all wrong for me, you forgot about something very important."

"What?"

"I need you too. Yes, I'm financially stable now, and I don't need your money or a free place to live, but I *do* need *you*. I need you to love me—and spend the rest of your life letting me love you."

My heart ached. My eyes filled with tears I was powerless to control. I shook my head, still fighting it.

"I can't. You know I—"

Kristal reached across the table and took my hands. "I wasn't finished yet, Mr. Bigshot Billionaire CEO. I don't *just* need you. I *want* you—more than anything I've ever wanted. I want your big ego and all your insecurities, your brilliance and the foolish ideas you've allowed to take root in that head of yours, your beauty—*and* the bits of ugliness that you carry around inside like *every person who's ever lived.* I want your family, your messy past. I want your future. Hunter, I want *all* of you. Forever. And I want to give myself to you. If you'll have me."

When I didn't answer immediately, Kristal got up and came to stand in front of my chair, gathering the skirts of her sundress in her hands in apparent preparation to kneel.

I stopped her, wrapping my hands around her waist and rising to my feet.

Our bodies were very close, her upturned face just beneath mine, the red heart-shaped lips parted in anticipation of my answer.

Instead of giving her one, I asked a question.

"Do you know how much I missed you?" I whispered.

Her smile was accompanied by tears. "How much?"

"Enough to give you what you're asking for... no matter how terrified I am it's a mistake."

"You know... being scared is not a bad thing," she told me.

"It isn't?"

Kristal shook her head and grinned. "It'll make for a great damsel-in-distress moment. Where's a camera when you need one?"

I laughed and blinked, trying to hold back the tears that insisted on spilling down my cheeks anyway.

"I love you so much. I can't believe you came back to me. And I, for one, am happy there are no cameras around. So no one can tell me to cut-scene when I do this."

Lowing my mouth to hers, I took it in a kiss worthy of Prince Charming.

All that was missing was the fairytale wedding.

THIRTY

The Fairytale Wedding

Kristal-- Five months later

Standing beside Cinda in the opulent ballroom of Seacliff, I watched my reception guests dance to an upbeat tune played by the live band on stage.

The French doors that lined the ballroom stood open to allow in the cool September night air and the welcome ocean breeze.

Having danced for an hour straight myself and feeling the pinch of my blue pumps and the restriction of my white strapless gown's snug bodice, I was taking a break. It would be only slow dances for me the rest of the night.

In front of us, just on the edge of the dance floor, AJ boogied in his tiny tux.

"Look at me Kristhal. Look at me, Mommy. I'm a dancer."

"Yes, you are, and you did a great job as ring-bearer, so you deserve to celebrate," I said.

"Those are some fancy moves there, buddy," Cinda said. "You're awesome."

Encouraged, AJ spun and jumped, pumping his little arms to the beat and making both of his admirers laugh.

Speaking of admirers, an attractive man I didn't recognize approached us, congratulating me on my marriage then asking Cinda to dance.

"Oh, no thank you," my friend said. "I'm afraid all my dances tonight are promised to this handsome gentleman."

She gestured to AJ, who ran over and wrapped his short arms around her knees possessively. Smiling at the stranger, Cinda said, "Enjoy the party."

The man nodded and gave her a tight-lipped smile before leaving, obviously disappointed. I couldn't blame him for his interest.

Men had been staring at Cinda all night. She looked gorgeous in the frothy pink designer gown that served as her maid of honor dress.

Her blonde hair was up in a chignon, and she wore a pair of my diamond earrings that sparkled like stars in the romantic low lighting of the antique crystal chandeliers and wall sconces.

"You're a great mom," I said to her when AJ had gone back to the dance floor and resumed his performance. "But you can't let that be your *whole* life."

"I also run a company," Cinda reminded me.

"Right. I know. And you do it incredibly well. I'm just saying, maybe it wouldn't be a bad idea to say 'yes' to some fun once in a while... like when a handsome man asks you to dance, or to dinner, or to lunch. You're the most loving person I've ever met. You should let someone love you too."

Cinda's nose wrinkled in distaste at the notion. "I already had love—with Alex. Look where that got me."

I looked around. "I don't know... things aren't so bad. You have an amazing kid. You're at a ball in a glamourous mansion, looking like a princess. All you need is a crown."

Cinda laughed. "Ha. As *if.* I do wish my mom could have

been here to see this night. She would have been in her glory. She loved you. And you know how she loved fairy tales. But I'm more like the "before" picture of Cinderella than a princess. Speaking of... where *are* my stepmother and my stepsisters?"

Cinda and I had bonded in high school over our respective "wicked" stepmothers.

Mine was doing time now in a low security prison, but Cinda's stepmother, Julia, had made sure to finagle an invitation for herself and her two biological daughters to the reception, convinced it would be the perfect place to find "quality" matches for them—which of course was code for "rich husbands."

"I haven't seen them in the past hour or so," I said, a smile growing on my face. "But I *do* see a handsome prince heading this way."

Hunter reached us and presented each of us with a glass of champagne.

"Hello ladies. Has my bride had enough dancing already?" he asked me.

"I haven't, but my feet have. I think I need to rest for a while."

A mischievous gleam entered those entrancing turquoise eyes. "You know, I think I might know the perfect place. Have you ever toured the second level of this mansion?"

Lowering his voice, he said, "There are some very dark, very private rooms upstairs, just right for resting—or stealing a *very long* kiss."

Then Hunter pushed my hair back from my ear and whispered what would come *after* the kissing.

A tide of scarlet heat rose from my chest to my hairline, and other more intimate parts of my anatomy were growing rather warm as well.

Cinda laughed as she took AJ's hand and started leading

her son away. “I think we’ll go check out the dessert table. Want a piece of cake, buddy?”

With a hand on the small of my back, Hunter urged me to walk with him toward the staircase to the second floor.

“Wait—you weren’t serious,” I said, blushing instantly as my pulse picked up speed.

“As a heart attack. I’m afraid one little kiss isn’t going to do it for me tonight. And *that* one had an audience. I’m ready for a few minutes alone with my beautiful wife.”

Laughing nervously, I looked around. “But all our guests... what if someone sees us going upstairs? What will we tell them?”

“Oh, I wouldn’t worry about that,” Hunter reassured me. “I’ll come up with a little white lie to cover it. I’m pretty good at that, you know.”

Epilogue

Alexander Wessex

I looked out the tall, domed window at the expansive grounds of the royal palace in Aubernesse.

Elaborately uniformed soldiers changed places in an age-old ritual that was very nearly a dance as delighted tourists watched and snapped photos on their phones.

Beyond the tall, iron gates, morning traffic snaked through the tree-lined streets of the European mountainside city-state, people on their way to work or school or one of the many pursuits open to the principality's citizens.

To those who were free to live their own lives.

Behind me, my mother set down her china teacup in its saucer. My father turned the page of the crisply ironed newspaper he still insisted on reading every morning, though I'd tried repeatedly to convince him to use the tablet I'd bought for the monarch's last birthday.

"But you used to love Eastport Bay when you were

younger. Why won't you ever go with us anymore?" Mum asked me.

Sighing, I turned to face my parents. "Because I'm not a child anymore. I have my own life. I don't have time to traipse off to America every summer."

"You're not *that* busy," my father said, his face still obscured behind the papers. "You make time to fly in that plane of yours. You spend more time in the air than you do on affairs of the state. You need to start learning the ropes so you're ready when I step down."

"You'll step down when pigs fly, and we both know it."

That got a chuckle from my dad, and I stepped over to lay a hand on my mother's shoulder, seeking to soothe her feelings as well.

"I know you love Eastport Bay, and we did have some good times there, but what would I do if I went along? Hang out at Kingsley Beach every day? Eat fish and chips at Flo's Clam Shack? I don't play polo anymore since I hurt my knee in that rugby game. I've outgrown it. There's nothing there for me anymore."

I didn't mention the real reason I'd avoided returning to Eastport Bay, Rhode Island for the past five years—my heart couldn't take it.

Too many memories.

"The America's Cup sailing race will be there," Father pointed out. "The race has only taken place in Eastport Bay twice in the past thirty-seven years. Wouldn't it be smashing to watch the racers from our lawn? We could make an occasion of it."

"A party," Mum exclaimed, clasping her hands in front of her. "Yes. Audrey's parents have been pressing us to make an announcement. And I've told her mother all about Eastport Bay—she's dying to see it, and fall is the ideal time. This will be perfect—we'll invite them to stay at the mansion, have a viewing party for the sailing race..."

Her expression became more and more animated as she went on. "And a ball!"

She clapped in glee. "Oh lovely. It's been ages since we had a ball at our estate there. We'll present you and Audrey at the ball, announce your betrothal then. Since your sister is right near there at university in Boston, she'll be able to attend. Perhaps your globe-trotting brother might even deign to make an appearance if he knows it's a special occasion."

I heaved a sigh, sensing a resounding defeat coming my way. I should have left the room the second they started discussing their annual trek to Eastport Bay.

But... the announcement had to be made eventually. Maybe this was the right time.

We could get it over with, and really, what did it matter when and where we did it? The whole thing was for the parents anyway.

"What day does the race start?" I asked my father, trying to drum up some enthusiasm for at least that part of the plans.

America's Cup racing *was* the premier event in yachting, after all, the oldest trophy in international sport.

His Royal Highness, Henry Wessex, Prince of Aubernesse, held out the newspaper, and I took it, skimming the article about the America's Cup then absentmindedly thumbing through the other pages.

On the sixth page, which typically featured celebrities and society happenings, a headline caught my eye.

Billionaire Tech Mogul Weds in Eastport Bay

Huh. Two stories about Eastport Bay, Rhode Island in one day? The "Village by the Sea" was coming up in the world.

Apparently, the founder of Chipp had wed an Eastport Bay socialite in a fabulous ceremony at Seacliff Mansion.

I remembered the place well. It was just down the street

from my family's estate. A large photo of the wedding party accompanied the article.

There was the groom, Hunter Bestia, his wife, a pretty brunette named Kristal Bianco, the best man, who looked so much like the groom it had to be his brother, and a small dark-haired boy, the ring bearer.

The woman beside the bride was especially eye-catching. I squinted at the photo, trying to get a better look. She was short and blonde, and her face was beautiful.

I know that face.

An explosion rocked my heart. The trembling of my fingers fluttered the pages, so I walked away from the table where my parents sat, seeking privacy.

Crossing the morning room, I settled on a small, uncomfortable sofa that had been intended, hundreds of years in the past, to accommodate two people. My large frame took up nearly the whole thing.

My eyes raced over the caption beneath the photo, seeking confirmation.

There it was in black and white. "Maid of honor, Cinda Brown."

Cinda. *I knew it.*

Of course I'd known it—the second I'd laid eyes on her image. You didn't forget a face like that one.

And the caption said *maid* of honor, not matron. I was finding it hard to breathe, and the lack of oxygen made me a bit light-headed.

Did she still live in Eastport Bay then, or had she just been visiting for the wedding?

I considered picking up my phone then and there and dialing this tech billionaire to ask. But no, tech billionaires probably had people screening their calls, just as I did.

If I called up claiming to be the prince of a small European principality… the screener would hang up on me without a second thought.

Setting the paper down, I looked at my parents across the room. They were acting as if this was just another ordinary morning while I felt like the earth had shifted off its axis in the past five minutes.

"You know, maybe I *will* go—it has been a long time. When are you leaving?"

"Three weeks from Tuesday," my mother answered. "Oh darling, I'm so happy you've changed your mind. This will be splendid. I'll contact the party planner in America right away, and I'll ask my secretary to book your ticket."

"Don't bother. I'll just fly myself," I said. "It's been a while since I made a trans-Atlantic flight. And that way I can arrive and depart whenever I need to."

Such as right away if I find out she's married after all.

"Just as long as you stay over Saturday night for the ball," my father said. "I'm not keen to spend a fortune to host a formal ball that never happens."

Reading my father's warning tone loud and clear, I stood and crossed the morning room again, returning his paper.

"Don't worry, Father. I made a commitment to you, and I'll honor it. That's what we Wessex's do, right?"

"Exactly." Father's thick gray mustache twitched with approval. "Duty first."

"Duty first," I repeated the family motto in a far less zealous manner. "After all… what else is there?"

* * *

Thank you so much for reading Bargain with the Bachelor. I hope you loved it! The Eastport Bay Billionaires series continues with The Baby and the Blueblood. It's another fun fairytale retelling and features Alexander Wessex and Kristal's best friend Cinda, in a secret baby/second chance/stranded together/royal hero romance with humor, heart, and hurricane force winds.

Sign up for my Tru Tales VIP list at https://bit.ly/Tru-Tales to make sure you're notified whenever I have a new book release. You'll get a FREE novella set in the world of the East-port Bay Billionaires just for joining!

Here's a bit about The Baby and the Blueblood:

She's risen from the ashes of heartbreak...

Cinda

As a single mom, I'm not looking for Prince Charming. The last time I fell for a handsome, sophisticated, wealthy guy, he left me at the worst possible time without a look backward or even a word of explanation.

He did leave me with a lovely parting gift though... which arrived nine months later.

With no way to reach him, I picked up the pieces of that shattered glass slipper and moved on. Now I'm running my own business—the Fairy Godmother Cleaning Agency. My hands—and all my hours—are more than full managing my employees (including my two hapless stepsisters) and keeping my four-year-old son AJ happy, healthy, fed, and clothed. It's not easy doing it all on my own, but I have zero interest in a new relationship.

And who has the time? My high society clients expect their mansions to be sparkling—on schedule—come hell, high water, or hurricane.

So when a flu epidemic sweeps through my agency the day before the royal family of Aubernesse is to arrive in Eastport Bay, I put on a uniform and pick up the slack, working furiously to make sure their gorgeous vacation home is immaculate and ready for the elaborate ball they're planning to throw.

He's looking for the perfect fit...

Alex

I'm back in Eastport Bay for the first time in five years—and let's just say I'm not happy to be here. There's a reason I've stayed away so long.

While the rest of the royal family has continued to vacation in the beautiful seaside American town every year, the place lost its magic for me long ago—the night the only girl I've ever loved proved beyond a shadow of a doubt she didn't feel the same.

But this trip is non-negotiable, a matter of duty. I'm planning to fly in, attend the ridiculous ball my mother is so insistent upon, then get back to my life in Europe as quickly as possible.

That is until I arrive at the family estate early and catch the cleaning crew still at work.

And get a look at the woman beneath that coating of dust, ash, and spiderwebs...

The Baby and the Blue Blood is a hot small town rom com take on Cinderella. It's available now in ebook, print, and audio. Turn the page for a note from Tru and a sneak peek at the first chapter!

Afterword

Thank you so much for reading Bargain with the Bachelor. I hope you loved it! If you did, please consider leaving a review on Amazon and if your fingers aren't too tired, at Goodreads, too.

Just a few words is all it takes, and reviews help other readers find great books!

I love to chat with my readers! Visit my website at www.trutaylor.com. You can also connect with me on Tiktok, Instagram, and Facebook.

Never miss a new release or special sales news by signing up for my Tru Tales mailing list at https://bit.ly/TruTales. You'll also get a free story and other fun welcome gifts!

The Eastport Bay Billionaires series continues with The Baby and the Blueblood. Keep reading for a sneak peek at the first chapter!

Next in Series Sneak Peek

You can't really grasp the full essence of the word "mortified" until you've stood face to face with the former *love of your life—covered head to toe in soot and cobwebs. – Cinda Brown*

I could hardly believe what I'd heard coming out of my stepsister's mouth.

"Both of them?" I gasped.

Olivia nodded at me from the receptionist's desk. "I guess the flu's going around."

The head of the cleaning crew I'd had sent over to 600 Oceanview Avenue this morning had just called and said two of her staff, Janice and Zoe, had started vomiting and were running high fevers. I'd sent them home.

It had been the right thing to do. The idea was to *sanitize* the clients' homes, not fill them with germs and viruses.

But with two fewer workers, there was no way the enormous mansion would be finished on time, and that wouldn't do. The royal family of Aubernesse would be arriving in Newport tomorrow for the America's Cup finals and expecting their stateside "summer cottage," as they called the twenty-four-thousand square foot home, to be sparkling and ready for the ball they were hosting next weekend.

Fantastic.

Flu season had the *worst* timing. Three other employees had already fallen ill this week, including my other stepsister, Traci, who'd called in this morning. She rarely made an appearance at work anyway, so I suspected her Friday "illness" was more along the lines of Netflix-itis than influenza, but still the business was critically short staffed.

That made it a challenge to get the regular homes on our list cleaned, not to mention the mega-mansions. This one, though, was non-negotiable.

The Wessex family was an excellent client. I couldn't afford to let them down. I sighed.

"I'll have to go over and help them finish up. Looks like it's going to be a late night."

I studied Olivia in her designer clothes and shoes. She

hadn't actually done any cleaning herself since we were teenagers and my father had made us all work—his daughter and his stepdaughters alike—in an effort to teach us the value of good, honest work.

But hey, some help was better than none. Olivia would no doubt gripe about putting on the serviceable company uniform, but she could at least do some dusting.

"Actually, an extra hand would be amazing if you don't have plans this evening," I said.

Olivia scratched her arm with one perfectly manicured hand. "You know, I'm not feeling so good myself. I think I'm developing a rash. Maybe I should go home before I infect anyone." She stood and picked up her Chanel handbag.

"Skin rash is not a flu symptom."

"Oh." Olivia blinked. "Well, it must be something else then."

Biting the inside of my cheek, I drew a long breath. "Fine. If you're not feeling up to it, of course I won't make you go. But if you can manage it, could you at least stay here till closing and lock up? We're so short-staffed."

Olivia's eyes widened in horror. "What about AJ? You're not planning to leave him here with me, are you? You know I'm terrible with kids."

I shuddered at the thought of leaving my helpless four-year-old alone with Olivia. "No, of course not. I'll call Kristal. I'm sure she'll come and pick him up."

Olivia visibly relaxed and sat back down. The phone rang, and she turned to answer it. "Fairy Godmother Home Cleaning Service. How may we help you today?"

Back in the manager's office, AJ lifted his head and looked up as I entered.

"Hi Mommy! Look what I made."

He pushed a sheet of copier paper toward me so I could

admire the drawing he'd created with the set of crayons I kept in my desk for him. I walked over and stood beside him, resting one hand atop his dark curls.

"Wow. That's a very exciting scene. Is it a knight fighting a dragon?"

"He's not a knight. He's a prince. But he's also a fighter. What's that called?"

He turned his little face up and stared at me with trusting brown eyes, certain I had the answer. Warmth saturated my heart, and I gave his button nose a light tap with one fingertip.

"I'm not sure. I think you'd still call him a prince. But a valiant one."

"What's valley-unt?"

"Valiant. It means brave, courageous, heroic."

"I like that. Yes. That's what he is. And he's protecting his family."

"Oh my—he is brave, then. And does he have a big family?"

I was endlessly fascinated by my son's intelligence and imagination. He was always begging me to tell him stories, but honestly, the ones he came up with were usually far better than anything I could imagine.

"No," AJ said. "A little one. He has a princess wife and a four-year-old boy. What's that called, Mommy? When a prince has a little boy?"

"The son of a prince is also a prince. I think. I'll have to check on that." I wasn't a royal-watcher. Hopefully I didn't have my facts wrong.

"The big prince protects the little prince and the princess. He takes care of them. They do everything together," AJ informed me matter-of-factly.

A wistful twinge twisted through my belly. It wasn't the first time AJ had drawn a family of three or concocted fantasies about a heroic father figure. I knew he longed for a daddy to do things with him, but I was doing my best to fill both parental roles.

"It's a wonderful picture," I said. "You'll have to show it to Kristal when she gets here."

"She's coming here?" Excitement lit his eyes, but it was quickly replaced by suspicion. "You said we were going to go home and make pizza for supper."

"I know I did, buddy, but I have to stay and work some more. You remember Janice and Zoe?"

He nodded.

"Both of them are sick and had to go home early. Maria and Anna are sick, too. So I have to go do the cleaning instead."

He pouted, resting one plump cheek on his hand. "Why can't the people clean their own houses?"

"Many of them work hard at their own jobs all day long and don't have time. And some of them have houses that are too big for them to clean all alone. It's a good thing for us that they do need some help because that's how we get money to pay for our house and food, right?"

He nodded reluctantly.

I brushed my fingers through his soft curls. "I'm sorry, buddy. I know you're disappointed, but I don't have any choice. I'm sure Kristal would love to make pizza with you. And then you and I can make waffles tomorrow morning."

That seemed to cheer him a bit. He looked up. "Yoda waffles?"

"Yep. And Darth Vader too."

"Okay." He gave me the sweet smile that always turned my heart into goo.

"Good. Now you get your backpack all packed up and ready while I go change into a uniform, okay?"

"Will you be home in time to tuck me in?"

"I should be," I said. "Unless something very unexpected happens."

* * *

Want to find out what happens next? Order your copy of The Baby and the Blueblood today!

About the Author

Award-winning author Tru Taylor writes small town romance that's hot and sunny (and a little bit funny.)

She runs on Coke Zero and dark chocolate, lives for lunches with her girlfriends, and drives to the town beach several times a week to watch the sun set over the water.

She loves LOVE and will attempt to turn any show or movie she's watching into a romance whether it is one or not. Star Wars? A romance. Lord of the Rings? Clearly a romance. The Expendables? Okay, well not even Tru can redeem that one.

When she's not writing, Tru enjoys watching movies and reading books with happy endings, spending time with her husband and two kids, and sneaking Hershey's Kisses from the top shelf of the freezer throughout the day. (Top shelf because... two kids. Enough said.)

Tru is the author of the Eastport Bay small town rom com

series and loves living in a small New England town where she's surrounded every day by the beautiful coastal setting you see brought to life in her books.

Want fun email from Tru? Join her Tru Tales mailing list at https://bit.ly/TruTales for true stories of small town romantic comedy, excerpts, sneak peeks, giveaways, and a free novella set in the world of Eastport Bay!

www.trutaylor.com

Oxford South Press August 2021

Editing by Judy Roth

Cover Design: Emily Cover Design

www.ingramcontent.com/pod-product-compliance
Lightning Source LLC
Chambersburg PA
CBHW050829190726
48286CB00007B/2013

9781946166302